Summer Kitchen

A SAVING HOME NOVEL

E.J. RUSSELL

Summer Kitchen

Cover art: Cate Ashwood, cateashwooddesigns.com
Edited by Catherine Thorsen; Meg DesCamp

ISBN: 978-1-947033-92-4

First edition
April 2024

Contact information:
ejr@ejrussell.com

Summer Kitchen

A SAVING HOME NOVEL

E.J. RUSSELL

With deep affection for Dorset, Vermont, where my life changed direction in the best possible way.

Chapter One

For Pete's sake, why was Beef Wellington so ridiculously *picky*?

Casey poked at the mess on the cutting board with the tip of his dad's chef's knife. Why should it matter if the sirloin was at room temperature before you seared it? As for the whole searing thing, how hot was a *hot pan* supposed to be, anyway? And then you had to stick it in the fridge *again*?

"Jeez, meat, make up your *mind*," Casey muttered.

If the meat wasn't bad enough, there were the mushrooms—oh, *excuse me*—duxelles, not to mention the whole puff pastry nonsense. Casey had sort of forgotten about the egg wash until the thing had been in the oven for ten minutes already, so the pastry case had split, and things had gone from *oops* to *oopser* when Casey lost his grip and half-dropped the pan when he was transferring the sorry result to the cutting board.

"Maybe I can convince Uncle Walt it's *deconstructed* Beef Wellington."

Except even a deconstructed dish was supposed to be edible. His father had featured enough of them in his Michelin star restaurant over the years, and those had always been beautifully arranged on the plate too, with sculpted vegetable garnishes and artistic smears of colorful sauces.

This thing was less Wellington and more Waterloo.

He sighed and tossed the knife aside. There was no point in cutting into the stupid thing. It would taste just as dreadful as it looked, because apparently Casey sucked just as much at presentation as he did at preparation. But all the fuss and bother just seemed so *pointless*. All this work for a meal that would be over in an hour—less than an hour, actually, even if the chocolate hazelnut soufflé hadn't fallen and the tomato-basil bisque hadn't curdled.

Well, at least the salad would be edible. Casey reached out to tweak a leaf of butter lettuce into a less precarious position in the bowl and froze.

An unidentifiable insect was waving its antennae at him, a decidedly judgmental expression in its beady little eyes. Casey marched out of the narrow kitchen into his tiny living room and threw open the sash window. Then he returned, and holding the bowl at arms-length, he crept back to the window, careful not to jostle its contents. If Mr. Judgy Antenna swan dived off the salad, Casey would spend all night tracking him down because sharing his apartment with insects? No. Just no.

He dumped the bowl's contents—including Mr. Judgy Antenna—into the window box, where the brilliant green of the lettuce mocked the withered brown remains of the violas Casey had optimistically planted in March.

Because, yeah. Casey wasn't any better at gardening than he was at cooking.

He closed the window and trudged back to the kitchen to wash out the bowl. Uncle Walt would be here in less than thirty minutes, expecting Casey to have recreated one of Chez Donatien's signature menus. Since the last seven times Casey had attempted to do so had been equally unsuccessful, Uncle Walt couldn't possibly be surprised, although he would be disappointed. And Casey *hated* to disappoint his uncle, who'd been much more devastated at the death of his twin than Casey had been over the loss of his father.

Donald Friel had never been a warm, paternal presence in Casey's life. Uncle Walt had always filled that role—attending school programs, taking Casey to playgrounds and amusement parks, arriving with special treats for every birthday and holiday—while Donald had been busy with the latest in his string of restaurants.

And frankly, Casey had been glad of that, because every meal with his father had been fraught with anxiety. If he didn't eat everything on his plate, if he talked too much, if he talked too *little*—and heaven forbid he dropped a fork—Donald would lay into him as though Casey had destroyed the Pietà.

Yeah, thanks for that, Dad. Casey had endured years of therapy to overcome an eating disorder, and while he didn't have trouble eating enough to stay healthy now, he still didn't like to eat in front of other people. Just in case.

His therapist and Uncle Walt had never figured out the reason he hated meals. They chalked it up to losing his mother so early. And since Uncle Walt loved Donald's food, and was as proud as any fond parent of his brother's success and notoriety, he'd never realized that Casey's experience had been vastly different.

Uncle Walt had found visits to Chez Donatien's kitchen exciting and inspirational. Casey had merely been terrified, although he had discovered one pertinent fact: His father was as terse, disparaging, and vicious to everyone in his restaurant kitchen as he was at home, so it meant he didn't hate *Casey* per se.

He was just a really unpleasant person.

If only Uncle Walt wasn't determined to re-open the restaurant.

But Uncle Walt had decided, in his fraternal zeal, that the best way to honor his twin—who'd collapsed with a heart attack in the middle of dinner service—was to stage a grand reopening of Chez Donatien.

With Donald Friel's only child as the chef.

This close to an MBA, Casey could admit that it was a solid idea from a promotional perspective. However, promotional gold would only go so far, because a restaurant couldn't exist purely on hype.

People might come once, as an homage to Donald and perhaps because they were nostalgic about his food and the Chez Donatien experience. But once they tasted Casey's attempts at his dad's signature dishes? They'd certainly never come back.

Glumly, he scraped the singed and flattened soufflé into the garbage pail, stuck the dish into the sink, and turned on the tap. Maybe if he let it soak for about four hours, he could chip the petrified chocolate off its fluted edges.

"Or maybe I should just toss the dish. It's not like I'll ever use it again. After all, three strikes and you're out."

That wasn't really fair, though. Today's trio of soufflé fails weren't the dish's fault, and it was really rather lovely, the porcelain a delicate rose shading to peach, like a tequila sunrise. Once he sandblasted the remains of the last choco-catastrophe off it, maybe he could use it as a planter or something.

He remembered the viola corpses. *Or maybe not.*

A key rattled in the front door lock, and Casey's belly plummeted. *Uncle Walt.*

He glanced wildly around the kitchen, but there was really nothing he could do to salvage the situation. Maybe if he made a quick call to the falafel restaurant downstairs—but no. Donald had always looked down on anything he labeled *street food*, and Uncle Walt, while he wasn't averse to taking Casey to a food cart or hot dog stand when Donald was alive, was fully embracing his brother's culinary biases now that Donald was gone.

"Casey?" Uncle Walt called, his voice cheerful as ever. "I've brought the wine."

Crap. He bundled Beef Waterloo back in the oven, curdled soup behind the cleaning supplies under the sink, salad bowl on top of the fridge. If only this place had more *hiding* places—aka storage. But what Casey's Chelsea apartment lacked in space and amenities it made up for in location and convenience. He shoved the soufflé dish into the fridge—managing to slop half the brown-tinged water onto the shelf—just as Uncle Walt appeared in the kitchen doorway.

Although they hadn't been identical, Uncle Walt had the same silver-shot brown hair as his twin, the same gray eyes, the same pointed chin that Casey shared with both of them. But unlike Donald, Walt wore a perpetual smile, and instead of chef's whites, he favored suits like tonight's charcoal gray number, tailored to camouflage a middle softened by years of enthusiastic consumption of his brother's cooking.

Casey closed the fridge and plastered his back against the door. "Hi, Uncle."

"Something smells…" Uncle Walt's smile faded as he took a tentative sniff. "Did something burn?"

Uncle Walt was always careful to avoid assigning blame to Casey personally, unlike Donald, who was as quick with a spatula to Casey's backside as he was with a cutting remark, even if Casey was only making a peanut butter sandwich. With Uncle Walt, though, it was as though the food and the oven and the stove were sentient entities with their own agendas, who were responsible for the latest carnage rather than Casey himself.

It was kind of Uncle Walt to make the effort, but his *there are no bad cooks, only unfortunate circumstances* attitude was a little divorced from reality, at least where Casey was concerned.

"A few things." Make that *all* the things, and seriously? Casey could never quite figure out how something could be both burned and raw at the same time.

Uncle Walt gazed at the dirty pans and utensils still littering the kitchen, and whereas Donald would have been furious, Uncle Walt just looked sad as he set the wine bottle on the counter. "Oh, Casey."

"How about this? Let's head over to La Trattoria Rosa for some pasta. We'll have a nice dinner and some conversation, and I'll clean up when I get home."

Uncle Walt shook his head and shrugged out of his Burberry raincoat. "Nonsense. I'll help tidy up and then you can whip up something from what you have on hand, just like your father used to do." He ducked out of the kitchen and returned without the coat. "I have faith in you, my boy."

"You shouldn't."

"What?"

Casey took a deep breath. "It's time to face the truth, Uncle Walt. I'm not a chef. I'll never be a chef. I'm barely even a cook."

"Don't be so down on yourself," he said heartily. "You just need more practice. Once you've mastered one of your father's signature dishes, you'll have the confidence to tackle the rest of them and they'll fall like dominos."

"Oh, they'll fall, all right, but maybe not the way you think." Casey linked elbows with Uncle Walt and led him into the living room to the love seat that was the largest sofa that would fit in the space. He sat down beside him. "How many menus does this make?"

Walt's brows drew together and he turned away, his throat working. "I don't know what you mean."

"You do. Every week, you've presented me with a menu from Chez Donatien, along with Dad's recipes. Have I ever succeeded in turning out anything remotely edible?"

"You've made valiant efforts, my boy. I'm sure with more practice—"

"Uncle, have you ever *looked* at one of Dad's recipes? The technical challenges on *The Great British Bake Off* have more detail."

"But—"

"I think it's time to admit that if you don't want Chez Donatien to close the day after it reopens, you need a different person running the kitchen. What about Dad's sous chef, Charity? She was with him for nearly twenty years."

Walt screwed up his face. "She's a competent craftsperson, but she's not an artist. Not the creative genius your father was."

"But I'm not either." Casey took one of his uncle's hands in both of his. "Furthermore, I'm *not* a competent craftsperson. Not even close."

"You could be, Casey. I know you could."

"Uncle Walt. I flunked out of two culinary schools, and a third one rejected me so fast I think they must have had a special email rule set up just for me. I'm not cut out for this. Call Charity and beg her to come back. It's your only hope."

"Nonsense. You were practically raised in the kitchen of your father's many restaurants. It's in your blood."

Maybe that's why I hate being in kitchens now. "Uncle Walt. Listen to me, please. I *hate* to cook."

Uncle Walt laughed, the deep, rolling chuckle that had accompanied every announcement Casey had ever made, from the time he was four and wanted to be a ballet dancer, to his eight-year-old firefighter ambition, to his intention to get an art history degree. "The only reason you hate it is because you haven't mastered your father's signature dishes."

"Exactly. Not only do I hate to cook, but I'm *bad* at it." *Or maybe I'm bad at it because I hate it.* Was he wrestling with some kind of passive-aggressive relationship with cooking? Casey sighed. It wasn't totally outside the realm of possibility.

Walt's face brightened, and he patted Casey's hand. "Ah, but you mustn't lose heart. I have some wonderful news."

Casey narrowed his eyes. Walt's *wonderful news* usually involved something else to do with this cockamamie idea of making Casey into a knock-off copy of his father. "Really?"

"Yes. Bradley Pillsbury has signed on as the silent partner. Furthermore, he's pitching the idea to a number of other investors. He thinks the whole package—the kitchen and front of house upgrades, the curated prix fixe menus, and the story of how Donald Friel's son is carrying on his father's legacy will net us more than enough capital to complete the renovations *and* open a bistro at a second site in the Village." He beamed at Casey. "What do you think?"

Casey stared at him, horror pooling like ice in his belly. "*You* didn't invest money in this scheme, did you?"

"Of course I did. I'm completely confident of our success. And anyway, I was able to get a very favorable rate on the refinance of my Westchester house."

Casey propped his elbows on his knees and dropped his head into his hands. "Uncle Walt. When it comes to money, you're shrewder than this, way too shrewd to bet on something this chancy. You need to stop this. Now. Before it's too late."

"Don't you worry. Things are already well on their way. Chez Donatien was always booked out weeks in advance, and its renaissance won't be any different. You'll see." He got a faraway look in his eyes. "It will be like he never left, like he's still with us, every day."

Oh, god, I hope not. "What I'll see is you losing your money and your home if you don't get a different chef."

"Now, now." He patted Casey's shoulder. "You've got plenty of time to bring yourself up to speed. We don't open until after Labor Day."

"Labor Day?" Casey felt as though he were sinking through the sofa. "But it's nearly June. That's only three months."

"Exactly! As I said, plenty of time."

"Uncle, I really don't think—"

"More on that in a moment." He gave Casey a reproachful look. "I have a small bone to pick with you first."

"As long as the bone isn't in something I have to cook—since I'd be sure to incinerate it—hit me."

Walt laughed again. "Nothing too dire. But Bradley told me you haven't responded to his messages. You really should make time to go out with him, my boy." He nudged Casey with an elbow. "You'd make a lovely couple."

Casey blinked. Was *that* why Bradley kept calling and asking Casey to meet him at various upscale restaurants around town? Casey had assumed it was just to show him the competition in a misguided attempt to inspire him to work harder. "Are you trying to set me up?"

"Why not? I only want you to be happy. Settled. Secure. Bradley's handsome. Maybe a bit older than you, but six years is nothing these days. He's got money, influence, connections."

Yeah, and he never lets anyone forget it. The one time Casey had met Bradley without Uncle Walt in tow, he'd seemed more focused on displaying his wealth and power than in anything Casey had to say—which was why Casey assumed it was a business-related snow job. If Bradley was trying to hit on him, he had to *seriously* work on his seduction technique.

"I don't think we're really that compatible."

"Nonsense, nonsense. You just need to get to know him a little better. The two of you could be the next power couple to conquer the international food scene."

"International?" Casey squeaked. "I can't even conquer my own *kitchen.*"

Walt's indulgent smile was tinged with triumph. "And that's my other news." He leaned over and snagged his raincoat from the ladder-back chair next to Casey's drop-leaf table—which was easy for him to do, since nothing in Casey's living room was more than an arms-length from anything else. "Those culinary schools were obviously not a good fit for you. Your goal is to recapture the magic of your father's food, and to do that, you need one-on-one attention and a curriculum that's centered around the Chez Donatien menu." He extracted a glossy brochure out of the coat's inner pocket. "Do you remember Sylvia Grande?"

Casey frowned, racking his brain. "Oh, yeah. I think I met her at one of Dad's birthday bashes when I was a kid. She had that cooking show, *Grande Style*, right? It went off the air when I was still in high school. Some kind of scandal, wasn't there?"

Walt cleared his throat. "Nothing *criminal*. She had a small problem with alcohol. But that's all in the past. She runs her own cooking school up in Vermont now." He handed Casey the brochure, which featured a white clapboard building nestled amid a stand of leafy trees. The words splashed across the top read *Summer Kitchen*, and along the bottom, *Culinary instruction by legendary chef Sylvia Grande*.

Numbly, Casey unfolded the brochure, revealing a photo spread of the kitchen-slash-classroom, a street view of a picturesque town, and—the most terrifying part—pictures of exactly the kind of elaborate food that Casey had spent the last few months failing to master.

"Uncle Walt, I'm not sure—"

"It's a summer program, so it's perfect for our timeline. The students all reside in a big house right next to the classroom."

Casey bit his lip, glancing down at the brochure again. A summer spent in—he squinted at the fine print—Home, Vermont? Summer Kitchen's surroundings looked lovely, and while Casey would be spending most of his time in the classroom, it had to be better than sweltering in his own kitchen until September, right?

Sylvia Grande had been a wonderful chef, by all Casey had ever heard. Even his father had praised her. Maybe she really could whip him into shape, if only so he could supervise the restaurant—he was almost an MBA, after all; he had management skills, just zero cooking ability—and leave the actual food preparation to the sous chef and line cooks.

He owed it to Uncle Walt to at least give it a try, since he was betting everything—including his home—on Casey coming up to scratch. Plus, bonus: Bradley wouldn't be there, so he'd have at least three months free of Walt's clumsy matchmaking attempts.

"When do I leave?"

Chapter Two

Dev Harrison slammed down the phone on his office desk. "Why the hell are Port-a-Potties so damned expensive?"

A chuckle sounded from the hallway. "Maybe because having people piss on the nearest tree doesn't play well with the tourist crowd." Dev's cousin Ty sauntered into the room, his pale green scrubs already dotted with dark threads of animal fur, and dropped into the chair next to the desk. "Plus, Pete would have a fit trying to mow around any open cesspits. And the smell?" Ty wrinkled his nose. "The dog runs at the clinic after a bout of puppy diarrhea've got nothin' on that."

Dev scrunched up his face. "That's disgusting."

"So is wrangling a crowd of tourists when you don't have the right bio break facilities."

"I know." Dev sighed, leaning back in the chair which, along with the desk, the house, and the town, didn't really *fit* him. Or rather, *he* didn't fit any of *them*, despite eighteen months of trying to shoehorn himself into his role. "I don't know how Garlan managed everything so well."

Despite the pang under his heart whenever he thought about the accident that had taken his brother and grandfather out of the world in one skid on the ice, he still found the room to be pissed at Garlan for dying.

He should be here. He was the Harrison heir. He was the one groomed for this.

But Garlan was gone, and without him, the mantle of Harrison heir, town manager of Home, and caretaker of Home's legacy fell straight onto Dev's unprepared shoulders.

Ty laced his fingers across his flat stomach. "If it makes you feel any better, everyone thinks you're doing a great job."

If only I felt the same. "By *everyone,* do you mean the people who are too stubborn to move away while the town dies around them? The people who are too stubborn to admit that Vermont winters suck all the life out of your bones? The people who are too stubborn to elect a town manager who isn't a goddamn Harrison?"

Ty narrowed his eyes as if considering the questions, and then shrugged. "Pretty much, yeah."

"Why don't they elect you?" Dev jabbed a finger in Ty's direction. "You're a Harrison too."

"Because whenever they threaten to put me on the ballot, I counter with the specter of a vet who won't make house calls because he's too busy with town business. Besides, my family isn't in the direct line of succession." He flicked a finger through his straight, black hair, inherited from his Korean grandfather. "Harabeoji was an *adopted* Harrison, remember. I dodged that bullet two generations ago."

"Adoptions count," Dev mumbled.

"Don't pout, Devondre. It's highly unattractive. Besides…" He shrugged.

Dev sighed. "I know." After Garlan's death, Dev was the only one of the remaining Harrisons who didn't have another useful occupation. His band, Persistence of Vision, hadn't been getting any traction, so despite being the primary songwriter and lead guitarist, Dev had left the band—and broken up with his lover, Nash, the lead singer—and returned to Home.

Nash had never forgiven Dev for what he considered the double betrayal, making sure to twist the guilt knife at the same time he gloated when POV finally hit it big the month after Dev's departure. With one of Dev's songs, no less.

Drowning in grief and self-reproach, Dev hadn't pushed for his share of the royalties. Yet. *Maybe I'll cash them in to fund the fucking Port-a-Potties.* Heaven knew the town's budget wouldn't cover them.

"You know," Ty said, his tone cautious, "nobody would blame you if you decided to leave again. Go back to the band."

Dev lifted an eyebrow. "I'm sorry. Have you *met* the people in this town?" He held up both hands, palms out. "No need to answer. Of course you've met them. So have I. We've seen the same people every fucking day from the time we were born."

"But the difference is I actually *like* it here. Home is... well, home. The whole time I was away at vet school, all I dreamed about was coming back and taking over Doc Patel's practice."

Dev smiled, despite his financial-doom-laden mood. "I think that dream dawned the first time you took a stray kitten to Doc and he let you watch while he set its leg."

"A point. But you were different, Dev. You had ambitions outside of Home, not to mention more talent in your little finger than Nash Tambling has in his whole manscaped, perfectly coiffed body."

"Talent isn't everything." Dev sighed again. "I never saw my place in Home, not the way you and Garlan did. But that doesn't mean I don't love the town. Its legacy. *Our family's* legacy. We've been diverse and welcoming from the town's founding, and that's something I'll always be proud of. It's worth preserving. Worth working for."

"Yeah, but that doesn't mean it should make you miserable in the process. Have you even picked up your guitar in the last year and a half?"

Dev pressed his lips together. "No time. Garlan's bookkeeping was what I'd call idiosyncratic, and trying to figure out how to pay the town's bills is like an eternal game of Whack-a-Mole. I might complain about the Port-a-Potties, especially since I have to pay for them now to reserve them for the antique fair before the vendor registration fees start rolling in, but can I say thank you to the powers that be for the antique fair? With the Inn shut down, Madame Ivanova closing her dance studio, and Summer Kitchen's enrollments down to almost nothing, it's the only thing we've got to lure tourists into town."

"Yeah. Too bad it's biennial."

"Please." Dev clenched his eyes shut. "Don't wish an annual event like this on me. I'm only thankful that Garlan and Grandfather had just wrangled the last one before the accident. I'd never have been able to get up to speed in less than six months."

"I guess." Ty tilted his head, and the way his bangs flopped over his eyes made him look like one of the dogs in the shelter he ran out of his vet practice. "Do you regret that we fought the bypass? If we'd allowed the road to run through Home, we'd at least get some drive-through traffic."

Dev shook his head. "Nope. Even a two-lane state road would have ruined the town's peace. We'll just have to figure out some other way to lure the tourists away from that damn resort."

"A resort which wouldn't have existed if Merrilton hadn't actively lobbied for the bypass."

"Well, they're welcome to it." Dev glared at his monitor, where the red numbers splattered across the budget spreadsheet looked like arterial spray. The town was bleeding out in front of his eyes—and on his watch.

"Knock knock?" Sylvia Grande hovered in the doorway in her usual summer uniform of black trousers and crisp white shirt, although her wavy silver hair was more flyaway than usual without her chef's toque. "Dev, could I have a word?"

Ty rose, ineffectually brushing at his shirt—the fur didn't budge. "I'll get out of your way."

She waved him back into the chair. "No need. It's not a private word." She carded her hands through her hair—which probably explained its state. "My student is arriving today."

Dev buried his wince. Student. Singular. True, the lone student would be paying for lodging in Harrison House, but Dev's grandfather had started the tradition of charging Sylvia rent on the summer kitchen where she held her classes based on enrollment. When she'd first arrived, fresh from rehab, invited by Grandfather who'd met her soon after her show was cancelled, that was actually a good deal for everyone: The student fees were generous, classes were full for all three sessions—summer, autumn, and spring, since nobody with any sense traveled to Vermont in the winter unless they were rabid skiers. Sylvia turned a nice profit, and Harrison House brought in more than enough for building upkeep and improvements.

But with the advent of so many TV cooking competitions, and the rise of younger, more social media-savvy chefs, nobody remembered Sylvia anymore, secluded as her school was up here in Home.

"Kenny's dropping a new nightstand off for the student's room today, but otherwise, everything's ready." Dev tried to keep the desperation out of his tone. "Will, um, other students be arriving later?"

She grimaced. "Sorry. He's the only one."

"Got it." Dev ought to be grateful. Until last week, there'd been nobody booked at all.

"I wanted to be here to greet him, but"—she bit her lip—"I really need a meeting."

Dev braced his hands on the chair arms, ready to stand. "If you need a ride into Merrilton—"

"No, no." She waved him back down, too. "Pete's driving me as soon as he finishes mowing the field behind the Inn. But could you look out for him, please? Show him his room? Take him over to the classroom? Since he's the only student and we've got a special curriculum, we'll be starting classes tomorrow. Oh!" She hauled her giant shoulder bag in front of her and started digging through it. "I need to pick up a couple of frozen ducks at Shaw's. My supplier didn't have any fresh duck. I just hope it has time to thaw before we have to bone it."

"Duck?" Ty asked. "You've never asked me to sample duck before, and I always make a point of walking the dogs by the summer kitchen at the end of the day. I didn't realize it was one of your specialties."

"It's not. Where the heck is that— Aha! Gotcha!" She produced her phone with a flourish. Her expression clouded as she keyed something in. "I have to arrange the wine delivery, too."

"Wine? What gives?" Dev peered at her lowered head and detected a flush on her cheeks. "None of your Summer Kitchen recipes ever involve alcohol."

"It's the special curriculum for this student. He has to master specific dishes and many of them involve liquor." She dropped the phone back in her bag and spread her hands. "Hence, the meeting."

Dev lowered his brows. "You shouldn't have to deal with that. It's your school, so you should be able to run it according to your rules."

She gave him a pitying look. "Dev, my dear, without students, there is no school. I need the money. So do you."

Dev glanced sidelong at Ty. "I get by just fine."

She hitched the bag's strap further onto her shoulder. "Perhaps. But I don't. I'll just make sure I attend more meetings this summer." She winked at Ty. "And hire Ty to do all the tasting for me."

"Sylvia—"

"If you wouldn't mind doing me another favor, Dev, could you take a look at the bookcase outside my office? That middle shelf collapsed again."

Clearly she was evading the issue, but Dev couldn't really call her on it. He'd become a master of evading lately himself. "No problem."

"Thank you, dear." She rounded the desk and dropped a kiss on Dev's cheek, and then waggled her fingers at Ty as she headed for the door. "I'll see you later."

Ty harrumphed as she walked out. "How come you get a kiss and I get a finger wiggle?"

"You get to taste the food."

Ty's expression cleared. "Good point. But don't think I missed that little hedge. What aren't you telling me about your finances, Devondre?

"I don't tell you anything about my finances, Tyrese, because they're none of your business."

"Dev." Ty reached across the desk and gripped Dev's forearm. "We're family. You've got a lot to shoulder, and although said shoulders are broad enough to cause all the twinks from here to Atlantic City to swoon—"

"Look who's talking."

"—they're not broad enough to carry Home and everyone in it. What's going on?"

Dev dropped his gaze to his hands. They used to speak— through his guitar, his songs, his music. But now? They couldn't even balance the damn budget. "Nothing."

"Dev." Ty's voice was edged with command.

Dev scowled up at him from under his brows. "Don't use that tone with me. I'm not one of the dogs in your training classes."

"Then stop acting like you need a trust refresher. Come on," Ty said, coaxing. "Tell me."

Dev scrubbed both hands over his face, the weight of his worries making him slump in the chair. "It's…" He dropped his hands into his lap and met Ty's concerned gaze. "The town isn't pulling in enough for its maintenance. I've, uh, kind of been supplementing it. Out of the Harrison estate account."

"What?" Ty punched Dev's biceps. "That's *your* inheritance. You can't fritter it away on the town."

"When you think about it, Home is our inheritance too. Do you imagine Persistence Harrison would have stood by and let the town and its people suffer if he could have done something about it? Hell, that's the whole reason he founded Home—so anybody who didn't fit in elsewhere because of who they were, or how they looked, or who they loved would be safe and happy."

"Even Persistence didn't pay everyone's bills."

Dev glared at Ty. "It was 1791. People were more self-sufficient then. There was no internet." He shifted his glare to the monitor. "And no Port-a-Potties."

"Granted. But how many times can your neighbor ask you to help them dig a privy before you tell them to bury their own shit?"

Dev pushed his chair back from the desk as though the distance would make him feel less trapped. It didn't. "I get what you're saying, Ty. I do. But times have changed. A couple of hams and a flat of strawberries cut no ice with cable companies or Vermont Electric."

"Maybe not, but that doesn't mean you have to foot the bill for bringing the services to town."

"No? If we want Home to survive, it needs to offer the kind of lifestyle that people can get in a bigger city."

"I'm *preeety* sure," Ty drawled, "that if people wanted a big city lifestyle, they'd be, you know, living in a big city. Part of the reason people come to Home is to get away from that fuckery."

"Tell that to all the kids who left for college and never came back. Our populace is aging, Ty, and even the aging populace is abandoning the place and looking for milder climates. If we can offer the charm of a small town with the conveniences of a city, then we might stop the hemorrhaging. Home has a history, a legacy, something that no other place in the country has. We just need to make sure other people know it. And to know it, they have to visit. And to visit, they need a reason." He resolutely turned off the monitor. The scary red numbers would still be there the next time he looked. "At least the antique fair will bring in some traffic. People have been coming back to it every other year since the mid-70s."

Ty screwed up his face. "Yeah, but last time the Inn was still open and they had a place to stay or catch a meal or grab a drink after a busy day of trying to talk vendors into reducing their prices. This time, the only thing in town is the Market, and while Kat's espresso machine is kick-ass and her wine aisle rivals Burlington's best, there's really nothing else to keep them here."

"I talked to Kat. She's planning to offer ready-made sandwiches. Some of the high school kids'll be helping her prep and serve."

"Yeah, but she can't offer anything more complicated than that. She's got a deli counter, not a kitchen. And while she can sell unopened wine and beer, she can't *serve* it. How likely is it that people won't stow their authentic Shaker chairs into their SUVs and high-tail it back to the resort where they can enjoy bottomless bloody Marys and a hot tub?"

Dev narrowed his eyes. "How do you know about the bloody Marys, let alone the hot tubs?"

"Relax. I haven't defected. But Pete's better than a paparazzo when it comes to nosing out gossip. He reports back every time he gets an Uber or Lyft fare in Merrilton."

The notion of Pete—Home's grizzled, curmudgeonly jack-of-all-trades—eavesdropping on his riders was more than a little disturbing. "That's another thing. Pete used to make a decent living here in Home. Now he has to hire himself out to people from the resort."

"You ever think he might enjoy it?"

"Pete? He hates flatlanders."

"He doesn't hate them. He pities them for not being native Vermonters. If you'd ever take the time to talk with him—"

"I talk with him," Dev protested. "I always have. The most he ever says is 'Ayup.'"

"That's because you only talk to him about the jobs. But never mind. My point is, we've got more trouble than the antique fair is likely to solve, no matter how many Port-a-Potties you order." Ty slapped his thighs and stood. "By the way, if you see Randolph Scott around, grab him and text me, will you? It's time for his rabies shot and he's avoiding me."

Dev lifted an eyebrow. "He's a cat. He can't possibly know what you intend."

"That's what you think." Ty sighed. "If we knew where he spent his nights, we could get his... his..."

"Host?" Dev said dryly.

Ty huffed a laugh. "That fits. We could get his host to detain him long enough for me to show up with the syringe. But he's slipperier than an eel when vaccinations are due, even though he's constantly underfoot the rest of the time."

"I'll keep an eye out."

"Thanks, man." Ty lifted a hand. "Later."

Dev frowned at his dark monitor for a solid five minutes after Ty left, but he couldn't scare up the courage to face the budget again. He stood up.

"Might as well get something accomplished, so I don't feel so fucking useless."

He could fix Sylvia's broken shelf, even if he couldn't fix Home's dwindling supply of both resources and residents. In fact, he'd construct a whole new unit, sturdier than the last one. Metal, this time, instead of wood. Something that would last. *Maybe longer than the town.*

Anyway, his basement workshop was the perfect place to hide from red ink, family obligations, and goddamn fucking Port-a-Potties.

Chapter Three

The trip to Vermont had been excruciating, despite the cushiness of the leather seats in Bradley's Lexus. Even if he'd wanted to—which he had not—Casey hadn't been required to contribute to the conversation since Bradley took care of that all on his own. He'd even ordered for Casey when they'd stopped for lunch in Hartford.

By the time they turned onto Home's Main Street, Casey could have given a master class on All Things Bradley Pillsbury, including the unabridged text of Bradley's prep school valedictorian speech, because if Bradley had left anything out, it was purely by accident.

Luckily, Casey had been blessed with a very efficient memory, and when they passed a tall hedge near the end of the street and he got his first look at Harrison House, he shunted everything Bradley had said to his mental Trash folder.

Because *wow*.

Not wow *fancy* wow, but just *wow*, because this was exactly the kind of house Casey had always dreamed of, growing up in Manhattan apartments that were either cramped and rundown (his early childhood) or spare, modern, and soulless (after his dad's first restaurant took off). This house—a conglomeration of Federalist, Victorian, farmhouse, and maybe a couple of other styles that Casey didn't recognize—had three stories in its central block, with single story wings jutting off each side. It looked like a place you could explore for years and still find an unexpected staircase behind a door you'd never noticed.

A trio of massive oak trees shaded a front lawn that had to be at least the size of a city block. That much grass needed the giant riding mower that was parked under one of the oaks, with a sturdy man in overalls, white hair peeking from under his ball cap, bent over its engine.

Bradley *hmmph*ed as he turned into the gravel drive that cut a semi-circle like a smile in front of the house.

"So inconsiderate." Bradley's mutter was barely audible over the Persistence of Vision playlist he'd had on a loop since they crossed the Vermont border. Casey liked POV's music well enough, but Bradley didn't seem to be listening to the songs. They simply served as a soundtrack to his monologue. "This gravel could chip the Lexus's paint." He looked down his nose at the mower. "Although I suppose they don't get many high-end cars up here." He pulled to a stop next to the steps that led to a wide front porch.

Casey didn't waste a minute climbing out. He took a deep breath, filling his lungs with the clean air redolent of new-mown grass and lilacs from the bushes massed along the porch railing and towering at the corners of the house in colors from white through lavender all the way to dark purple. The guy with the mower looked up and touched the brim of his cap. Casey grinned at him and gave a little wave as Bradley climbed out the driver's side door, still grumbling.

He crunched to the trunk, his loafers—*"Italian. Handmade for me in a village outside Naples."*—skidding a little in the gravel. Casey couldn't help feeling a tad smug over his trainers, which, along with his well-worn jeans, T-shirt, and faded red hoodie, had seriously offended Bradley when he'd double-parked in front of the apartment this morning. *"You could have dressed up a little for our first date."*

Casey had rolled his eyes. "It's not a date. You're making a completely unnecessary drive. I was perfectly happy to take the train and catch an Uber from the station in Merrilton."

But Uncle Walt had said it would make him feel better to know that Casey had made it there safely, so he'd given in. Now he wished he'd stood his ground, because over six hours of Bradley Pillsbury—if you counted lunch and two stops for lattes—was *way* more than enough.

Bradley unloaded Casey's luggage and slammed the trunk. "I'm surprised at your uncle."

Casey didn't answer. He'd learned by now that Bradley didn't require a response—he'd supply one himself regardless of whether Casey said anything or not. Besides, he'd just noticed a bird's nest tucked under the front porch eaves. A swallow swooped past him and perched on its edge, greeted by the frantic peeps of the babies inside.

So different from New York. Even if a swallow had nested outside his building, Casey wouldn't have been able to hear them over the noise of traffic and the gabble of endless crowds rushing, rushing, rushing, yet never seeming to be satisfied with their destination.

"Considering your pedigree," Bradley said, setting Casey's bags next to the porch steps, "he could have enrolled you in a culinary institute in Manhattan with no difficulty at all. Add in my connections, and—"

"I've already attended"—and failed—"Manhattan schools. Twice. Uncle Walt and I discussed it, Bradley. This is *my* choice."

Bradley gazed at a spot over Casey's left shoulder. *Would it kill him to look me in the eye?* "You realize that the distance will be quite inconvenient for me to visit you regularly?"

Oh, I certainly do. In fact, Casey was counting on it. "You definitely shouldn't *inconvenience* yourself, Bradley. In fact"—Casey picked up his suitcases—"I can take it from here."

"Don't be ridiculous." Bradley looked around, probably expecting a bellhop to materialize along with a valet. "Just look at this place. I doubt there's a decent latte closer than Merrilton. In fact, you ought to stay there instead. I'll lease a car for you and you can drive out here for your lessons while staying in marginally civilized lodgings."

"No." Casey might have trouble saying no to Uncle Walt, but Bradley was another story. "For one thing, I can't drive, so leasing a car would be useless. For another, the proximity to the classroom is one of the selling points of this place. For a third—" Casey smiled as he turned in a circle, checking out the other houses along Main Street, all different, all idiosyncratic, all set behind deep, emerald-green lawns. "—I like it here."

This time, Bradley *did* meet Casey's eyes, if only to stare at him with total shock. "Impossible. Just *look* at this place!"

Casey's smile grew. "I am." He widened his stance and folded his arms, blocking his suitcases from Bradley. "Thank you for the ride, but I'd like you to go now. I need time to get acclimated before I start classes tomorrow."

Behind Bradley, the mower guy gave Bradley a narrow-eyed stare, then winked at Casey, and fired up the mower, kicking a spray of grass over the Lexus's shiny silver hood—and probably inside its open driver's door—even though a giant canvas grass catcher sat right next to the mower's rear wheels.

"What the—" Bradley marched toward the car, glaring at the mower guy, who didn't seem the least daunted. Or impressed.

Casey grinned. *I think I like this guy.*

Bradley met Casey's gaze over the car roof. "I'll call you," he shouted over the growl of the mower's engine.

"Don't bother," Casey said.

"What?"

"I said—"

Mower guy revved the motor and Casey gave up. Instead, he just made shooing motions until Bradley climbed back in his car. Bradley's desire to get away from the mower was apparently greater than his fear of gravel-induced paint chips, because he took off along the curve of the drive, rocks spraying from his wheels. Several of them pinged off the mower.

"Oh my god." Casey hurried toward the mower, raising his voice to be heard over the engine. "Are you okay? Did that"—the engine cut out before Casey could moderate his tone—"idiot hit…" He blinked, clearing his throat. "I mean, did any of the rocks hit you?"

"Not so's you'd notice." He wiped his right hand on his overalls and held it out. "Pete Tucker."

Casey shook the callused palm. "Casey Friel. Sorry about"—he flicked his fingers at Bradley's disappearing taillights—"that."

"No skin off my backside." Pete resettled his cap. Closer to it, Casey could see that its logo wasn't from a ball club or seed company. Instead, it was the stylized, intertwined letters *POV*, the emblem that adorned Persistence of Vision's first album, from before their breakout success.

Casey gestured toward the house. "This is Summer Kitchen, isn't it?"

"Not so's you'd say."

"But…" Casey frowned, pulling the creased Summer Kitchen brochure from his back pocket. "The brochure—"

"This here's Harrison House. The summer kitchen's around back."

Casey blinked again. "So Summer Kitchen, the program, is held in an actual summer kitchen?"

He knew that in the days of wood stove cooking and before the advent of air conditioning, families who could afford it often built a separate structure for preparing meals in hot weather—a summer kitchen. For some reason, that bit of whimsy made him feel a bit better about spending his summer at remedial cooking school.

Not a lot better, but some.

"Ayup," Pete grunted.

Casey glanced around. There didn't seem to be anybody else around other than Pete. "I was supposed to check in with Ms. Grande. Will I find her in the classroom?"

"Nawp."

Casey frowned. "Inside Harrison House?" He cast another appreciative glance at the building. "I believe I'm supposed to room here for the summer." He couldn't help a little shiver of anticipation. If it weren't for, you know, having to *cook*, this could be a dream vacation.

"Nawp." Pete started up the mower and climbed onto its seat. "Day's wasting."

"But—"

Pete put the mower in gear and trundled off across the lawn. With its mower deck lifted, it made decent speed, enough that Casey would look like a fool running alongside to ask more questions. So he stayed where he was and raised his face to the dappled sunlight as a playful breeze teased his hair.

Back in Manhattan, summer humidity was already setting in, the skyscrapers creating canyons of exhaust and noise. But here? The sun and breeze balanced each other—the breeze cool enough to offset the sun's warmth and the sun hot enough to offset the breeze's chill.

In fact, Casey stripped off his light hoodie and tossed it over his largest suitcase. He'd needed it in Bradley's car because Bradley had the AC cranked up to eleven.

He paused with one foot on the bottom porch step. Presumably he'd find somebody inside to show him to his room and give him the rundown, even if Ms. Grande was unexpectedly absent. But with nobody around to look over his shoulder, he had the perfect opportunity to do a little reconnaissance—aka snooping—before somebody else took charge of his time.

Hands in his pockets, he strolled along the front of Harrison House, shamelessly peering inside. The porch shaded the front windows, cutting the sun's glare, so he was able to catch glimpses of well-worn furniture and floor-to-very-high-ceiling bookshelves stuffed full of everything from mass market paperbacks to what looked like gold-embossed, leather-bound hardcovers.

Casey made a pleased sound in his throat. The room, whether it was a living room, parlor, or library, had the air of comfort and use. Although his own apartment would probably fit in its center, the room had the same cozy ambience that Casey intentionally sought, probably because his father's style in decorating echoed his restaurant kitchens: all sharp angles, hard metal surfaces, and unforgiving white light.

In Donald's view, comfort was for the weak and lazy—two words that he'd thrown at Casey times beyond counting.

The drugging scent of the big lilacs at the corner of the house wound around him, tempting him closer. *This* was a place *made* for laziness, that invited a leisure that was its own reward. He'd leave the industry to the bees buzzing busily among the blooms.

Casey carefully broke off one spray of magenta blossoms. He held it to his nose and inhaled as he rounded the corner.

A smaller porch was tucked along the side of the house, its French doors opening onto that same living room-slash-library. Casey couldn't detect any movement inside, so since there was nobody to get freaked out, he climbed onto the porch and cupped his hands beside his eyes to peer through the glass. From this angle, he could see that opposite where he stood, up two steps, was an entryway, the foot of a wide oak staircase with a carved pineapple-topped newel post visible beyond an arch. Another room opened off the entry, and beyond that, another.

It was almost like one of those endless funhouse mirrors, and Casey had the notion that if he stepped into this room, he could keep going from one room to the next, possibly forever.

He stepped back with a sigh. Leave it to a guy who lived in an apartment with a bedroom the size of a bathtub—and no *actual* bathtub—to fantasize about square footage. Hopping down from the porch, he continued his circuit. When he got his first glimpse of the rear of the house, he stopped dead, his jaw sagging.

He'd thought the front lawn was huge, but the back lawn—or should he say *field*—had to be five times as big, easily as long as a football field and twice as wide. If Pete maintained this—and the open grass was neatly cropped—it was no wonder he drove a mower the size of a Humvee.

At the other end of the house, separated from it by a brick path, was another building of the same general style as Harrison House. But instead of three rambling stories, this was a single story with a steeply gabled roof and brilliant white clapboard siding, its many windows framed by forest green shutters. The door was a vivid scarlet.

"The summer kitchen, I presume," Casey murmured.

Its footprint wasn't huge, although it still made at least four of his apartment. Casey could understand the logic: For its original use, it would have needed space for those massive wood stoves, and enough room around them that the servants wouldn't be parboiled by the time dessert rolled around.

That red door called to him and repelled him at the same time. He trotted across the expanse of grass toward it. It only made sense for him to at least peek inside, right? After all, he'd be stuck there for the next three months. Might as well see what he was in for.

When he was halfway there, though, he slowed, his hand pressed against his belly. What would greet him inside? Would it be like the kitchen at Chez Donatien, all long steel prep tables and glaring halogen lights? Trying to cook his father's food would be bad enough if he had to try to accomplish it in a place that echoed his worst childhood nightmares.

He crept forward until he reached the walkway. Up close, he saw that the bricks were laid out in a herringbone pattern of random red, gray, and black bricks. He swallowed and squared his shoulders before marching up the path and onto the summer kitchen's stoop. He laid his hand on the shiny brass doorknob. It turned easily under his hand, so either locking doors wasn't a thing in Home or else Pete was mistaken and Ms. Grande was awaiting him inside.

He winced. If that was the case, would she judge him for poking his nose in before she invited him? Was she the same kind of kitchen martinet as his father had been? He'd never have another chance to make a first impression on her, and he didn't want to screw it up before she'd ever sampled the horror that was Casey's cooking. Time enough for bad impressions the first time he dropped a skillet or cut his finger on a chef's knife or mistook oregano for basil.

Hey, that could happen to anybody. They smelled *exactly* the same.

So instead, Casey backed away and continued on around the house. This side didn't have another little porch, but a set of metal bulkhead doors stood open about halfway along. As Casey drew closer, he detected sounds coming from the doors: the clank of metal, a fuzzy burr interspersed with pops like frying bacon, and—oddly enough—a deep, rich voice singing a song from the same POV album Bradley'd had on repeat during the drive from New York.

Intrigued, Casey peered past the doors. A set of wide plank steps descended into what was clearly a basement. Maybe whoever was down there could tell him where to find Ms. Grande, or else point him to his room.

He crept down the stairs, one hand on the cool cement wall. This section of the basement was lined with metal shelving. Some of them held jars of preserved food—Casey spotted pickles, tomatoes, peaches, and green beans. Others were stacked with building materials and hardware—boxes of nails, coils of electrical wire, lumber arranged neatly by size. But no singer.

Casey stepped past a retaining wall and froze with a strangled cry.

In the center of the floor stood the Iron Giant.

The Giant's metal head nearly brushed the exposed ceiling joists. He wore a leather apron, leather gloves, and held a torch tipped with blue flame in one hand. His blank glass eyes were focused on the cage of metal clamped in a vise on the waist-high table in front of him.

The Giant looked up, and the song died. "Shit," he growled.

Casey dropped the lilacs and bolted.

Chapter Four

"*Damn* it." Dev shut off the welding torch and ripped off his helmet, taking some of his hair along with it. *Fuck. On top of everything else, I need a haircut.* He shucked off his gloves and tossed them aside, along with his apron, and strode for the stairs.

How had he forgotten that Sylvia's student was arriving and that Dev was supposed to greet him like a civilized person? He'd only gotten a glimpse before the man had run. From what he could tell, given the dim and distorted view through the welding helmet, the guy was probably about Kenny's size—five-ten or so and slender, with a mop of wavy hair.

Dev had caught the wide-eyed shock, though. He needed to catch up with the guy before he ran all the way back to wherever he'd come from. Sylvia needed the income, and frankly, so did Dev.

When he reached the stairs, his boot heel slid on something. Was that... Yes, it was. He picked up the crushed lilac spray, his heart constricting. The guy had obviously been having a moment, enjoying the house, enjoying the town, enjoying Dev's *home*, and Dev had spoiled it, just like he'd spoiled these flowers.

And since he'd spoiled it, he needed to fix it. Pronto.

He set the broken blooms aside gently, took the bulkhead stairs two at a time, and burst into the sunlight. He glanced sharply right and left, shielding his eyes with one hand. The summer kitchen door was closed. Had the student taken refuge there? Dev hesitated, but pivoted and took off in the other direction. If the guy was hiding out in the kitchen, he'd still be there after Dev circled the house. But if he was already in his car and burning rubber on his way out of town, Dev needed to head him off at the pass.

Fuck. He was hot and sweaty and covered with metal shavings. He knew from experience that when a guy his size barreled toward someone, people tended to jump to the wrong conclusions. So he slowed down and stopped, shielded from view by the white lilac bush.

He listened carefully—he didn't hear a car engine, although the sound of Pete's mower drifted from further down the street. He waved a bee away, but then scratched his head, staring at the flowers. *Lilacs.* Dev had scared the poor dude into dropping the ones he'd picked, so maybe offering up a bouquet would be a way to defuse the situation. Besides, who tried to stage an assault when they were carrying an armful of lilacs?

He pulled out his pocketknife and cut several sprays, then tucked the knife away, plastered a smile on his face, and rounded the corner to face…

…Absolutely nobody.

The lawn was empty and no car stood in the drive. He was too late, after all. "Shit." Sylvia would be devastated.

He let the hand clutching the flowers drop to his side, thumping them on his thigh for good measure and sending a cascade of white petals onto his work boots. Head down, he trudged toward the porch steps, and then froze when he caught something out of the corner of his eye.

Suitcases.

He hurried forward. Two suitcases and a messenger bag, with a faded red hoodie draped over the largest one. The knot in Dev's belly unraveled. Maybe it wasn't too late after all.

Although… Where was the guy's car? No flatlander Dev had ever met wanted to be stuck in Home with no means of escaping to marginally more cosmopolitan Merrilton. All of

Sylvia's previous students had arrived in laden vehicles, from vintage MGs to minivans. True, Pete's Uber-slash-Lyft business made people a little more mobile, but fuck. If it meant holding on to the sole student, Dev would drive the guy around himself.

"It'd be a break from staring at the damn budget all day," he muttered.

Voices drifted through Harrison House's screen door, followed by a burst of recognizable laughter.

Kenny. Dev heaved a relieved breath. If anyone could talk somebody off the ledge—any ledge—it was Kenny Li. He'd been doing it from the time they were kids, his sunny nature and nonjudgmental inclusion de-escalating more playground squabbles than all the school guidance counselors put together.

Dev suspected Kenny had helped his best friend, Mitch, figure out his sexuality when they were in high school. Neither one of them had ever said anything about it, but right after graduation, Mitch had taken off for college and his career as an openly gay geotechnical engineer who specialized in working in developing countries. Kenny had stayed in Home, taking over his family's fix-it shop, Make It Do, when his parents had retired to Arizona.

Since Dev didn't want to undo Kenny's work and scare the student—the *only* student—*again*, he eased up the steps as quietly as his size fourteen boots allowed, wincing at the creak he hadn't managed to fix in the top step.

When the voices inside didn't stop suddenly, he crept across the porch, straining his ears to hear the conversation. Yeah, maybe eavesdroppers rarely heard anything good about themselves, but he needed more ammunition if he expected to encourage the guy to stay for the entire Summer Kitchen session.

Students had bailed before, either because they found the curriculum too grueling—Summer Kitchen was a serious training school, not a carefree way to pass the time, drinking mimosas with friends while you gossiped over the pastry.

Sometimes, Sylvia had expelled them, although that had happened more often in the early days when students were still vying for one of the limited spots.

Dev angled himself so he could peer through the screen door without being *too* visible from inside. He couldn't see the student from this angle, only Kenny, standing next to an angular knee-high object that must be the new nightstand.

"Really?" Kenny asked between his signature chuckles.

"I'm sorry to say that it's true." The other man's voice was light and pleasant—*a tenor*—and held an undercurrent of amusement. "I mean, I'm not *totally* divorced from reality. I knew it couldn't *really* be the Iron Giant."

"I expect it was Dev in his welding gear."

"Dev?"

"Devondre Harrison. He's—" Kenny caught sight of Dev lurking outside the screen, his eyes widening comically behind his tortoiseshell glasses. "How about that? Here he is now."

After that intro, Dev could scarcely refuse to come inside. He opened the screen and stepped onto the entry's weathered oak floorboards, somehow recovering the smile he'd lost when he thought he'd scared the guy away.

"Dev, this is Casey Friel," Kenny said. "I was just telling him that you don't commonly keep robots or monsters in the basement to scare away the flatlanders, but I'm not sure he believed me."

Dev tried to make a comeback to Kenny's snark—he'd had plenty of practice over the years—but somehow he couldn't make *words*. Because Casey Friel had to be the absolute embodiment of Dev's perfect man.

His impression of somebody Kenny's size was correct. Casey was the same height, and like Kenny, his body was wiry rather than muscled. While Casey had soft brown curls to Kenny's shiny, board-straight black hair, they both wore it a little overlong and shaggy rather than close-cropped like Dev's usual style.

But Dev had never felt the least stirring of lust for Kenny, maybe because they were practically brothers, growing up together as they had. Casey, though...

Dev belatedly shifted the lilacs to in front of his waist like a fucking bridal bouquet, because something about Casey's wide, guileless hazel eyes, the spray of freckles across his nose, the quirk of his mouth that made one side of his lips tilt up higher than the other... Well, Dev definitely needed the groin camouflage.

Casey's crooked smile faded—*no!*—and Dev realized he'd been holding out his hand for Dev to shake while Dev had been juggling lilacs and indulging in insta-fantasies. Casey started to drop his hand, but Dev lunged forward to catch it in his own.

"Hey. Hi. Welcome home." Dev grimaced. "I mean *to* Home. Welcome to Home."

Casey's smile returned, although it was a little shaky. "Thank you." He cut a sidelong glance at Kenny.

Shit. Was I too weird? I was too weird. Dev thrust out the lilacs. "I cut some flowers. For you." As Casey gazed at the lilacs, and Kenny gave Dev a *what is* wrong *with you?* stare, one of the clusters fell off its stem and dropped onto the floor at Casey's feet. "They, um, looked better a couple of minutes ago. They had an unfortunate encounter with my leg."

"Yes," Kenny drawled, amusement dancing in his dark eyes. "I always pick flowers with my feet too."

Dev glared at Kenny. "My *leg*. Not my feet."

"Contrary to what you might think, Dev, that doesn't sound any less ridiculous." He turned to Casey. "I promise that Dev is ordinarily much more lucid." He grinned at Dev. "Welding mask too tight, Dev? Bring it down to Make It Do and I'll adjust it so it's not squeezing your brain."

Dev did *not* glare at Kenny, although he sent him a mental *shut the fuck up*. "Sorry. Got a lot on my mind at the moment." Like what Casey's ass might look like when he turned around.

"No worries. It was really nice of you to pick these for me, considering I *did* kinda barge in on you. I'm sorry about that, by the way. But what can I say?" He spread his hands, palms up. "I'm nosy, and since nobody was here to tell me I couldn't, I decided to explore."

"No, *I'm* sorry about that. Sylvia asked me to look out for you, but she also needed a shelf repaired in the summer kitchen —"

"A repair?" Kenny frowned. "Why didn't she ask me to do it?"

"Maybe because it's in my house?" Dev said dryly, "and I'm not totally incompetent? Besides, you fix movable *things*. Not buildings."

Kenny wrinkled his nose, causing his glasses to rise toward his eyebrows. "Technically, a shelf is a *thing*, even if it's attached to the wall, but I'll concede that you know your way around a hammer."

"I decided to fabricate a metal unit, anyway." He glanced at Casey. "That's why I was in my welding gear. I'm sorry I frightened you."

Casey chuckled, a warm, infectious sound that made Dev want to join in. "If I hadn't already been feeling guilty about snooping, I doubt I'd have fled the way I did." He reached out and took the flowers. "Thanks for these. I confess I picked one of the magenta ones, but I dropped it." He lowered his face to the blooms and inhaled, his eyes fluttering closed. And really, was it *legal* to have eyelashes that long? "They smell heavenly." He looked up, grinning. "Way better than the average Manhattan stairwell."

Dev returned the grin. "Anything would be better than that. Although I understand some city folk actually prefer it."

"Don't say *anything*," Kenny said with a shudder. "Remember when the wind shifted right after that faux-organic farm over the border in Massachusetts spread a load of fresh manure on their forty-acre field?"

Casey's eyes widened. "Is that, er, something that happens often?"

Kenny shook his head, his smile sly. "No. Our town manager"—he made a gesture to Dev worthy of a game show host—"had a little chat with them about alternative fertilizers and we haven't had a recurrence."

Casey's smile dawned again. "You're the town manager? Wait... Dev *Harrison*. As in Harrison House?"

"Guilty," Dev said. "And for the rest of the summer, mi casa es su casa."

Casey's sigh could only be described as delighted. "I *love* this house." His smile faded and his eyebrows pinched together. "I should ask, though. Are there places that are off-limits? I warned you I was nosy, but I'm capable of respecting boundaries, too."

"Everything in Harrison House is fair game to anyone residing here."

"But what about your room? Shouldn't that be private?"

Dev shook his head. "I don't live in the house. I live in a cottage on the other side of the back meadow, behind that stand of birch and maple. I've got an office here in the house, but unless you're fascinated by very depressing spreadsheets, you won't find anything interesting there."

The smile that lit Casey's face was kid-at-Christmas worthy. "This whole house to myself for three whole months? Outstanding!"

"I should warn you that the place has been mostly shut up for a while. My brother had plans for some major renovations, so the third floor is basically gutted, and unless you're a fan of spiders, you probably should steer clear. But the common areas on the first floor are habitable, as are the second floor bedrooms for the most part. Laundry facilities in the basement"—Dev grinned—"accessed from the kitchen stairs, not the bulkhead. The bedroom you'll be staying in is in pretty good shape, except it needed a new nightstand."

"Which I have right here." Kenny patted the satiny top of the two-drawer Shaker-style unit next to him.

Dev studied it, eyes narrowing. "Kenny," he growled.

"What?" Kenny's innocent tone wouldn't fool anybody. The flush along his cheekbones was a giveaway, too.

"That is not the nightstand we agreed on."

"We never *agreed* on anything, Dev. *Agreeing* presupposes a *conversation* and a mutually accepted conclusion. You just pointed me to a website and said, '*This one.*'"

"Which this definitely is not."

"No, it isn't. Seriously, Dev. IKEA? I have standards, you know."

Dev ran a hand through his hair. No way could he afford this, not with the specter of Port-a-Potties looming over his head. "Kenny."

Kenny ignored Dev and turned to smile at Casey. "I spotted it at an estate sale and knew it would be a great fit for Harrison House."

"An estate sale? Really?" Casey traced a swirl in the wood grain on the nightstand's top. "It's so perfect that it looks brand new."

Kenny cleared his throat. "Well, that's kind of my business. My grandparents named the shop Make It Do because of that old New Englander motto: Use it up, wear it out, make it do, or do without."

"This isn't just making something do," Dev said, pointing at the little chest of drawers. "It's beautiful. Way too good for Harrison House."

Kenny rallied, propping his hands on his hips. "Are you saying it's too good for Casey's bedroom?"

Dev retreated a step. "N-n-no. Of course not. Nothing's too good for Casey's bedroom. I mean, for our guests."

Casey shook his head, chuckling again, and Dev was reminded of water running over the stones in the creek behind his cottage. "You don't have to make much effort for me. I'm not that hard to please. Although I think you're wrong about it being too good for Harrison House." His eyes widened and he flailed, scattering lilac florets on the floor. "I'm not saying that the nightstand isn't gorgeous, because it is. I'm just saying that this house deserves all the love anyone can throw at it."

Kenny held out both hands in a *see there?* gesture. "What have I told you? You see Harrison House through the eyes of familiarity, Dev. But other people see it as the remarkable thing it is." Kenny stuck his nose in the air. "So suck it up. You're getting a nightstand upgrade."

Dev grimaced. "There's a reason I asked for that specific unit, Kenny. There's no way my budget can stretch to anything this nice."

Kenny waved Dev's protest away. "Same price as the soulless IKEA kit."

Dev shared a conspiratorial glance with Casey. "He *never* charges people enough."

Kenny glared at him. "My rates are perfectly fine."

"They were fine for your *grandparents*. Your parents should have raised them years ago."

"Let's not talk about that. Make yourself useful, Iron Giant —"

"Oh, don't," Casey cried.

"—and carry the nightstand up to Casey's room."

"I can do that." Dev glanced through the screen door at the luggage still sitting at the foot of the porch stairs. "I'll haul your bags up too."

"You don't have to do that. I mean, I can't ask the *town manager* to carry my beater suitcases."

"I don't mind."

And I need to get my head on straight. Because as attractive as Dev found Casey, he had enough on his plate without adding a time-boxed relationship to the mix. In fact, the more distance he kept between them, the better. As of tomorrow, Casey would be Sylvia's responsibility. Best begin as he meant to go on.

"Kenny, why don't you take Casey with you and show him the sights of Home?"

"All two of them, you mean?"

"I mean, give him the nickel tour. Show him the Market. Your place. Ty's clinic."

"The shuttered Inn?"

Dev lowered his chin and glared at Kenny from under his lowered brows. "Kenny. Behave."

"Right, right." He gestured to Casey. "Step right up for the official Home tour. Don't worry. You'll be back in ten minutes."

Casey glanced from Dev to Kenny. "Are you sure?"

Dev smiled at him as he hefted the nightstand, which was—*oof*—heavier than it looked. The damn thing must be solid oak. "I'm sure. I probably won't be around when you get back, but make yourself at home." He nodded at the stairwell. "Your room is the first on the left at the top of the first flight."

"Okay," Casey said, sounding doubtful. "Thank you very much."

"No problem. And Kenny? If you see Randolph Scott around, Ty's looking for him."

Kenny scrunched up his face. "Let me guess. Vaccinations?"

Dev nodded. "Rabies."

"Well, with all the rodents Randolph Scott massacres, we can't skip that, now, can we? I'll keep my eyes open for him."

"Thanks, man." Dev nodded at Casey. "See you around."

Despite his arms shaking with the weight of the nightstand, Dev waited at the foot of the stairs until Kenny and Casey walked out the door, and as a result, had a perfect view of Casey's backside.

His ass was just as perfect as Dev had imagined.

I am in deep shit.

Chapter Five

Casey kept pace with Kenny as they trotted down the wide porch steps, managing—just barely—not to glance back for another Dev ogle. "Randolph Scott?"

Kenny laughed. "I guess you could call Randolph Scott the town cat, a big ginger longhair. He seems to belong to everyone and no one at the same time." Kenny shoved his hands in the pockets of jeans even more worn than Casey's. "Nobody knows where he spends his nights, but you're likely to see him just about anywhere around Home during the day."

They followed the curve of the drive, their shoes crunching in the gravel. "So. Dev?"

Kenny grinned. "He's siiingle," he caroled, "if that's what you're asking."

Heat rose up Casey's throat. The only upside to his tendency to blush at the drop of an innuendo was that it camouflaged his freckles. Sort of.

He couldn't deny that he *had* been fishing, though, but who could blame him? Dev was a *fine* hunk of man: those broad shoulders, those golden-brown eyes, the black hair just long enough to curl, the warm brown skin. *Yum.*

Casey would be the first to admit that he had a definite thing for big men. Some of his friends his own size or smaller questioned him about it constantly: "Dude, he could crush you like a bug!"

But Casey had never associated big men with danger. In fact, the pastry chef who'd been his champion and protector in his dad's kitchen had been even bigger than Dev. It was men his own size—like his father—who represented danger to him.

Conditioning. What could you do?

Just as Donald's rigid rules about food had fueled Casey's eating disorder, so had Donald's physical intimidation colored Casey's taste in men. Sue him, he was a product of his environment, and while his therapist had helped him with the eating aversion, the two of them had never discussed Casey's attraction to big protectors.

Probably because that wasn't something she expected to address with a ten-year-old.

However, Dev's relationship status hadn't been the only thing Casey was curious about, and Kenny seemed inclined to spill the tea. Did it make Casey a bad person that he intended to take full advantage?

"Thanks for that—I mean, really. Thanks. But I was actually wondering about the bigger picture. Harrison House, for instance. Dev mentioned his brother. Is he away? Is that why the third floor renovations are on hold?"

As they stepped out onto the sidewalk, Kenny grimaced. "You could say so." He pointed to the sidewalk, which wasn't concrete like New York pavement, but slabs of veined white stone. "Watch out for the sidewalks in the rain. It's marble from the old quarry and slippery as all get-out."

Marble sidewalks. Seriously? "Noted, and again, thanks. But why do I get the feeling you're dodging the question?"

Kenny heaved a sigh. "Dodging the feelings, more like. Garlan died a year and a half ago."

Casey froze mid-step and turned to Kenny. "I'm so sorry. You don't have to talk about it if you don't want to."

He shook his head, gesturing for them to continue down the street, although he set a pace so leisurely it almost qualified as slo-mo. "No. You'll be in Home for the summer, living right in Harrison House, so it's best if you know the story." His gaze lifted, and he seemed focused somewhere over the treetops at the end of Main Street. "Home is... unique. The town was founded in 1791 by Dev's ancestor, Persistence Harrison, a minister whose interpretations of the scripture were decidedly unpopular with his Boston community."

"Was he fire and brimstone?"

"Quite the opposite. He never believed in the punitive school of religious zeal. He fell squarely on the side of love-your-brother and do-unto-others. He also fell in love with a Pequot woman and ran afoul of the Massachusetts law against interracial marriage. So he and his congregation pulled up stakes and moved out of Massachusetts and into Vermont, where they could make their own community, their own rules." Kenny smiled crookedly. "Did you know that Vermont is one of the few states in the US that's never had anti-miscegenation laws on the books?"

Casey blinked. "No. I did not."

"Well, Persistence accepted anyone into his flock who was ready to live and let live, and his descendants fully embraced his vision. Harrison House was even a stop on the Underground Railroad. His great-great-grandson married one of the former slaves who decided to stay."

"Really? That's... wow."

Kenny grinned. "I know, right? They've always offered a home to anyone who didn't belong elsewhere—hence the town's name. It's actually written into the town charter, the original of which hangs over the fireplace in the Harrison House living room, right opposite a cross-stitch sampler that Dev's mother made with the town's *un*official motto: *Welcome Home. Don't be a dick.*"

Casey laughed. "Nice."

"Totally." Kenny held out his fist for Casey to bump. "The only people who were refused residence were those who weren't willing to follow that fundamental principle. Persistence's wife's sibling was two-natured, so there was queer representation as far back as the first settlers. That openness, that welcome, as well as the diversity, has continued ever since."

Casey swallowed against a throat gone tight. A whole town dedicated to *acceptance*. How cool was that? Man, his father would have *hated* it here.

"We had an influx of new residents after the World Wars, for instance," Kenny continued. "German-Americans who were run out of towns they'd lived in all their lives. Japanese-Americans released from internment camps with nowhere else to go. That's when my great-grandparents moved here. They were Chinese, but after the war, most people tarred any Asian with the Pearl Harbor brush."

"Wow."

"From the beginning, there's always been a Harrison at the helm." He wrinkled his nose. "Persistence was blind in one area, though—stupid primogeniture traditions. Ownership of Harrison House and responsibility for the town always goes to the eldest son. Dev is the younger of two. Since their dad was killed in action in the Gulf, his elder brother, Garlan, was groomed by their grandfather to take over from the time they were kids."

"Ouch. That sucks."

Kenny chuckled. "Actually, it suited them both just fine. Garlan, as first-born kids often are, had a definite control-freak side, and Dev… Well, he had other ambitions, other plans, that didn't include becoming the de facto Daddy to a town full of obstinate eccentrics." Kenny sighed. "All that changed when a semi skidded on the ice out by the quarry and plowed into Garlan's car, killing him and his grandfather instantly."

"That's awful."

"Yeah. The roads around here can be… Well, let's just say it's a good thing you're here during the summer and leave it at that. Anyway, Dev's been taking care of the place ever since. Which" —Kenny's smile was *definitely* sly—"is why Dev's single. His boyfriend objected strongly to Dev's decision to come home."

"Then I'm guessing said boyfriend wouldn't be welcome, anyway."

Kenny shot Casey a puzzled glance. "What do you mean?"

"He failed the unofficial motto test, of course. I mean, what's more dickish than not standing behind your partner when they experience hardship?" Casey caught a movement out of the corner of his eye and dared a quick look behind them. "Don't look now," he whispered, "but we've got a tail."

Kenny, to his credit, *didn't* look. "Randolph Scott?"

"Mmmhmmm. Unless Home's got another feline resident with a tail like a ginger squirrel's and a notch out of one ear."

Kenny bit his lip, brows bunched, then gave a tiny nod. "Okay. I was planning to take you to the Market and introduce you to Kat, the proprietor, but since we've collected a different sort of cat? Change of plan." Kenny veered off the sidewalk and cut across the wide lawn in front of a yellow Victorian with pristine white trim and a discreet sign that read *Home Historical Society.* "He still following?"

Casey dared another glance. "Yup. Where are we going?"

"Harrison Veterinary Clinic. It's on East Road."

Casey matched Kenny's casual amble. "Another Harrison?"

"Dev's cousin Ty."

"But if there was already a Harrison in town, why did Dev have to come home to run things?"

Kenny snorted. "Primogeniture, remember? Ty's not in the main hereditary line. He's actually Dev's second cousin. His grandfather was Dev's grandfather's adopted brother. He wouldn't be on the hook unless something happened to Dev, too."

"Why don't you change that rule? It seems like you risk getting saddled with poor or corrupt government when you're operating under a divine-right-of-Harrisons thing."

"Oh trust me, they've tried—the family, not the town. But every time the current Harrison-in-charge brings it up, the town votes it down again. It's almost a superstition with them now. As long as there's a Harrison at the helm, Home will be okay."

They emerged onto a narrower street, also tree-lined and shady. This side held several houses, but opposite them was a rambling, single-storied structure and behind it, a fenced area that ran the length of the short street. Barks, yips, and the occasional howl permeated the air, and Casey spotted several dogs racing along the fence.

"Harrison Veterinary Clinic, I presume?"

"Yep. Randolph Scott still there?"

"Yes, but he's got misgivings if the judgmental tilt of his ears is anything to go by."

"Hmmm. He's quicker than he looks, so we need to plan this." Kenny pulled his phone out of his back pocket and touched the screen. "Ty? We're out front with Randolph Scott. What's the game plan?" Kenny glanced back at the cat, who had sat down and shot out a rear paw, digging between some extremely impressive claws with his teeth. "Seriously? *That's* your plan?" He sighed. "Fine. But don't dawdle." He disconnected the call. "We're supposed to detain him."

"Us and what army?" Casey glanced down at the cat, who had moved on to the other paw. "Unless you've got a machete in your pocket, he's way better armed than we are. His feet are enormous."

"Polydactyly," Kenny said. "He's got six toes on each front paw."

Just then, Randolph Scott looked up and met Casey's gaze with wide golden eyes. "Uh oh. I think we've been made. Should we run for it?"

Kenny laughed, although it sounded to Casey as though there were an edge to it. "Nah. If he had it in for you, you'd know. He tends to express his disapprobation with dismembered rodents."

"Good to know." Casey glanced sidelong at Kenny as Randolph Scott sauntered forward, his tail in the air. Casey had never had a pet—his father claimed cats shed, dogs were too needy, and fish belonged on a plate with lemon.

While he was gathering ammunition to try to change his dad's mind—which had never happened, and not just about pets—Casey had watched a ton of videos on all kinds of domestic animals. He remembered that cats were evolutionarily wired to expect danger from above, so he took a sustaining breath and lowered himself to his haunches. Slowly.

"Hey, boy." He held out his hand, palm down, careful to keep it below the level of Randolph Scott's eyes. "I'm Casey."

The cat dabbed at Casey's fingers with his nose, then ducked his head under Casey's palm and nudged it imperiously, a purr that rivaled Pete's mower vibrating Casey's hand. Smile dawning, Casey obeyed the order and stroked the ginger fur, scratching behind the notched ear. "Wow. His fur is so soft."

"It is now." Kenny knelt down next to Casey. "Wait until the end of summer when the grasses go to seed. He gets covered in burrs. It takes Ty forever to get them out, since Randolph Scott scorns brushes."

"If I'm still around, I'll help. I don't mind. I like—"

A light brown hand reached over Casey's shoulder and scooped up the cat. By the time Casey registered what had happened, Randolph Scott was already on the ground again, shaking his leg before casting one baleful glance over his shoulder and darting off under a hydrangea bush. Casey rose reluctantly to face the owner of the hand, who was capping an empty syringe.

"Thanks, guys. He's been dodging me all week." He held out a hand. "Ty Harrison. You must be Sylvia's student."

Casey shook, trying not to be too obvious about comparing Ty to his cousin. While he was about Dev's height, or maybe an inch or two shorter, his eyes were more almond-shaped, his skin a couple of shades lighter, and his black hair straight, not curly. Their broad cheekbones were the same, however, as were the golden-brown eyes.

"That's me. Casey Friel. Nice to meet you." He glanced at the bushes, which were shaking alarmingly. "Is he going to hate me now?"

"Nah." Ty brandished the syringe. "He knows who to blame. You, he likes, or he wouldn't have let you pet him. Be careful or you'll find him underfoot constantly now."

Casey smiled. "I don't mind. I always wanted a pet when I was a kid, but my dad wouldn't allow it."

Ty gestured to his office. "I run a no-kill shelter out of my practice and I'm always looking for volunteers to socialize with the animals, so if you're ever in need of some one-on-one furbaby time, you're welcome to stop in."

Casey shrugged apologetically. "I kind of doubt I'll have much free time, but if I do, I'll keep it in mind."

"Excellent. Now, since you two have done me a signal service, allow me to buy you the beverage of your choice from the Market." Ty patted Casey's shoulder. "I'm impressed with how you charmed Randolph Scott, but if you can work the same magic on Kat Hathaway, I'm nominating you for sainthood."

Chapter Six

Sylvia hadn't returned after her meeting, which wasn't unusual since she often met with her sponsor afterward before returning to her home outside Merrilton. Her absence had given Dev the perfect excuse for avoiding the summer kitchen—and its tempting new student—for the rest of the day, although he could pinpoint the exact moment Casey entered his room in Harrison House.

Not that I'll ever admit it out loud.

He wished he could convince Sylvia move to Home—he had at least half a dozen Harrison properties with no current tenants —but Sylvia insisted she wanted to keep where she lived separate from both work and her ongoing recovery.

Maybe someday, if Dev could figure out how to bring more activities to town that were interesting but still maintained the town's atmosphere, Sylvia would reconsider. Since he'd been racking his brains for *that* Holy Grail from the moment he'd arrived following Garlan's death, however, he didn't really expect to have a sudden epiphany.

It was still on his mind, though—along with that tantalizing glimpse of Casey's ass—as he pounded down the street at dawn the next day on his morning run. He'd made the circuit of West Road and was on his way back, slowing to a stop as usual by the small marble plaque that marked where Garlan and Grandfather had gone off the road.

As he crouched to run a finger across the date carved into the surface, Ty emerged from the path down to the flooded quarry, shirtless, his skin still glistening with water from his swim and, for some reason, holding a battered cardboard box and wearing a thunderous scowl.

"Hey." Dev stood and nodded at the box. "People leaving trash by the quarry again?"

Ty grunted. "Give me your T-shirt."

"What?"

Ty thrust out his hand. "Just give me your damn T-shirt, Dev."

Clearly, Ty was in one of his moods. "Fine." He skinned off his T-shirt—he was overheated anyway—and handed it over. "Although if you're chilly, you should bring your own shirt next time. Or, you know, a towel."

Ty snatched the shirt with another grunt—he never wasted his bedside manner on actual humans—and hunkered down, setting the box on a patch of coltsfoot. Instead of donning the shirt himself, however, he laid it inside the box and lifted out—

"Holy shit. Is that a kitten?" The little scrap of sodden fur was smaller than Ty's palm and seemed composed entirely of a wide, pink mouth and tiny white teeth.

"Yes. I scared the asshole away before he could toss the rest of them in."

"The rest?" Dev knelt next to Ty. Two other kittens—a brown tabby and a black and white tuxedo—peered up at him with round blue eyes. Their ears hadn't migrated to the tops of their heads yet, so they had to be young. "Christ. Are they even weaned?"

Ty cradled the wet kitten against his chest as he blotted its fur. "Not a chance."

Dev swallowed against a surge of anger. "The mother?"

"Don't know. I didn't see a body in the water, but that doesn't mean much. He could have weighted her down. It's happened before. People from as far away as Rutland use this as a dumping ground." Ty glared down the road toward Home. "The shelter is *literally* half a mile away. There's no reason for this kind of cruelty unless you're a fucking serial killer in the making."

"Did you get a good look at the guy?" Dev's own scowl deepened. "It wasn't someone from Home, was it?"

Ty fried him with his death glare. "Of course not." He placed the mostly dry kitten—another brown tabby—in the box with its siblings and tucked Dev's T-shirt around all three of them. "I didn't recognize him. I don't suppose you saw an unfamiliar car on the highway?"

"I stayed off the highway until just now, so no." He waited until Ty hefted the box again. "Have you got enough volunteers to bottle-feed three more kittens?"

"I'll manage." Ty didn't look at him, which probably meant no. Most of his volunteers were high school kids, so round-the-clock care would fall on him again.

"If you need help…"

Ty shot him a wry smile. "You know I can hear the terror in your voice, right?" He gave the box a gentle pat. "You don't need to sacrifice yourself. Between Val and me, we can wrangle the livestock. You've got enough to do handling the human contingent."

"I wouldn't mind, you know. I don't have your deep and abiding love for all things furred and feathered—"

"Don't forget scaled. I don't discriminate against fish and reptiles."

"—but I'm not down with animal cruelty either."

Ty's smile turned fond. "I know. And if I *really* needed help, I'd ask. Which favor, by the way"—his eyes narrowed—"I'd expect you to return. We're family, Dev. You need me? I'm there."

"Thanks, man. Appreciate it."

"Appreciate it all you want as long as you actually *take advantage* of it."

As they rounded the corner onto East Road and Ty's clinic came into view, a familiar furry orange form stood up on the porch and trotted down the steps. Randolph Scott stopped right in front of them, blocking the sidewalk, and looked up, his gaze riveted on the box, ears twitching at the frantic cheeping coming from inside.

Dev bent down to give the cat's ears a skritch. "I thought you said he was avoiding you because of the S-H-O-T?"

Ty lifted a brow. "I'm not sure whether to be worried that you think it's necessary to spell out *shot* in front of him or that you don't realize he understands it when you spell it out anyway. Besides, that's taken care of." *Now* his smile was definitely evil. "Kenny and your new boarder stepped in. Mission accomplished."

Dev's skin heated more than he could blame on the early sunlight. "He's not my boarder. He's Sylvia's student." *Whom I'm avoiding like a lovesick junior high kid.*

"But he's living in Harrison House, and you own the place, so he's your boarder." Ty's grin grew. "And may I say that the scenery around Harrison House is definitely looking up?"

"Why? You looking for a date?" Dev growled, and then he grimaced. *Make that a* jealous *lovesick junior high kid.*

Ty scoffed. "Not me. I'm happy on my own. Anyway, sex is overrated." He tapped the box with one finger. "Look at the trouble my patients get in because of it. But you?" He knelt down and lowered the box so Randolph Scott could inspect the kittens. "You aren't meant to fly solo."

Dev snorted at Ty's comment as well as at Randolph Scott's expression of outraged betrayal. "I tried the duo flight once. Didn't work out."

"It didn't work out because Nash Tambling is a fucking narcissistic diva with a much higher opinion of his own talent than it deserves. Casey seems like someone who isn't blinded by the glow of his own self-importance. He's nice." Ty waggled his eyebrows. "And has an ass even finer than Kenny's."

Dev peered down at him, eyebrows climbing. "You're checking out Kenny's ass?"

Ty stood up again and tucked the box of kittens under his arm. "I told you. I can enjoy the scenery even when I have no desire to do anything about it. Besides, Kenny is off-limits."

"Why? Because he's practically our brother?"

"Because, oh oblivious one, he's already taken." Ty walked up the steps to the clinic, leaving Dev standing with his jaw sagging.

"Kenny's seeing somebody? Who? How did I not know this?" Ty didn't turn around, so Dev raised his voice. "Is the guy good enough for him? He's not good enough. He can't be good enough. That's why you didn't say anything."

Ty stood in the open door. "If Kenny wants you to know, he'll tell you. Now go home. You've got a boarder to ogle." He stepped inside and shut the door.

"I don't ogle," Dev muttered. He took Randolph Scott's *mew* as agreement and stalked off down East Road, cutting through the Historical Society side yard to Main Street with Randolph Scott trotting along at his heels. "Although if I *did*," he said to the cat, "Casey would be a prime candidate."

He came out onto the sidewalk next to the Market just as Casey was trotting down its steps, a to-go cup in his hands. His steps slowed when he spotted Dev and his eyes widened, a blush painting his cheeks.

Shit. Heat rushed up Dev's throat too. Had Casey heard Dev talking to the cat about him? *How about did he hear me talking to the cat, full stop?*

"G-good morning." Casey lifted his cup. "I was just fortifying myself with a latte for my first day in Summer Kitchen."

Dev winced. "Shit. I didn't give you the house orientation last night, did I?" He'd been so fixated on, well, *not* fixating, that he'd completely neglected his duties to Casey as a Harrison House guest. "You've got free use of the House kitchen. Since you're the only one staying there now, the fridge is all yours, and the pantry—"

"Don't worry." Casey took a sip of his latte. "I found the House manual when I was snooping. That's a great idea, by the way, having all the information collected and accessible like that."

"Thanks. That was my mom's idea, actually." Dev chuckled despite the usual pang under his heart over his mother's absence. "She got tired of everybody asking her where the sugar was."

"Well, she deserves a medal."

"She did."

Casey blinked up at Dev. "Oh. I'm sorry. I didn't realize she was—"

"She's not." When Casey flinched at the sharpness of Dev's tone, Dev cringed himself. "Sorry. Didn't mean to snap. Mom's not gone. I mean, she's gone from Home, but still living." Maybe someday Dev could convince her to come back, if only during the summer. After Garlan and Grandfather's accident, coming so soon after the one that led to the Inn's closing, she'd declared she never wanted to see ice and snow again. Dev cleared his throat. "You heading back to the house?"

"To the summer kitchen, yes." He began edging down the sidewalk. "I should probably get moving. Wouldn't want to be late."

Dev fell into step beside Casey, who blushed even rosier before shifting his gaze to his feet. "Nervous about your first day?"

"You have no idea." Casey clutched his cup in both hands, cradling it against his chest. "This whole thing has disaster written all over it."

"What whole thing?" Dev bristled a bit. If Casey was talking about Home…

"The whole thing where I'm supposed to become a Michelin-worthy chef in three months." He gazed around at Main Street, with its retro streetlamps and wide greensward dotted with maples and wooden benches. "If I never had to actually cook anything, this would be like heaven."

Dev frowned. "Wait a minute. You have to do what?"

"You heard me." Casey heaved a sigh. "You ever heard of Donald Friel?"

"The chef?" When Casey nodded, Dev smacked his forehead. "Friel. Casey Friel. You're related?"

Casey nodded. "His son. His flagship restaurant closed after his heart attack. Having the chef drop dead in the middle of dinner service has a deleterious effect on reservations. Go figure. But my uncle, who's Dad's twin, is determined to reopen it with the same menu and another Friel at the helm. In other words—" He pointed to himself, wrinkling his nose, which was... ridiculously adorable. "—me. Apparently, it's a publicity goldmine. Or it will be until the diners get a taste of my cooking."

They'd reached Harrison House, and Casey hesitated by the front steps.

"Good luck then," Dev said.

"Thanks. Thoughts and prayers wouldn't hurt either, if you've got any to spare." Casey glanced at the walkway that led to the summer kitchen with what looked like real trepidation. "Or maybe spells and incantations. Because trust me, I need all the help I can get."

Chapter Seven

His morning latte heating one hand and a frosty bottle of water chilling the other, Casey loitered by the Market's screen door, counting down the seconds.

Three... two... one...

"Bye, Kat," he called to the Market's prickly proprietor. "See you tomorrow."

Kat, arranging artisan Scottish shortbread next to the Oreos on her eclectic cookie shelves, merely *hmmph*ed, but he detected a twinkle in her eyes above her cheaters.

Yeah, he wasn't fooling her for a second.

As he had for the two weeks since he'd arrived in Home, Casey stepped out onto the porch at precisely 7:35, the exact time Dev trotted into view next to the Historical Society building.

Gotta love a man committed to a routine.

Casey didn't bother to pretend it was an accident, the way he had the first couple of days, because, for one thing, water bottle. For another, there was no point. Nobody could be here at exactly the same time every day without some effort.

When he was feeling optimistic, Casey dared hope that Dev timed his runs to end at 7:35 just so they'd run into one another, but he figured that was wishful thinking. After all, Dev probably made this same run every day of the year. Casey had only been privileged to catch the end of it for fourteen days.

"Morning, Dev." He held out the water. "Good run?"

Dev grinned and accepted the bottle. "Yep." He uncapped the water and gulped about half of it down. Casey forbore from sighing at the way his throat worked, the sheen of sweat that made his dark skin glow, the curls rumpled by his workout. Sadly, he hadn't been shirtless since that first day. Casey wondered if there was some way to encourage a repeat, but since he didn't know what had caused it in the first place, he contented himself with appreciating the play of Dev's muscles under the snug fabric.

The two of them fell into step as usual, heading back toward Harrison House and Casey's daily purgatory. Mid-June in Home was even more glorious than the end of May had been, the air softer, the breeze lighter, the grass greener. Also as usual, Randolph Scott appeared out of nowhere to trot along between them like some kind of furry ginger chaperone.

Dev glanced down at the cat and chuckled. "He's really taken a liking to you."

"I think he's taken a liking to the treats I slip him, not me per se." Casey bit his lip. "It won't hurt him, will it? People food?"

"I don't think so, although Ty's the one you ought to check with." Dev chuckled again, a seductive burr that made Casey want to join in. "I've lost count of the times he's informed me that cats are obligate carnivores."

"They're what now?"

Dev grinned down at Casey and Casey had to suppress another sigh. "Means they need meat to survive. You should have heard him ranting at the vegan couple who were insisting that everyone in their household—including their newly adopted kitten—eat vegan too."

Casey laughed. "I'm guessing it didn't go well."

"Not for the couple. Ty accused them of animal cruelty, which, considering, you know, *vegan*, was quite the shock for them."

"Did they agree to feed the cat meat?"

"They didn't get the chance. Ty rescinded their adoption, took the kitten back, and found a different home for her."

Casey shook his head. "I've gotta say that always surprises me."

"About Ty getting militant? You've been here long enough to know how he feels about his patients."

"No. I mean how much everybody in Home *cares*. About their friends, their neighbors, their jobs. I bet something like a poorly matched kitten adoption happening in New York would pass unnoticed."

"Maybe, maybe not. But the people who live in Home are invested in the place, in what it's always stood for."

Casey smiled up at him. "Making Home a home, whether you have two legs or four."

Dev grimaced. "Although the six-legged residents can be a big pain in the ass. Black fly season is no joke. And the mosquitos? Well, let's just say that Ty's bat house initiative got a *lot* of support!"

They reached Harrison House's drive, and Casey sighed, shoulders sagging.

Dev's brows pinched together. "Something wrong?"

"Cooking," Casey said glumly.

"What's Sylvia got you whipping up today?"

"It's actually her day off. I'm using it to practice, because goodness knows I need it." He forced a laugh, although it was a pretty poor effort. "She's been very patient with me, but I think she's secretly appalled at what she's undertaken."

"I'm sure it's not that bad." Dev's tone could only be described as *hearty*. "I mean, the summer kitchen is still standing. Which reminds me. I finished building that shelf unit. Would I disturb you if I came over and installed it today?"

"Not a bit." *I'll be grateful for the distraction.* "Come on over any time."

Dev lifted his water bottle. "Thanks again for the water. Hope you put it on my Market account."

Casey merely hummed in response, because of course he hadn't, despite Dev's insistence. The eye candy and the company more than compensated for the cost of the water. Casey needed the boost to face the ordeal ahead.

Dev loped off across the field toward his cottage, and Casey watched him go. Not only because the view was spectacular—and the meadow dotted with wildflowers wasn't bad either—but because it meant he was free from the summer kitchen for a few more precious minutes.

That red door had started to loom in Casey's nightmares since his first day, when Sylvia had conducted what she called some basic evaluations.

She'd had him dice an onion—and had to lead him to the eyewash station when he'd absently wiped his streaming eyes with an onion-tainted finger. When he'd tried caramel, it crystalized in the pan three times and burned on the fourth. A basic roux should have been simple, she'd said, but Casey managed to set off the kitchen's smoke alarm. Twice.

On the bright side, Dev hadn't been home to witness it, and the firefighters from the county station were very nice and not at all judgmental.

After his abysmal attempt at a galette de rois, she'd sat him down for a little chat.

"Casey." She folded her hands on the marble pastry board, which was still littered with the remains of Casey's puff pastry fail. "What the hell are you doing here?"

He grinned weakly. "Learning to cook?"

She studied her hands for a moment, sighed, and then met his eyes again. "My dear, there are people who are born to cook. People who can achieve reasonable competence. But you?"

"If we're going all Shakespearean here, you could say I've had cooking thrust upon me." He toyed with a scrap of pastry that resembled shoe leather. "I know I've got a lot to learn—"

"Sweetheart, you have *everything* to learn."

"I know," he said humbly.

She half stood and grasped his wrist with a floury hand. "Cooking at the Michelin level isn't like the alphabet or basic math. For one thing, mastery and success aren't as well-defined. For another, you can survive perfectly happily in the world without it. There's no reason you should spend so much time and..." She let go and sat back on her stool with a sigh. "I probably shouldn't say this because I need the tuition, but why spend so much money on something that you quite obviously hate? It might be better for you to call it a day and go home."

Casey flailed, sending flour *ploof*ing into the air like bleached dust motes. "No! I'll try harder. I promise. I owe it to Uncle Walt to make the effort. He's done so much for me, and my father's death was devastating to him."

"But not to you?" she asked gently.

He didn't meet her eyes. "Of course to me. He was my father, after all."

"Casey, you don't have to pretend with me. I met the man, remember? I know what he was like. But why can't your uncle reopen Chez Donatien with a different chef? Why do *you* have to be in the kitchen?"

Since Casey had no good answer to that, he'd simply hedged and promised to do better. Sylvia had agreed—albeit reluctantly —and set him on a course of basic kitchen skills that had lasted the first week. The second week, they'd worked on the same things he'd failed on that first day. He'd yet to produce an acceptable caramel or a puff pastry that actually puffed, but Sylvia had commended him on his knife skills, so that was something. And he'd managed to make a roux that wasn't singed around the edges. Or at least not much.

Today, though, he was going to attempt one of his father's recipes. He'd waited until Sylvia's well-earned day off because she didn't think he was ready yet. Well, Casey didn't think he was ready either, but he wanted to see *how* not ready he was after two weeks of full kitchen immersion.

He let himself into the summer kitchen and took a deep breath. A whiff of burned sugar still lingered from yesterday's caramel attempt, underlying the scents of vanilla, rosemary, and lemon cleanser.

When he'd stepped into the summer kitchen that first day, he'd been surprised it didn't resemble any of his father's restaurant kitchens in the least. Donald had always been adamant that there was only one way to outfit a kitchen properly. Sylvia apparently hadn't gotten the steel slab memo or else had tossed it in the trash, because her school had a totally different vibe.

The countertops at the six student stations were a combination of end-grain butcher block and marble, which Sylvia said had been specially crafted from local materials. Each bench had a sink, a four-burner gas cooktop, a double oven— one with a broiler—and a grill, capped by a refrigerator at the end next to the wall. And those appliances? Rather than the brushed chrome Donald demanded, they were all coordinated in bright colors named for foods: peach, carrot, lavender, lemon, avocado, tomato. The stations were named for their colors too, ceramic plaques announcing Peach, Carrot, Lavender, Lemon, Avocado, and Tomato hanging above each fridge.

Casey imagined that serious cooking students, or even hobbyists who were in it for fun, would be thrilled with the setup. While it wasn't as stark and intimidating as his father's kitchens, it still made Casey's belly clench. Because every one of those components—from the sink to the fridge—represented another place Casey could screw things up.

"Today will be different." He gulped down the last of his lukewarm latte and tossed the cup in the trash.

He marched past the Peach station where Sylvia had been working on her own projects while Casey had been sweating bullets at Tomato. Appropriately enough, a bowl of peaches sat on the end of the bench, their aroma tickling his nose as he flung open the pantry next to Sylvia's office.

"Today I shall conquer Marjolaine Donatien if it's the last thing I do."

His father had always shouted that Casey could cook properly if he'd just pay *attention*, although Donald had never acknowledged that his presence looming over Casey's shoulder and watching his every move was one sure way to draw his attention from the task at hand. Today, though, there'd be no distraction, not even Sylvia's unobtrusive pottering or the noise of the Manhattan streets.

"First things first," Casey muttered. He patted the sheaf of folded papers in his back pocket. He'd had to do a lot of research, because Donald's recipe said unhelpful things like *make the ganache* and *make the meringue* and *make the Italian meringue buttercream*—seriously, couldn't they come up with names that weren't so *similar?*—but didn't actually say how to do it.

He collected the ingredients and schlepped them to Tomato, although he needed to make several trips, because between all those meringues, this thing used fifteen egg whites.

"I can do this."

He extracted the bundle of instructions and smoothed them out on Tomato's marble countertop. All he had to do was follow the steps, one by one, and he'd surely end up with a decent result. It might not be as pristinely perfect as anything served at Chez Donatien, not yet. But if it tasted good, that was the most important thing, right?

Besides, the line cooks could make anything look good with the right garnish.

He pulled out a heavy All-Clad saucepan and glanced at the first page. "Step one. Make the caramel."

I'm doomed.

Chapter Eight

Somehow, the budget spreadsheets had acquired even more red than they'd had yesterday. How did that even happen? Garlan had clearly hooked the books up to some kind of automated billing system—more than one, had to be—but Dev still hadn't figured out where all the transactions were coming from. They all hit the check register, but from where?

The low-key panic that simmered in his belly whenever the numbers danced on the screen in front of him was back again. Because what if he missed something? What if there was a critical bill—like that mysterious *Maintenance: DO NOT SKIP* thing that showed up every month from somewhere Dev still hadn't tracked down?

Banks. Fuck, don't get me started. They wouldn't talk about their accounts with you, even whether or not an account existed. Garlan had put him down as a transfer-on-death beneficiary, so at least he was able to access the accounts he knew of. But the ones he didn't? After eighteen months, things were still popping up.

He sighed and picked up the empty water bottle from this morning's run, not bothering to suppress the smile as he set it on the credenza behind the desk with the others. Thirteen empty water bottles. He shouldn't be sentimental about freaking *plastic bottles*, and in fact should recycle them right now. But Casey had presented each of them to him, the first one on the day after Ty had found the abandoned kittens. Somehow, Casey had been at the Market again when Dev finished his run.

Then Kat had mentioned casually that Casey had told *her* that since he started classes every day at eight he'd arranged his schedule so he could get one of Kat's lattes every morning at 7:30, and after that Dev had timed his runs so he arrived at the Market at exactly 7:35.

They'd met there every morning since. Walking back to Harrison House with Casey gave Dev the fortitude to face another day attempting to save Home.

He scowled at the monitor and brought up the records for the antique fair, the reddest of the red pages, since many of the expenses—*damn Port-a-Potties*—had to be paid before vendor registration fee balances were due. A couple of the dealers who never missed Antiques at Home had already paid in full, but most of the money wouldn't arrive until the deadline at the end of June. Dev couldn't blame them. They had cash flow issues just like he did, but understanding the delay didn't make staring at that ever-growing red bottom line any easier.

Was it too soon to head over to the summer kitchen with the shelf unit? Sure, he *could* go more than an hour without seeing Casey, but if he didn't have to? Didn't he deserve something good—*really* good—to balance the financial bad news? Besides, installing the shelf was a totally legit excuse. Maybe if he—

An ear-piercing klaxon shrilled from outside, sending Dev's heart directly into his throat: the summer kitchen smoke alarm.

Casey.

Dev leaped out of his chair, sending it crashing against the credenza and toppling the empty bottles like ninepins. He sprinted out of his office and down the hall toward the kitchen. When he burst out the back door, he sucked in a breath. At least flames weren't licking out the windows or dancing along the roof.

When he yanked the door open, though, smoke billowed out, sending him into a coughing fit.

"Casey!" he called between coughs. "Are you"—*cough*—"okay?"

The *strrsssh* of a fire extinguisher answered him, and his pulse dialed down a notch. *At least he's ambulatory.*

The smoke cleared enough that he spotted Casey at the Avocado station, his T-shirt pulled up over his nose, just setting the canister by his feet. At the Tomato station, a metal pan dulled with the extinguisher's potassium acetate mist burped sullen black smoke, a cocktail of burned sugar and something indefinable but acrid that caught in his throat and made him cough again. But Dev didn't spot any actual flames, so he threw open all the windows and switched on the exhaust fans at each of the other stations.

After the smoke alarms stopped shrieking, Dev pulled out his cell phone and speed dialed the firehouse. "Hey, Cap. It's me. False alarm at the summer kitchen. You can stand down."

She chuckled. "Thanks, Dev. Casey again?"

"Yeah."

"You sound a little hoarse. Need me to come by with the oxygen?"

"I think we're good, but I'll let you know if Casey's in need of assistance." Dev disconnected the call and turned to face Casey, whose eyes were red-rimmed and mournful above the T-shirt collar still stretched across his nose.

"I'm a menace," he said, voice muffled by the cotton. "I turned my back on the stupid caramel for literally *seconds*—"

"Seconds?"

Casey's shoulders drooped. "Well, I intended it to be seconds, but the yolks in half my eggs refused to be parted from their whites, so I had to get more eggs, but then"—he flung out a hand at the Tomato counter which was littered with the shells of at least two dozen eggs under the fire extinguisher residue—"*they* had separation anxiety, too."

Although a laugh threatened to climb up his throat, Dev pushed it down, because he didn't want to make it seem like he was belittling Casey's obvious distress. His own heart had resumed its usual spot, but since residual adrenaline was still making his muscles twitch, Casey had to be experiencing something similar.

"Don't worry about the eggs."

"Are you *kidding*?" Casey's voice squeaked on the last word. "I'll probably be targeted by vigilante hens out for vengeance."

"I'm pretty sure we don't have any of those in Home," Dev said, his voice strangled.

"Not only that, but I've *destroyed* this pan and *wrecked* the summer kitchen." He nudged the extinguisher canister with his toe. "And now the fire extinguisher has to be replaced, too."

"Hey." Dev sidestepped the canister and gripped Casey's shoulders. "Extinguishers are intended to be used and replaced. That's what they're for. The fire damage looks like it's restricted to the pan. Tomato's countertop isn't even singed, and since it's at the end of the room, all the stations past Avocado are totally clear."

Casey glanced to the side. "You really think so?"

"Absolutely. A little cleanup, and even Tomato and Avocado will be good as new." Dev made himself release Casey, although he wanted more than anything to pull him in for a hug. "Better to replace the pan and the fire extinguisher than the whole building or, you know, *you*."

Casey's smile was wan. "Thanks." His gaze traveled from the blackened pan to Tomato's cluttered bench, all of it coated in residue. "I'm never going to manage this. Not in three months. Not in three years. Not in three freaking *decades*."

Dev took Casey's arm. "Come on. Let's head outside and let the smoke dissipate a little more." Casey nodded and let Dev lead him outdoors. Once they were on the lawn by the lilac bushes, Dev turned Casey to face him. "If you don't mind my asking, what exactly do you expect to accomplish in three months?"

Casey gave him a surly glare, which, on his open, freckled face, was fucking adorable. "Clearly nothing. Unless you count untold egg death and fire extinguisher destruction."

"I'm serious. Why are you here? Sylvia said she's offering a curriculum tailored to your needs, but what are they?"

"I told you before. I'm supposed to be able to step into my father's shoes. Headline the restaurant. Recreate Chez Donatien for a new generation."

"Do you want to do that?" When Casey pressed his lips together and turned away, Dev gently rested his palms on Casey's shoulders again. "Casey. Come on. Tell me. Do you want to do that?"

He heaved a sigh that lifted Dev's hands. "I want to make my uncle happy."

"That wasn't my question."

"Maybe not. But it's the only answer I've got. The gala opening is set for September twentieth, the anniversary of the day my father opened it, and I'm expected to be in the kitchen, turning out Dad's signature dishes." He gestured to the summer kitchen's open door. "At this rate, the only thing that'll turn out is Hook & Ladder Company 8."

Dev bit the inside of his cheek to bury his smile. "What were you making this morning?"

"I was trying to make Marjolaine Donatien, one of his desserts that people used to come all the way from Philadelphia for. Since it's complicated, I figured I'd need extra practice, so best start on it early."

"Don't you think it would make more sense to work up to it gradually?"

"I don't have *time* for gradual. It's the middle of June, Dev, and I haven't managed to make anything that wasn't singed, raw, bitter, or consumed in actual flame."

"Why do you suppose that is? Is it because the recipes are too complex?"

"That doesn't help. But mostly I don't see the *point*." Casey's arms flopped at his sides. "I mean why spend hours concocting some showstopper that people will spend at most ten minutes demolishing, or maybe leave most of it on the plate because they've spent the last thirty minutes scarfing down half a dozen other dishes that *also* took hours to make. The ROI between cooking and eating has just never made *sense* to me."

Dev chuckled at Casey's bewildered tone. "Haven't you ever enjoyed a leisurely meal with family? Spent a fun afternoon making holiday cookies with friends? Relaxed over drinks and appetizers after a hectic day?"

Casey's glare could have peeled onions. "There was no such thing as *enjoyment* at any of my family meals, and they were sure as hell never *relaxing*. And as for fun in the kitchen?" He scoffed. "My father treated our kitchen at home the same as one of his restaurants. He barely let me do more than make a sandwich and even then, it was never *fun*."

If Donald Friel hadn't already been dead, Dev would have been tempted to punch his lights out. The man had obviously been a bully who should never have been trusted with a child. If the only reinforcement Casey had ever had with regard to cooking and food was negative, no wonder he was having trouble.

"Tell me, Case. Is it that important for you to make Marjolaine Donatien today?"

Casey looked a little startled at Dev shortening his name, but he didn't pull away. "At this point, I'd settle for anything that's marginally edible."

Dev released Casey's shoulders and grabbed his hand. "Then come on. We'll clean up first, but I spotted some peaches in there that were way out of the line of fire. We're gonna make rustic fruit tarts."

"We?" Casey let Dev draw him back into the summer kitchen. "You mean you'll help?"

"Why not? I'm not exactly a Michelin-starred chef, but I can put together a decent meal when I have to."

"But if I don't make it myself, does it count?"

"Do you enjoy cooking by yourself?"

Casey shuddered. "No."

Placing a finger under Casey's chin, Dev lifted his face enough to gaze into those hazel eyes that were nearly amber in this light. "Do you think you'd like doing it with me?"

Casey's pupils dilated. "D-doing it with you?"

Dev leaned closer and murmured into Casey's ear. "Cooking, Casey. I'm talking about cooking."

That delectable flush painted Casey's cheeks. "Oh. Right." He stepped back. "If I must cook, I'd rather do it with somebody else, I guess. As long as you go into this with your eyes open." He pointed to the Armageddon on his workstation. "Don't say you weren't warned."

Dev grinned. "You don't scare me. I run the monthly town meetings. Nothing could produce more carnage than Kat and Sylvia snarking at each other over the coffee urn. Besides, you're not the first student whose work required fire extinguisher intervention. Follow me."

After a half hour's work with rubber gloves and a bucket of hot soapy water, Tomato and Avocado were back in fighting trim. Nevertheless, after he'd set the bucket outside for safe disposal of the tainted water, Dev headed for Peach, at the opposite end of the room.

"How are your food processor skills?"

"Food processor?" Casey sidled nearer. "For what?"

"For the tart crust."

Casey's brows drew together. "Isn't that cheating? Aren't you supposed to"—he made pinching motions with his fingers—"work the cold butter into the flour with your hands?"

"In my book, if you've got a tool that'll do the job faster and easier, why not use it?"

Casey snorted. "Said my father precisely never."

Dev paused with the flour canister in his hands. "Casey. Your father's gone. Whatever he told you in the past, however he made you feel, none of that is relevant anymore. We're making rustic fruit tarts. They're not going to be perfect. They're not going to be fancy. But trust me when I say that they'll be delicious, and that's all that really matters right now." He plonked the flour on the counter. "Now, measure out a cup and a half of that into the food processor bowl."

Casey frowned. "Shouldn't we do it by weight to be more precise?"

"Rustic, remember? Just fluff the flour with a fork, scoop it into the measuring cup, level it off, and call it good."

"Okay." The way Casey drew out the word made his skepticism clear. "If you say so. But on your head be it."

Chapter Nine

Casey had to admit that Dev's method of making tart crust was a lot more enjoyable than the way his father had declared was the only way to do it. For one thing, Dev had been standing at Casey's shoulder, murmuring, *"Pulse. Pulse. Again."* until the flour and butter had reached the correct consistency.

While Casey had visions of other ways he'd like to *pulse* with Dev, he couldn't help the little bloom of satisfaction when they'd wrapped the dough in plastic and set it to chill. It had looked *exactly* like his dad's dough and had taken much less time and effort.

"Now," Dev said as he closed Peach's fridge door. "How are your knife skills?"

Casey gestured to the knife block with a flourish. "Sylvia has actually given me a passing grade—not an A, but a B+—so I feel like I can meet your expectations."

Dev's soft smile perked Casey's cock up again, right after he'd gotten it under control from all the *pulse*-ing. "The only expectations I've got are for you to have a good time. Is it working?"

I'll tell you how I could have a good time... But Casey nodded rather than blurting out inappropriate comments.

"Good. Could you fill that bowl halfway with ice and top it off with cold water?"

Casey hefted the big ceramic bowl. "What does that have to do with knife skills?"

"Nothing yet. But after I dunk the peaches in boiling water and then into the ice bath, I'll slide off their skins and you're going to slice them. Think you can manage?" Dev waggled his eyebrows.

Although *slide* and *skin* conjured up images hotter than the boiling water, Casey lifted his chin and gave Dev a wink. "Just watch me."

Give Casey a specific task with a defined purpose and a measurable result and he had no problem, especially if he had a chance to practice. The ice-water bath was ready by the time Dev lifted the first of the peaches out of the hot water.

"Look at this." Dev scooped the peach out of the bowl, and with a few swipes of his big, deft fingers, removed the skin and handed the peach to Casey. "Voila."

"Wow. That's amazing."

"Same thing works with tomatoes. You never did that?"

"My father never trusted me near boiling water. Or tomatoes. Probably with good reason." Casey set the peach on the cutting board. "How thin should the slices be?"

"Maybe a quarter of an inch or so?"

Casey eyeballed the peach, nicking its flesh at about a quarter of an inch and slowly carved off a neat section, rather proud of himself until he looked up and caught Dev's dumbfounded expression. "What? You said a quarter of an inch." He pointed with the tip of the knife. "That's a quarter of an inch. Get a ruler and I'll prove it."

"I said a quarter of an inch *or so*. Rustic tarts, Casey, remember? There's no need for pinpoint accuracy. I think these are freestone peaches, so split 'em in half and slice each half into six or so crescent-shaped sections, okay?"

Still inclined to be a little defensive, Casey muttered, "If you say so." But he did as instructed, hoping Dev was serious about that *or so* and that Casey wouldn't be judged on precision, because peaches were dang *slippery* and his sections were not identical by any stretch of the imagination.

But Dev just grinned and said, "Perfect. Now dump 'em in that bowl with a little lemon juice while we roll out the crust."

Casey's nerves returned as he squeezed half a lemon over the peaches. The only time he'd tried rolling out any dough in the kitchen at home, his father had yelled at him, taken the rolling pin to Casey's backside, and ordered him to his room.

Get over yourself, Friel. Nothing else has been like Dad's kitchen, so why should this?

Dev retrieved the dough from the fridge and, on the lightly floured marble counter, cut it into four parts with a bench knife. "I'll wrap two of these up and stick 'em in the fridge while you roll that one out."

"Right." Casey's hand trembled as he grabbed the rolling pin. *I don't even know where to start.* Hoping for the best, he placed the rolling pin on the top of one dough ball and rocked it back and forth, making a little valley. The sight of the wooden cylinder cradled between two dough mounds... *Gah! Why does everything in this damn kitchen make me think about sex?*

"Casey?" Dev peered at him from across the bench, which didn't help, since *Dev* was the main thing in the kitchen that made him think about sex. "Haven't you ever done this before?"

He huffed out a breath. "Not really. I'm more or less a rolling pin virgin since the only other time I tried it, I never achieved" —heat rushed up his throat—"um..."

Dev lifted an eyebrow. "Completion?"

Casey let go of the rolling pin and flailed. "I'm sorry. I just don't want to screw it up. I mean, the peaches smell really good. What if I ruin everything? I doubt even Randolph Scott will eat charred fruit tarts."

"Don't bet on it. But also, don't worry about it. We've got the dough for four tarts. They're not gonna be big." He held up one palm. "About the size of my hand. If we mess up one, we've got three other chances to get it right."

"It's kind of you to say *we*, but I think we both know that any failures will be totally on my end."

"Then let me help." He motioned for Casey to move closer to the counter. "Put your hands on the balls and bear down. Press 'em down into a flatter disk." Casey did, trying not to think about *balls*. Or *bearing down*. "Good. Now pick up the rolling pin."

"I don't know. That might be dangerous. Isn't this the weapon of choice in most cartoon kitchen altercations? Maybe you should don a saucepan helmet, just to be safe."

Dev grinned. "I'll take my chances. Go ahead."

Casey gingerly lifted the rolling pin, laid it on one of the dough disks, and moved it back and forth a couple of times with no apparent effect.

"Don't be so tentative. Grab the handles in a tight, firm grip. Like you mean it."

All these smooth round hard *objects are giving me ideas that are so not appropriate for food preparation.* Nevertheless, Casey took hold of the handles, forcing himself not to imagine how much better Dev's cock would feel.

"Work from the center out. You don't have to be shy. Quick, hard strokes. The dough likes it a little rough." Dev moved behind Casey and placed his hands over Casey's on the rolling pin. "Like this."

He guided Casey to press down hard and quick. But despite the distraction of Dev's big body, solid and warm at his back, Casey couldn't help being enchanted by the smooth, round disk growing under the rolling pin.

"I'm doing it!" Well, technically, Casey was along for the ride, but the result was right there for anyone to see.

"Yup. I like rolling out the dough on the marble board because when you can see the veining through the dough, you know it's thin enough. Tart pastry can be a little thicker than pie crust, so we don't have to go too crazy. This one looks good. Now the other. Ready to go solo?"

Casey bit his lip and peered up at Dev through his lashes. *Okay, so I'm going to hell. The journey will be worth it.* "Maybe show me one more time?"

"My pleasure."

They shaped the second crust too quickly for Casey's liking. He heaved a tiny disappointed sigh when Dev stepped back, but now he was invested. This was farther than he'd *ever* gotten in his father's kitchen, and he wanted to see how these turned out.

"How about we each take one of these and lay the fruit out?" Dev said. "You can follow my lead until you get the hang of it."

Casey wanted to ask if Dev would guide him in handling the slippery fruit, but that would be pathetic, and he'd already risked eternal damnation by asking for unnecessary rolling pin assistance. "All right."

"Start in the center, making a little spiral. See? That's why we wanted them crescent shaped. The slices can spoon up against each other. Keep going until you're about an inch and a half, two inches from the edge."

Despite the suggestive *spooning*, Casey concentrated on laying out the peach slices neatly. And really, it wasn't hard. Their shapes were conducive to the circular dough disks, and the brilliant orange peaches, their inner curves edged with bright red, were so pretty that he nearly forgot Dev was standing next to him.

Okay, so maybe he wouldn't go *that* far, but he could admit to a surge of satisfaction when his tart didn't look too different from Dev's.

"Alright, now we'll pinch 'em."

"Pinch? Why?" Casey lowered his voice. "Have they been… bad?"

Dev smirked. "Pinching isn't always bad."

Did Dev's gaze flick to Casey's chest? *Probably just my imagination.*

"So, good pinching. Got it. Why?"

"We're creating the edge to keep the fruit contained while the tarts bake. Slide your fingers underneath and raise the edge. Then pinch the dough between your fingers to keep it up."

"Slide, raise, pinch. Keep it up. Got it," Casey muttered, although keeping certain things *down* was becoming more difficult. Was Dev using suggestive descriptions *on purpose*?

"Then we'll brush 'em with cream, give 'em a hit of raw sugar, and they'll be ready to go."

He's totally doing it on purpose. However, Casey gritted his teeth and carried on. Ten minutes later, the four tarts were in the oven.

"They won't take too long." Dev washed his hands at Peach's sink and dried them on one of Sylvia's ubiquitous tea towels. "We'll check 'em in about twenty minutes. I'll set the timer, but since we're not working from a recipe, we should probably hang out here and keep an eye on them."

Casey nodded as he washed and dried his own hands. "Working without a recipe. Isn't that like walking a tightrope without a net?"

Dev chuckled. "Nothing so risky. Besides, how do you think people develop their dishes? Trial and error, plus a little knowledge about food chemistry and flavors."

Casey's dad had always made it seem so much more... mystical. As though nobody should be allowed near a kitchen who hadn't been blessed by the food gods. He settled on a tall stool next to Dev, where they had a clear view of the oven. "So you're a welder *and* a baker?"

"And the town manager. Let's not forget that." Dev's expression turned a little bleak. "Lord knows nobody else ever does."

"If you don't want to be town manager, why do you run?"

"I don't."

Casey squinted at him. "Wait. You're not elected?"

"I didn't say that. I'm elected. I just don't run. It doesn't matter. Having a Harrison as town manager is a tradition that refuses to die, so every year on Town Meeting Day, they elect whichever Harrison happens to be on deck. At the moment, that's me."

"You could refuse to serve, you know."

Dev shook his head. "Who'd take care of the place then? My ancestors sacrificed to make the town a safe and welcoming place to anyone who didn't fit anywhere else. These days, it seems like we need that more than ever." He smiled wryly. "And it's up to me as the last Harrison in the line to figure out some way of saving Home."

Chapter Ten

With an eyebrow quirked and his head tilted, Casey looked like one of Ty's inquisitive rescue pups. "Two questions. Why does it need saving, and why is it all on you to do it?"

Dev scrubbed his hands over his hair. "I shouldn't gripe or make it seem like nobody else steps up. There's a three-person Selectboard. A town clerk."

"Then why not let them carry some of the weight?"

"They do. Kenny's the clerk. Kat and Pete are on the Selectboard, and they wrangle business and maintenance issues, respectively."

"What about the third person? Don't they do anything?"

"He… ah…" Dev cleared his throat. "Well, there are issues. We're all family, really, and everyone does their best. But when Persistence founded this town, he promised that he and his would always take care of it."

"Yeah, but it's not a law, right? What's the population?"

"Including the outlying properties that are still part of the town, about five hundred, give or take. It's been quadruple that in the past, before we started bleeding residents in the last couple of decades."

"Regardless of what it used to be, that's still five hundred people who could step up to the plate rather than let you carry the can for them."

Casey sounded so indignant on Dev's behalf that Dev couldn't suppress a smile. "Tell me something. If someone you were fond of, someone you'd known all your life, was in trouble and needed help, would you tell them to suck it up and deal?"

Casey's gaze slid away, pink flagging those high cheekbones. "No. Of course not."

Dev winced. "Sorry. I didn't mean that as a dig at you."

"I know. But me helping my uncle with his dream isn't quite the same scope as five hundred people expecting you to... to..."

"Be a good town manager?"

"*Fix* everything for them." He gestured to Tomato. "Although I probably shouldn't talk. You swooped in and fixed things for me, after all." Casey sighed as he stared mournfully at the blackened saucepan in the drainer. "I doubt even you could save that pan, though."

"If it can't be saved, Sylvia can replace it. Just like she could replace anything in the summer kitchen, because they're just *things*. It's the people who are irreplaceable. The people who are important."

"Dev." Casey laid a gentle hand on Dev's arm. "You're a person too. You're important too. Who takes care of you?"

Dev was about to spout his usual denial, the one he'd become so practiced at in the last year and a half, but the look in Casey's hazel eyes, the concern in his expression, stopped him. *God, I want to kiss him.*

Casey was such a sweet guy, loyal to his family legacy, to the point of learning to cook even though he had zero aptitude, just to make his uncle happy. If anybody could understand Dev's drive and determination to keep Home afloat, it was Casey.

I really want to kiss him.

His gaze riveted to Casey's, Dev leaned forward. Casey's eyes widened, lips parting as he sucked in a sharp breath. *Yes!* It was going to happen. Dev's chest felt twice its usual size but light, buoyant, as though he could drift up to the ceiling and float there with Casey, leaving all their problems below them. When Casey swayed toward him, Dev reached out and—

Beep beep beep beep

Both of them jerked back at the timer's shrill alarm. Casey licked his lips. "That'll be the tarts. I guess we should check on them. I mean, *two* kitchen fires in one day are a little much, even for me."

The sudden return to reality made Dev almost dizzy. Yeah, kissing Casey would be a bad idea. They both had responsibilities, and it wasn't as though Dev would ever leave Home or Casey leave Manhattan, especially once he was planted in Chez Donatien's kitchen.

"Right." Dev flinched at his own over-hearty tone. "Well then. Take a look through the window. How do they look to you?"

Casey bent over—*gah! That ass!*—and peered through the glass. "They look kind of like the plaster of paris hand print I made when I was in kindergarten." He glanced up with a crooked smile. "I don't mean in goopy clumsiness. But they're kind of uneven and hand-shaped."

"They looked like that when we put them in."

"Oh. Heh. Yeah, I guess they did."

"How does the crust look?"

Casey squinted at the tarts. "I can't... The gray glass makes it hard to tell the actual color."

Dev handed Casey a potholder. "Then open the door and take a look."

When Casey twisted to glance up at Dev, a frown pleating his brow, his T-shirt rode up, exposing a strip of skin above the waistband of his skinny jeans, and *oh, hello*, he was wearing purple underwear. Dev's tongue stuck to the roof of his mouth.

"You can do that?" Casey asked.

"W-why not?"

"Won't all the heat rush out? I thought once you shut the oven door, you couldn't open it or"—he flapped his hands—"death and untold destruction would ensue."

Dev's chuckle was a little strained as he attempted to keep his gaze from straying to the curve of Casey's ass and that tantalizing strip of skin. *He has freckles there too.* "There aren't a lot of dishes that will be totally ruined if you open the oven to check on them. Popovers, maybe. Some souffles. Sure, the temperature in the oven will drop a bit, but these are rustic tarts, remember? There's no leavening in them, nothing to fall. And if the browning is a little uneven, who cares?"

"This is so weird," Casey muttered. When he stood, the hem of his T-shirt caught on his waistband as though to tease Dev with what it revealed—Casey's ass—and what it concealed—that freckled skin. "It's like going against everything my father ever told me."

"From what you've said, it's not like he told you much. Go ahead. Just be careful not to burn your hand."

Casey shot him a look. "Despite all evidence to the contrary, I'm not a total klutz. Trust me. I learned all about oven mitts and potholders at a very early age." He brandished the potholder and opened the oven door, releasing the aroma of browned pastry, then pulled out the rack and peered at the tarts.

Their rims were nicely golden, winking with flecks of raw sugar, and the peaches glistened with released juices. "Here." Dev grabbed a spatula and lifted the edge of one tart. "Nice and browned on the bottom, too. I think they're good to go."

With a look of near awe on his face, Casey lifted the pan and set it on a cooling rack. "Wow. I can't believe it. They're so... so *approachable.*"

Dev lifted an eyebrow. "Approachable?"

"Yeah. *Friendly* food. So much of what my dad created was about impressing the diners, wowing them, implying that the dish was classier than they would ever be." He grinned up at Dev. "These tarts are definitely non-judgmental."

Dev laughed. "I don't think I'd ever want to face judgmental food."

"Then it's a good thing you never ate at one of my dad's restaurants. God knows I wish *I* never had." Casey's grin turned mischievous. "Can we taste one?"

"Usually we'd wait until they cooled a little more. They'll probably burn your mouth."

"So I'll blow on them." Casey's gaze darted away and he blushed. "But I don't want to wait."

Dev shrugged. "Okay. But let's transfer them off the pan first. Then at least the others can be cooling while we singe our tongues."

Casey pointed to the spatula. "You do it. I'm afraid I'll drop it and then it'll all be for nothing."

"I thought you said you weren't a total klutz?"

"No fair tossing my words back at me." Casey fairly danced in place. "I don't want to take any chances, that's all."

So Dev moved three of the tarts onto the cooling rack and the fourth onto the cutting board. With a chef's knife, he cut it in quarters and nudged one of them toward Casey.

"After you. Don't burn your fingers."

Casey ignored him, picking up his piece and shifting it quickly from hand to hand as he blew on it.

Fuck. Casey's puckered mouth was more delectable than any tart could be. Dev snatched up his piece, counting on the heat on his palm to derail the heat in his dick.

Casey took a bite, then rounded his lips and sucked in air, cheeks hollowing, which made Dev shove his piece in his mouth too because *that's* what Casey would look like with his mouth around Dev's dick. The burn on his tongue didn't ease the tightness in his groin, though, and the look of bliss on Casey's face just made things worse. Or better, depending on whether Dev could ever *do* anything about it.

"Oh," Casey breathed, his eyes closed. "This is the best thing I've ever had in my mouth." He opened his eyes, so bright and full of wonder. "And I made it. *We* made it." He popped the last morsel into his mouth, eyes closed again. "Mmmm." Then he met Dev's gaze, blurted, "*Thank* you," and threw himself into Dev's arms.

Casey's mouth on his, lips soft and a little sticky with peach juice, was sweeter than anything Dev had imagined. But before he could wrap his arms around Casey and soothe both their tongues with a little mutual massage, Casey leaped back, clapping his hands over his mouth.

"Sorry. I'm sorry. I didn't mean to— You probably don't want — And anyway, I should have asked."

"Come back here," Dev growled, and planted his hands on Casey's waist, drawing him close. "I've been wanting to kiss you for days now."

"Really?"

"Oh yeah." Dev carded his fingers through Casey's curls, which were just as soft as they looked, even dusted with flour. With Casey's head cradled between his palms, he bent his head, but Casey met him halfway. When Casey's tongue teased Dev's lower lip, Dev opened and *yes!* Casey's tongue met his at the same time the bulge in Casey's jeans pressed against Dev's dick.

He didn't take the kiss up a notch, not yet. He wanted time to explore, to taste, to savor, to delve beyond the taste of peaches to the *Casey* taste underneath.

And as enticing as Casey's erection felt against his, Dev had no intention of taking things any farther here. This was the summer kitchen, for fuck's sake. It was Sylvia's place of business. Besides, he'd never been the kind of guy who wanted to lay his partner out over a hard surface, because that had to be painful for the guy on the bottom. He wanted his first time with Casey to be *comfortable* as well as exciting. In the kitchen, there were too many sharp and hot things to get in the way, to threaten. Casey deserved better care than that.

But then Casey groaned into Dev's mouth, his hands roaming down Dev's spine to cup his ass, and made a pleased sound low in his throat as he pressed closer.

Hell, yeah. Despite his intention to keep things soft and sweet this time, Dev wanted more, wanted deeper, wanted hotter, and ate at Casey as though his mouth were the chef's special of the day. Casey didn't protest. In fact, he met Dev's assault with equal fervor as Dev backed him up against the peach fridge.

Got to feel him. Dev's fingers fumbled with Casey's zipper, with Casey humming in encouragement as he nibbled on Dev's lips. *I'll clean everything up. I'll clean* him *with my tongue. He can lean there, no stress involved, not if I'm on my knees.*

"Dev," Casey murmured. "Please." Then he dove for Dev's mouth again.

Dev eased the zipper down, tongue warring with Casey's— no, not warring. Not sparring. *Mating.* He slid his hand into Casey's briefs and as his fist closed around Casey's hot, perfect dick, he moaned.

Decisions, decisions. Casey's mouth or Casey's cock? Maybe both? He could keep kissing while he stroked for a bit, and then he could kneel and—

"What the *hell* are you doing with my fiancé?"

Chapter Eleven

Dev sprang away from Casey so fast Casey nearly face-planted next to the oven. Still dazed from the sensual onslaught of Dev's mouth and his hand on Casey's cock, it took a minute to figure out what was happening.

For one thing, his cock was jutting out of his briefs. For another, Dev was halfway across the kitchen, glaring at him with a look of near hatred. For a third, *Bradley* was standing in the doorway, arms crossed, his face twisted in an expression of outraged self-righteousness.

"B-Bradley? What are you doing here?"

Bradley lifted an eyebrow. "I could ask you the same, but the answer is glaringly obvious. You've clearly lost your mind."

"Excuse me," Dev muttered and practically sprinted out the door.

"Dev!" Casey called, but his forward momentum was slowed by the need to tuck his privates away—not easy, because his cock was taking its time wilting after Dev's touch—and by Bradley stepping into his path.

"Really, Casey. Consorting with the help? Have you no self-respect?"

Casey glared at him. "He's not the *help*, not that there's anything wrong with that. He owns this estate. Plus, he's the *town manager*." He propped his fists on his hips. "And anyway, where do you get off with this *fiancé* business? We're not engaged."

"Don't be ridiculous, Casey. Of course we are. Your uncle and I have it all planned as the second boost for the restaurant. December first, right before we introduce the new holiday menu." He peered at the tarts, distaste flickering across his face to land on his down-turned mouth. "Which will definitely not include anything this downscale." He cast a dismissive glance at Casey's midsection. "Just to be perfectly clear, I expect you to conduct your... *liaisons* with more discretion. Cheating is one thing, but flaunting your infidelity with clearly unsuitable partners is something else entirely."

Casey stalked back to Peach's counter and picked up the cooling rack, shielding them from Bradley's unappreciative gaze. *He doesn't deserve anything this wonderful.*

"Newsflash. I can't cheat on somebody I'm not even with. We've never even dated. Not," he shot over his shoulder as he set the tarts inside the antique pie safe with its pierced tin panels, "that I would have ever accepted a date if you'd asked. Which you didn't. You *never* ask, Bradley. You instruct. You assume. You... you *pontificate.*" He shut the pie safe door carefully, because he wasn't mad at *it.* He double checked to make sure the oven was turned off. "You'll have to excuse me now. I need to go find Dev."

He marched toward the door, dodging around Bradley, who had planted himself stolidly in the middle of the room like an Armani-suited boulder. Once outside, he scanned the field for any sign of Dev.

Nothing.

He raced down the path and alongside Harrison House, rounded the corner by the lilacs, and scattered gravel under his feet as he ran down the drive.

"Casey!" Bradley called. "We have things to discuss."

"No, we don't," Casey muttered. He spotted Dev just passing the Market on what had to be an Olympic record pace, something Casey could never match even if Dev hadn't had a quarter mile head start. "Damn it." He kicked at a rock and turned around, only to come face to backside with Bradley. "Go away, Bradley. I mean it."

Bradley, as usual, ignored him, his gaze fixed speculatively on Harrison House. "Do you know the extent of this estate?"

Bradley's tone slowed Casey's headlong rush toward the front porch. When he turned back, Bradley was scrutinizing Harrison House, from its multiple chimneys and the dormers that made the third story roofline so quirky, down the scalloped shingles that gave way to clapboard siding on the second floor, to the river rock that formed its foundation.

A knot seethed in Casey's middle, because he recognized the speculative look in Bradley's narrowed eyes. He'd seen it whenever Bradley and Uncle Walt had discussed restaurant investors and possible expansion.

"Why do you want to know?"

"The place has obviously seen better days, and could use serious upgrades from an architect who could create a more"— he sniffed—"cohesive aesthetic, but there might be something…" He shifted his gaze to Casey. "We have lunch reservations in Merrilton in twenty minutes. How long will it take you to pack?"

Casey frowned. "Pack? Why would I want to pack?"

Bradley shook his head with a smile that was the definition of *patronizing*. "Clearly you can't stay here. I told you so on the first day. I've made arrangements for you at Green Mountain Shadows, along with a car service that will shuttle you here for your lessons. You'll share my suite—"

"*Your* suite? You're staying at that resort? Why?"

Bradley waved a hand, dismissing Casey's questions as he strolled toward his Lexus. "Business, Casey. Nothing you'd understand."

Casey gritted his teeth. "Need I remind you that I actually attended *business school*? I'm a semester away from my MBA."

"Yes, yes. But you needn't worry I'll chide you for not completing your studies, particularly since your role in our enterprises will be different."

"Our enterprises." Casey was surprised his molars weren't ground to nubs. "*Our* enterprises? This is *exactly* what I mean. I've never agreed to be a part of any *enterprise*."

"No?" Bradley cast a glance around him. "Then why are you here?"

Casey flexed his fingers, curling his hands into fists. "I'm here for Uncle Walt. Not for you."

"Your uncle and I are business partners, Casey, you know that. And you misunderstood. When I said *our* enterprises, I was referring, of course, to Walter and myself. You needn't concern yourself with the bigger picture. All you need to do is cook."

Casey growled and turned on his heel, yanking the screen door open and letting it slam behind him. As he stomped up the stairs, Bradley entered with much less force.

"Twenty minutes, Casey," he called.

Casey leaned over the banister. "I am *not* going to pack. I am *not* leaving Home. And I am *not*—not now, not tomorrow, not ever—your fiancé. Do I make myself clear?"

Bradley shook his head. "Stop being a child. Even you must see that this is the best path. The one that will deliver the optimal outcome for all concerned."

"It's not the optimal outcome for *me*."

He stomped the rest of the way up the stairs. The door to his bedroom was slightly ajar, which meant that he had a more welcome visitor: Randolph Scott was adept at operating the paddle-type door handles and had taken to napping in Casey's room in the afternoon. *Good.* Maybe a half hour or so of petting a cat would cool Casey's temper down to a low simmer.

When he walked into the room, the snarl in his belly eased immediately. He'd left the windows open this morning, so the breeze ruffled the curtains and the scent of lilacs filled the air.

He drew his brows together as he pivoted in place, because Randolph Scott wasn't curled in the middle of the big four-poster bed, nor was he perched on one of the two wide windowsills, or basking in the sunlight that spilled across the desk in the corner.

"Randolph Scott?" he murmured. "Here, kitty, kitty."

Ty claimed referring to the big orange bruiser as *kitty* offended his dignity, but he always came when Casey called him. Well, until now, that is. Then he spotted a pair of ginger ears poking above the cornice of his oak armoire.

"Ah, there you are."

But as he reached up to scratch Randolph Scott's head, he spotted something else that hadn't been there this morning.

A painting hung over the desk, where this morning there had only been a framed sepia photograph of a rather severe looking farmer cradling a lamb in his beefy arms.

Casey stepped closer, the painting drawing him in. He was no art expert, so he didn't know what this style was called. It wasn't hyperrealistic, but it wasn't abstract either. He had no trouble recognizing the subject: Home's Main Street. The perspective wasn't one that Casey had seen in his two weeks of residence, though. It was as though the artist were looking down on the town from above—but not too high. Maybe a house's second or third story? But that angle—the slice of the Market's roof, the tops of the lilacs massed in the greensward that ran halfway down the street, Harrison House's chimneys peeking over the tops of the oaks and sycamores.

He peered closer. There was a figure on the sidewalk, half hidden by the leaves of a maple, and foreshortened by the angle.

"Holy crap," he murmured. "That's me." Or at least someone wearing the same trainers and whose brown curls were as seriously in need of a trim as Casey's.

"Casey." Bradley stood in the doorway. "If you don't hurry, we won't make our reservation, and as someone raised in the restaurant business, you should realize how rude that is."

Casey tore his gaze away from the painting to glare at Bradley. "I wasn't raised *in* the restaurant business. I was raised *adjacent* to it. And I told you. I'm not leaving."

Bradley, once again, ignored him. Instead, he moved further into the room, his gaze lingering on the bed—although not from any amorous intent, since he was wearing that same appraising look he got when he was reviewing the linen and tableware choices for the restaurant. His gaze shifted to the bedside table, the one Kenny had delivered Casey's first day in Home.

He ran a finger along the lustrous surface. "Who's the artist?"

"I'm sorry. What?"

"The woodcraft artist. The one who created this nightstand and the bedstead." He turned to view the armoire. "This." He nodded toward the desk. "And that."

"I don't think they were built by the same person. Or they might have been originally, but they were restored by the man who runs the repair shop here in town."

Bradley stood and looked down his nose at Casey. "I know that you're naïve, but anyone with a modicum of knowledge about antiques could tell that these are recently constructed, and by the hand of a true master." He flicked a finger toward the window that overlooked the summer kitchen. "That oak and tin monstrosity in the cooking school was as well, unless I miss my guess, and I never do."

"The pie safe? No, Sylvia said Kenny found it at an estate sale and refurbished it for her."

Bradley's smile somehow hit an equal balance of condescending and avaricious. "If everybody in this place is as ignorant as you and this… this *Sylvia*, then it's clearly my duty to…"

His smile faded and his eyes widened in the closest to shock Casey had ever seen on his face. "That's a Rafe Wetherell. An *original* Rafe Wetherell. What in blazes is it doing here, of all places?"

Casey followed the direction of Bradley's gaze. "The painting?"

"Yes, the painting," he said testily. "Where did it come from?"

"I don't know. There's an artists' collective in town, so maybe he's part of it?"

Bradley gave him a withering look. "Really, Casey, I know you're naive, but no artist with Rafe Wetherell's stature would be part of a backwoods artists' collective. The last privately held Wetherell sold at auction last year for nearly three hundred thousand dollars. Most of them are in museums. No new canvases have surfaced for at least two years." His expression altered, turning decidedly sly and smug. "This puts an entirely different spin on things."

The knot in Casey's stomach was back, because while he didn't trust Bradley at the best of times, he *really* didn't trust him when he got that look—like Randolph Scott after he'd stolen a trout from Pete's fishing creel. Casey was surprised he didn't rub his hands together and cackle.

As though thinking about Randolph Scott had conjured him, the cat poked his head over the edge of the armoire and peered down at Bradley with slitted golden eyes. He reached down with one six-toed paw and slowly, so delicately that Bradley didn't notice anything, hooked a claw in Bradley's perfectly arranged quiff, and pulled up one lock so it stood like a question mark atop Bradley's head.

Casey choked back a laugh. *He looks just like the Tastee-Freez guy. Should I say something? I should say something.* Casey opened his mouth, but then Bradley cast another proprietary gaze around the room.

"Since you're determined to act like a child, I'll tender your regrets to the developer who's even now awaiting us at the resort and hope that I can convince him that our enterprises deserve his serious consideration." He nodded, causing the little loop to bob jauntily.

Nah.

He let Bradley parade out of the room and then grinned up at Randolph Scott. "*Good* kitty."

Chapter Twelve

Running later in the day was a royal pain in the ass.

The weather had warmed enough now that the sun was almost too hot on his head and shoulders, whether he was wearing a shirt or not. But if he wanted to avoid Casey—and Dev had been on a mission to do just that for the two days since the *fiancé* bombshell—he had to make sure Casey was already ensconced in the summer kitchen with Sylvia before he headed out.

With every pace, every *thwap* of his trainers against the asphalt, Dev's inner litany was *damn damn damn*. He'd always prided himself on his ability to judge a person's character. It was a Harrison family trait. They all had it, although Ty preferred to exercise his abilities on animals, not people.

Dev had never been so wrong before. For instance, he'd spotted Nash's inner self-centered asshole from the moment they'd met, but his voice and stage presence had been worth it at first. Their relationship had been secondary to the music for Dev as well, so he could hardly fault Nash for his reaction when Dev left the band.

He'd always suspected that Nash felt *that* betrayal, his abandonment of POV, more deeply than their own breakup. If Dev were honest with himself, he hadn't been that different. He'd missed the band more than Nash, but both those aches had been buried under the loss of Garlan and Grandfather.

So why had Dev picked up his guitar last night for the first time in months and started picking out a song—an *unrequited love* song, for fuck's sake—about Casey?

Damn damn damn.

Dev had been certain—as certain as he'd ever been about anything—that Casey was a stand-up guy. Loyal. Honest. Hopeless in the kitchen maybe, but a good man.

How could I have misjudged him so badly? So far from being a good man, Casey was a guy who'd cheat on his fiancé, who'd had no trouble putting Dev in the position of being a dirty little secret.

He slowed his punishing pace outside the Market, resting his hands on his thighs. *Okay, so I'm a dirty* big *secret.*

The Market door banged open. *Shit!* Had Casey figured out his avoidance strategy? Dev forced himself to rise slowly and grabbed one foot to stretch his quads. *Nothing to see here. Just an average run. At an average pace. On an average route.* At the wrong time of day.

But when he glanced sidelong at the Market porch, it wasn't Casey who stood there with a bottle of water and an undoubtedly lying smile on his stupid, adorable face. Nope. Kat Hathaway was planted on the top step, right next to a vintage Ben & Jerry's Eat the Weirdness poster, her arms crossed, the usual couple of pencils poking out of her salt-and-pepper bun.

"Morning, Kat." Dev stretched his other quad. Might as well bury himself in the part.

She narrowed her eyes at him from behind her cat's-eye glasses. "Never known you to run like this, Devondre Harrison."

"What can I say?" Dev spread his hands. "Had stuff to do around the house early this morning, so I got delayed."

"I'm not talking about your little jaunt around town."

"Little?" Dev slapped a hand to his chest in mock outrage. "Five miles every day, Kat. All summer without fail."

"Don't mince words with me. I changed your diapers."

"Thanks for announcing that to the whole street as though I'm still fucking *wearing* them. Besides, I doubt you ever came anywhere near any of us when we were babies."

"Well, I could have done, if I'd a mind to." She jerked her chin in the direction of Harrison House. "He's been by at the usual time, you know. Yesterday and today both. Bought water for you, same as ever, then stood out here on the porch, looking up and down the street, waiting for you to show your cowardly ass, until he had to run hisself or be late for that woman's silly school."

A sudden wash of Sally Field euphoria—*he likes me!*—nearly swamped the anger and disgust wrangling in Dev's chest. Resolutely, he pushed it down. *Deflect.*

"Sylvia's been running Summer Kitchen here since the first Obama Administration. Don't you think it's time you referred to her by name?"

Kat squinted at him, lips pursed. "I'll treat her like one of us when she starts acting like she is. But you"—she jabbed her finger at Dev—"need to stop running and face your problems."

"See?" He thrust his arms out, palms open. "You admit he's a problem, too."

"*Casey* isn't the problem. Your *attitude* is the problem."

Dev frowned. "Wait a minute. You won't call Sylvia by name after fourteen years, but you call Casey by name after he's been here less than a month? What the fuck, Kat?"

"The *fuck*, Dev, is that I can tell when somebody belongs in Home. Casey does. 'Bout time you figured that out, too."

She turned and marched back into the Market, letting the screen double-bump closed behind her.

"Great," Dev muttered as he stalked down the sidewalk toward Harrison House. Just what he needed—matchmaking services from his friends, who'd apparently been hoodwinked by Casey just as effectively as Dev had been. He strode past the hedge at the Harrison House property line and stopped before his feet hit the driveway.

A latest model silver Lexus was parked directly in front of the front door—but on the lawn, not the gravel. Dev peered at the grass inside the curve of the drive. Sure enough: tire tracks.

"Seriously?" he growled. "What the fuck do you think the driveway is *for*, asshole?"

Although the sky was clear this morning, they'd had a thunderstorm overnight, so the ground was soft and the tires had left twin runnels in the grass Pete was so proud of maintaining. Water had pooled in the tracks and the tires had kicked up a couple of divots.

Dev marched toward the car. There was no driver behind the wheel, and nobody in sight other than Randolph Scott, who was crouched under a hydrangea bush, eyes half-lidded, a clump of chickweed brushing his nose.

Dev reached down and worked his fingers into the mud to uproot the plant. "Thanks for pointing out the invader, but I'm still not planting any catnip for you."

"There you are."

Dev's fist clenched around the chickweed, because even though he'd only heard it once, he recognized the entitled arrogance in that voice. He turned slowly. Sure enough, Casey's fiancé was strolling toward him, a tablet in one hand, his khaki chinos creased within an inch of their lives and a pair of designer sunglasses hooked in the collar of his navy polo.

"I believe you know me."

Dev shrugged. "Can't say as I do." *Since Casey never mentioned he happened to be engaged.*

"Bradley Pillsbury." He glanced pointedly at the chickweed in Dev's muddy fingers, then dismissively over his sweat-dampened T-shirt, and didn't extend his hand to shake.

Good thing, since Dev would have refused it, anyway.

"The driveway's here for a reason," Dev said stonily. "To drive on."

Bradley shrugged. "The gravel could chip the paint." He made a note on his tablet. "That's one of the first things that will have to change."

Dev's scowl deepened. "What are you talking about?"

"I understand you're the owner of this place," he said, without looking up.

"That's right."

"Then we have some things to discuss." He raised his head, but his gaze didn't land on Dev. Instead, it swept Harrison House before returning to his car. His eyes widened and his jaw dropped in an expression of absolute horror. He hurried over and peered at his hood.

"What is *that?*"

Dev strolled over to take a look. Muddy paw prints looped across the hood, up the windshield, and over the roof. That much mud couldn't have been on the cat's paws at one go. He'd had to have made several trips.

Dev glanced at Randolph Scott, who gave him a slow blink. *Good kitty.*

Dev buried a smile and put on an exaggerated New England drawl. "Looks like a crittur's been investigatin' your fine vehicle." He deliberately wiped the mud off his fingers on his T-shirt while he rocked from his toes to his heels. "Can't blame 'em, you know. Somethin' that shiny's bound to attract the wildlife."

"Well?"

"Well what?"

Bradley crossed his arms and lifted his chin. "What are you going to do about it?"

"Me? Nothing."

"The least you can do is wash it off."

Dev narrowed his eyes. "Since A) I'm not your lackey, and B) I can't control the animal population"—*especially Randolph Scott* —"and C) I didn't invite you, I don't see how the state of your vehicle is my responsibility."

For some reason, instead of backing down, a hint of a smile relaxed Bradley's pinched mouth.

"I expect you'll change your tune shortly." He tapped his tablet. "I've done some research, and I'm prepared to offer you a fair price for the place, including the outbuildings." He glanced down at the screen. "And all contents, of course."

Dev crossed his arms. "It's not for sale."

Bradley smirked, although since he was a good four inches shorter, he had to look up at Dev to do it. "Everything's for sale, for the right price."

"Not Harrison House." *Not anything, not to you.*

Bradley's smirk took on a self-satisfied edge, and although Dev wasn't a believer in violence as a solution to anything, he was strongly tempted to smack this guy upside the head.

"I told you. I've done some research, *Mr. Town Manager*. The population of this place is decreasing by double digit percentage points every year, so the tax rolls are likewise shrinking. Its businesses are suffering from the lack of tourist traffic thanks to your short-sighted decision to refuse to allow the bypass to run through town. You personally may be land-rich, since your name is on multiple properties in and around Home, but I suspect you're cash-poor. Many—in fact, most—of those properties are vacant, and consequently they're a financial drain rather than an income stream." He made another note on his tablet. "I might be persuaded to take some of those off your hands as well, with the proper incentive."

Heat beat behind Dev's eyes. "Listen, Mr. Whoever-you-are —"

"Pillsbury. Of *the* Pillsburys."

"I don't care if you're the fucking Doughboy himself, Harrison House is not for sale. My other places aren't for sale. And Home is most fucking definitely not for sale."

Pillsbury's smirk faded, to be replaced by a hard stare out of pale blue eyes colder than the dead of a Vermont winter. "We'll see about that."

He unhooked his sunglasses and settled them on his nose. Then he stood there and waited. And waited. And waited, clearly expecting Dev to move aside. Since Dev chose not to oblige, Pillsbury was forced to walk around him, his loafers skidding on the gravel.

With his tablet tucked under one arm, he pulled a handkerchief out of his pocket and buffed a couple of muddy cat footprints off his hood. He made a disgusted sound at the soiled fabric and then angled his chin toward Dev. He was probably glaring behind his sunglasses, but since Dev couldn't see through the dark lenses, he didn't give a fuck.

Not that he had fucks to give even if he *could* see Pillsbury's glare, but plausible deniability and all that.

"Just so you know?" Bradley opened the driver's-side door and tossed the handkerchief inside. "I always get what I want. Things. Places." He gave Dev a smug, tightlipped smile. "People."

He climbed behind the wheel and started the engine. When he squirted wiper fluid on the windshield, the wipers didn't do much more than smear the mud around, which, yeah, Dev could admit his resulting smile was a little malicious. When Pillsbury gunned his motor and kicked up divots in the lawn as he launched the car forward, though, Dev winced. *I'm gonna owe Pete big time.* Or maybe Casey would owe him, since it was his fiancé who was being a dickhead.

Randolph Scott sauntered over and sat at Dev's feet, the tip of his tail twitching and tickling Dev's ankles as Pillsbury's Lexus disappeared beyond the hedge. Dev bent over and scratched behind the cat's ears.

"Tell you what, Randolph Scott. You claw your way up that idiot's trousers next time you see him, I just might plant that catnip for you after all."

.

Chapter Thirteen

"You call them what?" Val, Ty's assistant, leaned their arms on the ledge of the cat meet-and-greet room's half-door, grinning down at Casey where he sat on the floor being swarmed by all three kittens. "And why?"

"I named them in honor of Randolph Scott. They're named after characters in *Roberta*, a movie the human Randolph Scott starred in with Fred Astaire and Ginger Rogers." Casey detached the brown tabby female from the front of his shirt. "This is Lizzie, named after Ginger's character." He sat her down next to the black-and-white male. "And that's Huck."

"Since he's in a tuxedo, I'm assuming he was named for Fred's character?"

"Yup." Their brown tabby brother hopped over sideways, stiff-legged and arched-backed, ears flattened. "And that's Alexander Petrovich Moskovitch Voyda."

Val chuckled. "Quite a mouthful, considering he's no bigger than a minute."

"He'll grow. But in the meantime, we can call him Xander for short."

Xander wiggled his little butt and pounced on Lizzie. The two of them rolled over, collided with Huck, and all three kittens devolved into a ball of fur, rolling across the blue and gray tiles.

As soon as the wrestling match started, it ended, the three of them sitting with backs toward each other, washing random paws, obviously pretending they were all *far* too superior to participate in anything as undignified as a kitten pile-up. Casey sighed and ran a finger down Huck's spine, igniting his little baby purr.

Ty appeared beyond Val's shoulder. "Kenny brought in Fro and Travisher for their vaccines. They're in Exam One."

"On it, boss." Val saluted and trotted off down the hallway.

Ty smiled down at Casey. "Thanks for hanging out with them."

Casey returned the smile. "Don't pretend I'm not the one getting the benefit here. Kitten therapy is remarkably soothing."

"Very true. But you really are doing me a service. Doing *them* a service, too, since socialization is very important when it comes to adoptability."

Casey stood up and brushed off the seat of his jeans, although he doubted he made a dent in the kitten fur. He'd need to change before class so he wouldn't contaminate the summer kitchen.

"Do you have homes for them yet?"

"They won't be ready for another couple of weeks. I'll put the word around then. We usually don't have trouble placing kittens." Ty's expression darkened. "Which is another reason I'm still royally ticked that some asshole would try to drown them."

Casey winced as he unhooked Lizzie's claws from his inseam before she could reach his balls. "Ugh. Despicable. I can't even." He dropped a kiss on the kitten's fuzzy forehead. "Need help returning these monsters to their enclosure?"

"Appreciate it."

Casey passed Lizzie to Ty, then scooped up the other two. Ty opened the gate for him and led him down the hall and into the cat room, which was divided into three main sections. Two of them amounted to floor-to-ceiling feline parkour courses: carpeted ramps, shelves, columns, and cubbies, with cushy beds tucked in corners and shielded by overhangs.

An enormous black cat, his fur sleek and shiny, drowsed on the highest shelf, his chin on a rainbow-hued toy with a feathered tail, but he was the only current resident other than the kittens.

Because they required a different level of care, they had their own enclosure on the opposite side of the room. As Casey deposited Huck and Xander in their bed—which they immediately hopped out of and started chasing each other—Casey glanced at the gorgeous black cat.

"Do you have a home for him yet?"

"Who?" Ty followed Casey's gaze. "Oh, Explorer's not a rescue. He's just visiting. His family's off on vacation, so he's hanging with us while they're gone."

"So you board animals as well as rescuing them and providing medical care?"

Ty shrugged. "What can I say? It's a living."

Not a living. A calling.

As Ty set Lizzie in with her brothers, Randolph Scott trotted in. He glanced dismissively at Explorer, flicked his tail once, and then leaped over the gate into the kittens' habitat and stretched out like a ginger sphinx.

The kittens immediately descended on him, Lizzie batting at his tail and the two boys scrambling over his back.

"I've been meaning to ask you," Casey said as he skritched Randolph Scott's ears. "Do you think he could be their father? He's awfully good with them."

"Nah." Ty mimed a snip. "His fathering days are long gone, plus these babies didn't come from around Home. I'd have known."

Casey grinned at him. "What, are you an animal psychic, too? Tuning in with your crystal ball?"

"Nothing so unreliable." He winked. "My high school volunteers. Nothing gets past them, and none of them heard anything about a pregnant female. She might have been feral, but if so, how'd that asshole get ahold of her and her kittens?"

"Well, I appreciate the time with them." Casey's expression turned wistful. "If I weren't heading back to a teensy Manhattan apartment in September, I'd be tempted to adopt one of them myself."

Ty made an odd noise, something like *Mmmphmmm*, which Casey had discovered was the universal Home response when any of the residents wanted to avoid verbalizing their reaction.

Casey narrowed his eyes. "All right, Ty. I've heard that same response from almost everyone in Home at some point."

"Have you?" Ty asked blandly.

"I have. It's like the town's verbal version of a sonic screwdriver. You use it for everything from *yes* to *no* to *you're a freaking idiot*."

"Mmmphmmm."

"Seriously?" Casey threw up his hands. "What's that supposed to mean?

"Nothing." Ty turned and sauntered out of the cat room.

"Ty!" Casey followed him into the hall. "I mean it."

Ty pushed the door nearly closed, but left it ajar, presumably so Randolph Scott could escape. "Seen my cousin lately?"

"Nice segue." Casey crossed his arms and fixed Ty with a glare in the brightly lit hallway. "But since you ask, no, I haven't, because the big dope has been *avoiding* me." He pointed at Ty's nose. "And don't say he hasn't been."

"Okay. I won't. Although if you wanted to give me a clue as to why…" Ty's voice rose in hopeful invitation on the last word.

From the way Casey's cheeks heated, his face probably looked like somebody had flung a handful of cherry jujubes on a snowbank. "There may have been an… incident."

Ty grinned, his eyes sparkling. "Really? An incident? Above the neck? Below the belt? Please tell me it was below the belt."

"Seriously?" Casey shook his head, his blush burning hotter. "I say *incident* and you immediately jump to sex?"

Ty scrunched his face. "Sorry. Call it wishful thinking. Dev hasn't really had any action since he broke up with his boyfriend and left the band to come back to Home."

"Wait." Casey fell into step beside Ty as they headed toward the shelter lobby. "Band? Dev's a musician?"

"He was. A damn good one. Songwriter too, but he hasn't picked up his guitar since... well, since."

Casey stopped in front of the plate-glass window with its view onto the road past the blocky *Harrison Veterinary Clinic* lettering. "Guitar? I had my bedroom window open last night and I'm pretty sure I heard somebody playing. It was faint, and I couldn't tell what direction it was coming from, but I'm sure it was a single acoustic guitar."

The look that flickered across Ty's face combined disbelief with a hope so desperate it pinched Casey's heart.

"Could you identify the song?"

Casey shook his head. "No. It wasn't familiar. But it also wasn't complete, you know? Just bits that broke off and then repeated, or stopped in the middle and jumped to another phrase. That's why I figured it was somebody playing guitar and not just someone who needed to turn their stereo down."

"Holy shit," Ty breathed.

Then he whooped and grabbed Casey around the waist, dancing across the lobby with him, much to the amusement of Val and Kenny, who'd emerged from an exam room with two mid-sized dogs of indeterminate breed.

Pain lanced through Casey's instep and he stumbled. "Ow!"

"Shit. Was that your toe?" Ty released him and stepped back. "I'm usually better than that. Must be out of practice."

"It's fine. Although if you're considering a career as a ballroom dancer? Don't quit your day job."

"I'm sorry, Casey." Ty's tone was sincere but a smile broke through, banishing his expression of regret. "Really."

"Yeah?" Kenny snapped leads on both the dogs. "Then why are you grinning like a loon?"

Ty turned his shining face to Kenny. "Because Dev's playing again. He's *writing* again."

Behind his glasses, Kenny's eyes widened. "What?" He dropped the dogs' leads, grabbed Ty, and danced *him* around the lobby, the dogs hopping around them like backup dancers.

"Ow!" Kenny let go of Ty and knelt, looping his arms around the dogs' necks to settle them. "Not that I mind sacrificing my toes for the greater good, but Casey's right about the day job. I think Fro and Travisher stand a better chance of dancing with the stars than you do."

Ty showed his palms and angled his chin away from Kenny. "I'd point out that you were leading that time. Not even those hurtful words can bring me down, though, because hot *damn*, Kenny. He's playing again." He turned to Casey, all snark vanished from his face. "It's gotta be because of you. *Thank you.*"

Casey smiled crookedly. "Considering the *incident,* and the fact he's been dodging me since it happened, I find that hard to believe."

"Ooh, an incident?" Kenny stood up. "What incident? Care to share some details?"

Casey glanced sidelong at Val, who had retreated behind the reception desk but was watching all the antics with their chin in their fist. They made a *get on with it* gesture.

"Don't hold back because of me. I'm a huge fan of oversharing. And don't worry. What happens in the clinic, stays in the clinic."

Clearly Casey wasn't getting out of this without some kind of admission. But then he considered: These people knew Dev. Maybe they'd have an insight into how to approach him.

So he took a deep breath. "It was a stupid misunderstanding, that's all. And I could explain to Dev if he'd stop impersonating the Invisible Man and *talk* to me."

"Brother," Kenny muttered.

Val heaved a sigh. "Typical."

"He can be a stubborn cuss, I admit," Ty said, "and has some residual trust issues after his last boyfriend." He gripped Casey's shoulder. "But don't give up on him, okay? If I have to, I'll lock him in the butler's pantry at Harrison House and you can shout at one another through the door."

"As charming as that sounds—"

"Uh, boss?"

Ty let go of Casey and gave him a last pat. "Yes, Val?"

They pointed at the window. "That same car has been cruising the street for the last twenty minutes."

"Maybe they're looking for an address."

Val scoffed. "This is Home. They don't need to drive up the road more than once to see all there is to see."

Curious, Casey stepped to the window and peered out. A silver Lexus was just disappearing around the corner at the end of the one-block street. His heartbeat throbbed in his ears, masking the others' conversation.

He'd been in Home for almost three weeks, and the only silver Lexus he'd ever seen was Bradley's. He stood frozen at the window, and sure enough, the car nosed around the opposite corner, as though it had circled the block and was making another pass.

It's a coincidence. It has to be. There's no reason for him to—

But as the Lexus passed the shelter, Casey got a good look at the driver.

Bradley.

What the heck was he doing back here? He couldn't be cruising around looking for Casey, could he? Their imaginary relationship couldn't be important enough for Bradley to make that much effort. He had to be up to something else, and it couldn't be good.

Casey was torn between wanting to hide behind the reception desk and storming out onto the sidewalk and demanding to know what Bradley was doing. The old Casey, the Manhattan

Casey, would definitely have opted for the reception desk hideout, because *conflict*. *Ugh*. It was the absolute *worst*.

But the new Casey, the Home Casey, wasn't about to let another *incident* get in the way of his relationship with Dev. Assuming there *was* a relationship.

There could be. Casey was sure of it. If only the infuriating man would *listen*.

Ty moved to Casey's side as the Lexus disappeared around the corner again. "You recognize that guy?"

Casey sighed. "Unfortunately."

Ty regarded him, head tilted to one side. "Does he have anything to do with the *incident*?"

"He *is* the incident, and he has no business here." Casey straightened his shoulders and shot what he hoped was a confident smile at Ty, Kenny, and Val. "So I guess it's up to me to find out why he seems to be casing the joint."

Ty caught Casey's arm as he was about to walk out the door. "You know what? Screw that guy."

Casey shuddered. "No thank you."

"I mean ignore him. Let him putter around town as long as he likes. You need to talk to Dev."

"I can't. I have to go feed my sourdough starter."

Ty glared at him. "Is that the baker's version of *Sorry, can't go out with you tonight. I've got to wash my hair*?"

Casey rolled his eyes. "No. It's actually a thing. Sylvia's adding a few recipes to my curriculum, and first up is rustic sourdough bread. But apparently to make sourdough bread, you need a starter, and starters need feeding on a regular basis or they die."

"Kind of like relationships?" Ty said with a wry smile.

"Yeah." Casey glared out the window, where Bradley was making another pass. "Although some *non*-relationships simply refuse to die." He smiled at Ty. "I promise I'll talk to him, assuming I can find him."

"I'll nail his shoes to the floor for you." Ty's eyebrows bunched in thought. "I know you're tied up with your classes all day, but the best time to catch him is mid-afternoon. He's usually in his office at Harrison House then, wrestling with the accounting for the town and the estate."

"I'll see what I can do." Casey sighed. "After the starter's little snack, I've got to tackle duck with apricot chutney, so I suspect today will be a washout." *In more ways than one.*

Maybe if Casey set off the fire alarm again, it would at least catch Dev's attention. But he didn't want this hoped-for relationship to be based on arson.

"Yeah, and I expect he'll jet out of the office before five and head into Merrilton, same as he's done for the last couple of days," Ty said. "Tomorrow maybe?"

"Tomorrow." He waved at Val and Kenny. "See you later. And, Ty? Thanks again for the kitten therapy."

"Any time, buddy. Any time."

Casey slipped out the door. He stood on the porch for a moment and focused on taking calming breaths.

It didn't work.

Fine. Borderline murderous rage was probably better for facing Bradley, anyway. He marched down the porch steps and waited at the curb, arms crossed, foot tapping.

And waited. And waited. And *waited.* After ten minutes, Casey finally gave up. Confronting Bradley would have to wait.

He had a sourdough starter to feed.

Chapter Fourteen

Dev peered at the invoice for the library roof repair. It couldn't be that much, could it? They only had to replace about a dozen shingles. He sighed and keyed in the amount, wincing as the red number at the bottom of the screen grew enough to gain a comma.

"Damn it, Garlan," he growled. "Why the hell did you have to die?"

Immediately, guilt washed through him, turning him hollow. Because of course Garlan hadn't intended to be in the path of that semi when it skidded on the ice. His death and Grandfather's had been an accident, nothing more, and certainly hadn't been some conspiracy to derail Dev's life, too.

He'd never been as close to Garlan as he had been with Ty or even Kenny and Mitch, who weren't blood relations, because Garlan was a decade older. Half a generation removed from them.

The *Maintenance—DO NOT SKIP* entry popped up as pending in the automatic payments again, and Dev cursed under his breath, wishing that somewhere in that half a generation, Garlan had learned to make better notes about estate finances.

Dev's fingers hovered over the keypad. What would happen if he *did* skip it? If it was so important, surely he'd get some kind of warning or inquiry. In response, he could apologize for the late payment and put it back on autopay, but at least he'd have a clue what he was autopaying *for*.

His gaze caught on the time display in the corner of the monitor. Half-past two. He'd be safe from encountering Casey for at least another two hours because he'd checked in with Sylvia this morning to find out what today's lesson was. Roast duck? No way would Casey be free from *that* until well after six, possibly later.

Just to be safe, though, Dev could close up here by four and head into Merrilton. Maybe pop in at the resort and chat with Shira, the manager, about the antique fair. Green Mountain Shadows had only been open for the last two biennial fairs, but in both instances, Shira directed resort guests out to Home for the event, promoting it as a local activity. In fact, she'd told Dev several times that occupancy was at a peak during the weeks before and after the fair because some guests were repeaters, and planned their vacations around the fair.

Then he could mope into a beer for a couple of hours while he listened to whichever local garage band was murdering Queen and Beatles covers onstage at the Station Tavern.

He rubbed the tips of his fingers absently. He'd lost his guitar calluses long ago, and the hours he'd spent the last two nights playing and composing had left them tender. He hadn't noticed it then, falling into the zone, immersed in the music as he hadn't been since Garlan and Grandfather died and he'd left POV.

In truth, the hours had passed in a heartbeat, just as they always had, and his sore fingertips were the only evidence of exactly how much time he'd played.

God, he'd *missed* music. If the debacle with Casey had done nothing else for him, at least it had brought him back to his guitar. Sometimes the only way he could process any strong emotion was by writing about it, singing about it, and he hadn't done that even once since the accident.

Fuck, had he ever really grieved?

He'd gotten the call from Ty as the band was rehearsing for a gig at the biggest venue they'd yet played. He could still recall Ty's voice, choked with tears. The shape of his cell phone in his hand, the pressure of it against his ear. The scuff mark on the toe of his left boat shoe. The snort of Eli's laughter over one of Owen's incessant pranks, backed by Nash's petulant demand for Dev's attention.

But he couldn't remember crying. He couldn't remember anything at all, from the call until he'd arrived in Home. It was almost as though he'd stepped into a time warp: One minute he'd been at the rehearsal studio and the next he'd been stepping out of Pete's truck in front of Harrison House, the snow crunching under his feet.

He'd forgotten there would be snow.

The cold seeping in through his Sperrys, the wind cutting through a denim jacket suitable for LA in January but not for Home—those he remembered. And his fingers, so stiff in the icy darkness that he'd been certain if he tried to move them, even to do something as familiar as fold them around the neck of his guitar, that they'd crack. Break right off at the knuckle.

Ty had been waiting for him on the porch. So had Kenny. Kat. Sylvia. Dev had hugged each of them in turn, their tears dampening the denim of his jacket, the cotton of his T-shirt, making him colder still.

But his own face had stayed dry and unmoving, as though paralyzed at the moment of Ty's call.

Because the one thing he remembered feeling then was anger. Anger at Garlan for passing the burden of Home onto Dev's shoulders, shoulders that could never be broad enough to carry the weight. Anger at his grandfather for schooling Garlan in estate management, but not Dev. He'd even been angry at Ty, at Kenny, at Sylvia, at Pete—hell, at the whole *town*. At everyone who expected him to step in, take charge, be *enough*.

He'd never had *time* to grieve.

"Christ," he muttered brokenly. "Did I really never cry for them?"

He scrubbed his hands over his face, because he didn't have time for it now either. Because Casey's fucking fiancé had brought up something Dev had been trying to ignore for the last year and a half.

The town was dying. On his watch.

Land-rich and cash poor. That's what that asshole Pillsbury had said, and it was true. Persistence's grandson had started the tradition: If anyone who lived in Home decided to move on, to seek a different life elsewhere, the Harrisons would purchase their land, their dwelling, and keep it in trust to let or sell to the next person who needed Home.

Dev had sixteen properties on the estate rolls now, and only five of them were occupied. The eleven empty places returned nothing to the coffers yet continued to consume maintenance and upkeep resources.

Grandfather had always insisted on that. All Harrison properties must be meticulously preserved, so they'd be ready for the next person who moved in, the next person who needed a soft landing. Summers spent on repairs and renovations, autumns raking leaves and cleaning gutters, winters chopping wood and shoveling snow, springs pruning trees and prepping garden beds—Dev had done it all.

He hadn't done it alone, though. There'd been his dad and Ty's dad, Garlan and Grandfather, Kenny's folks, Mitch's mom, to work alongside him and Ty and Kenny and Mitch.

But all the Harrisons except Ty and Dev were gone now, as was Mitch's mom. Kenny's folks had retired to Arizona—about as opposite from Vermont as you could get. Ty and Kenny had their own businesses to run, and Mitch had left more than a decade ago, hightailing it out of Home like his ass was on fire right after high school.

Without them, Dev was hanging on by his fingernails. Barely. Home needed *people*, but his family had always maintained that some people—the right people—needed Home more. That's who they kept those houses ready for. But without the funds to maintain them, they would be just as unusable as if they didn't belong to the Harrisons anymore.

Would it really be so terrible to sell off a couple of those places—not Harrison House; never Harrison House—but maybe the places furthest out, the ones closest to Merrilton? Dev could use the money to hire *real* contractors, a real property manager. The vacation rental game had changed completely in the last few years. Maybe enrolling one or two properties with one of those outfits would at least bring in some very necessary income.

But what if somebody really needed those places? Dev snorted. It wasn't as though Home would suddenly be overrun by displaced people, like it had been back in the day. Didn't he owe it to the people who *were* here, the ones who already belonged, to preserve the town for them?

He remembered Bradley's shiny car, his disregard for the lawn, his disparaging remarks about *change*. If Dev sold any of his family's properties to that dickhead, they sure wouldn't be preserved. The guy was a slick operator, for sure. He'd probably find some way to circumvent the zoning laws, subdivide the land, tear down the buildings that were his family's heritage and throw up something as soulless as a meat locker.

Those red numbers bored into him and he pressed his fingers against his eyes. If he didn't do *something*, the situation might be moot. Home would be gone, because Dev couldn't find a way to save it.

Do the needs of the many outweigh the needs of my own fucking ego?

As much as he hated the notion, selling off some of the property—although not to Bradley Pillsbury, not if he could help it—might be the best way to rescue the town.

Last resort, though. Totally last resort. Who knew? Maybe this year's antique fair would fill in the cash flow gap, at least long enough for Dev to get a better handle on things. It always had before, and the deadline for vendor registration fees was Friday.

Yeah, that was the answer. All he needed was a little patience. A little patience and it would all work out. Dev could totally be patient—although Nash had always claimed what Dev called patience was really self-denial and pigheadedness.

Unbidden, the feel of Casey's cock in his hand returned, the taste of Casey's kiss, like peaches and honey, the tickle of Casey's curls. If Dev had been more patient before he'd taken that leap, if he'd had an ounce of self control, maybe he'd have caught the signs, the signs that Casey wasn't who he seemed to be.

Christ, Casey wasn't just *engaged*, he was engaged to Bradley fucking Pillsbury. Anyone who'd be willing to tie himself to *that* asshole for life wasn't somebody who could ever be happy in Home, who could ever be content with someone like Dev.

Patience. That's all it takes. Casey would be gone in two months, and then Dev could return to his regularly scheduled life.

He glared at the spreadsheet. "The life with leaky library roofs, mysterious autopayments, and goddamn fucking Port-a-Potties."

Oh, yeah. Good times.

Chapter Fifteen

"Casey, my dear." Sylvia settled onto the stool at the end of Casey's station. "You seem more than usually distracted today. Is there something the matter?"

Casey surveyed the carnage on his bench, the poor duck that was somehow burnt on the outside and raw in the middle. "Other than this, you mean?" And how did *anybody* curdle chutney?

Sylvia chuckled. "I suspect you would have made a better job of the chutney if you'd actually been paying attention to preparing it."

She had a point. He'd been so focused on cornering Dev in the middle of the afternoon that he'd rushed through the recipe. Apparently, you couldn't get duck to roast faster by glaring at it or upping the oven temperature every five minutes.

Who knew?

"Sorry, Sylvia. I'll try harder next time." He glanced at the clock. Nearly three. It had taken over six hours to get this far. If he had to start this stupid recipe all over again, he wouldn't get out of here until after nine if he was lucky. Sylvia was being incredibly patient with him, considering he was taking up all her time too, and learning how to cook these recipes was the reason he was here. He needed to put his own wishes on the back burner. So to speak.

She pursed her lips and folded her hands in her lap. "I wonder if there should be a next time."

The bottom dropped out of Casey's belly. Was he about to be expelled from *another* cooking school, one Uncle Walt had paid a mint for, one where he was the only freaking student? "I promise I'll pay closer attention. Please don't kick me out."

"What?" She slid off the stool and hurried over to him to enfold him in a hug. "Of course I'm not kicking you out. Not if you truly want to stay."

He sagged within her embrace, returning the hug carefully. She was nearly seventy, after all, and her bones seemed as fragile as a sparrow's.

"I'm not sure why I can't get this." He patted her gently on the back and released her. "I mean, billions of people cook every day, right?"

"That's a safe assumption, since people do have to eat if they expect to survive. But not everyone attempts this level of complexity, at least not on a daily basis." She flicked a finger at the canister that held the sourdough starter, which they'd named Carl. "Take Carl, for instance. Tomorrow we can use a bit of him to make a rustic sourdough loaf. Considering your success with those tarts—"

"I had help with those." Casey dropped his gaze to the floor, scuffing the toe of his trainer through a scatter of flour. "I can't claim credit for how they turned out."

"Nonsense." She gestured to the pitiful duck. "You had help with this too, with all the recipes we've tried so far, and yet those rustic tarts are the only things that... that..."

"Didn't either destroy the summer kitchen or make you want to hurl?"

She chuckled. "I was going to say the only things that you were pleased with. You know, simple food isn't shameful, neither eating it nor preparing it. In my book, a perfectly grilled cheese sandwich, browned nicely and served with a nice, crisp pickle, is just as admirable as roast duck. They both feed the body, but touch different parts of the soul."

Casey picked up a bench knife and scraped chutney detritus off the cutting board. "Somehow, I can't see Uncle Walt agreeing to change the Chez Donatien menu to offer grilled cheese and rustic tarts instead of Beef Wellington and Marjolaine."

"Perhaps not. But Casey, my dear, perhaps he should offer those dishes with another chef at the helm?"

"But I *promised* him." Casey's voice shook. "He never once broke a promise to me"—*unlike my father*—"so how can I renege? He's so set on this, on continuing the family legacy—"

"Piffle," she said. "What legacy? Donald was the first chef in your family. If I recall, Walter is in finance. Yes, Donald opened a string of restaurants, all of which were successful *for a time*. But of those, only Chez Donatien was in operation at his death. And frankly? I suspect he would have moved on to another project before long if his blood pressure, temper, and refusal to moderate his diet hadn't gotten to him. That's the danger in believing in your own omnipotence." She smiled wryly. "Humility in the face of our own mortality is a lesson we all have to learn. Unfortunately Donald's came too late."

Casey blinked at her. Nobody, not his father's sous chef, his line cooks, the food critics—and certainly not Uncle Walt—had ever spoken about his father like that. *Like he wasn't the patron saint of haute cuisine.* Guilt niggled at Casey because he found it such a *relief* that he wasn't the only person in the world who didn't worship at his father's altar.

"Um…"

"Oh, Casey, I'm so sorry." She grabbed his hand and squeezed. "I lack the least modicum of tact. That's one of the things that got me in trouble before. I didn't mean to upset you."

"You didn't." He smiled at her as he returned the squeeze. "I was just surprised that *somebody* finally saw a different side of my father." *One closer to the one I knew.*

She chuckled. "Well, I was his rival, not his employee, friend, or family, so perhaps I had a different perspective. I remember once when—" Her cell phone buzzed in her pocket. "Drat. I thought I silenced that for our lesson. I do beg your pardon."

Casey picked up the bench knife again and waggled it in a shooing motion. "Go ahead and answer it. I'll be cleaning up this mess for a while anyway, before I can start again."

She held up one finger as she pulled out the phone. "Hold that thought. We haven't finished this conversation." She connected the call and paced toward the end of the room and the door to her tiny office. "Hello?"

Casey turned back to his cleanup, with Sylvia's low-voiced conversation as a soundtrack. He poked at the duck's charred skin. If only he hadn't gotten so impatient. If he'd just let it roast at the right temperature for that stupidly long time, he'd be finished by now and on his way to confront Dev. Instead, he had the whole mess to do over, probably to fail again, and the idea of all the *waste* made his stomach cramp.

Hmmm...

Val had told Casey that some of the food they used for the animals at the shelter was duck-based. He had no idea whether that meant duck-based kibble or actual duck, but it wouldn't hurt to check. This could be just the ticket for obligate carnivores.

If Casey couldn't manage edible *people* food, maybe he could serve up treats to Home's animal population. After all, *somebody* should benefit from all this effort.

As he was packing the duck for transport, Sylvia's voice rose.

"Nazariy, you guaranteed I'd have those black truffles by tomorrow. My lesson depends on them."

The combination of that name—Nazariy—and black truffles caught Casey's ear. Sylvia had to be talking to Nazariy Sobol, who ran Sobol Food Traders in New Jersey. Casey left the half-wrapped duck and inched closer. Yeah, maybe it was rude to eavesdrop on Sylvia's conversation, but the seed of an idea was taking root.

He peeked into the office. Sylvia was squinting up at the ceiling, phone pressed to her ear with one hand and the other hand gripping her hair so tightly it had to be painful.

"This is insupportable. I pay your ridiculous surcharges specifically so I can get the ingredients I require. How you can sell my order out from under me—"

Casey could hear Nazariy's harsh squawks, although they were noise, not actual words. Judging by the way Sylvia's brows snapped down, whatever he was saying wasn't welcome news.

"No, I will not pay extra. I'm *already* paying extra." Her expression turned bleak as the squawking went on, and she let the phone drift down to her lap.

Casey reached out and took it gently, cutting off Nazariy mid-squawk. "That was the guy from Sobol Food Traders, wasn't it?"

She nodded. "It's days like this that make me wish I hadn't quit drinking. Which, according to Nazariy, nobody in the industry believes, anyway."

"My dad had trouble with him all the time." He took her elbow and led her back to his pristine station. "Sit down and I'll make you a cup of that cardamom tea you like."

"Thank you, dear, but you needn't go to the trouble."

"It's no trouble to help a friend." He switched on the electric kettle and retrieved two very large mugs from Peach's cupboard. As the water boiled, he sat down facing her. "Was he very horrible to you?"

She laughed weakly. "Other than selling those black truffles for your Beef Wellington to that new bistro in Soho and insinuating that I wouldn't be hiding out in the backwoods of Vermont if I were sober, nothing out of the ordinary."

"What a dickhead." He winced. "Sorry."

"Don't apologize. He is, without a doubt, a huge dickhead."

Even though the water hadn't boiled, Casey rose and shuffled to the counter. He stared down at the blue lights on the kettle's power base. "It's my fault."

"How did you reach that astonishing conclusion?"

He bit his lip as he filled two tea balls with the cardamom tea and dropped them in the mugs. "How can it not be?"

"Casey—"

"Those black truffles were for me, just like all the other rare ingredients you've had to buy." The kettle beeped, and he poured water over the tea. "If it weren't for my lessons, for Dad's stupidly fancy recipes, you wouldn't have to deal with Nazariy."

She sighed as he passed her the steaming cup. "If it wasn't him, it would be someone else. None of my old suppliers are quite as eager to keep me happy as they were when I still had influence."

Casey leaned against Peach's counter and took a sip of his tea. "So why keep using them?"

"I beg your pardon?"

"Why not source your ingredients locally?"

She lifted an eyebrow. "Do you really think I could waltz into the Market and pick up black truffles?"

"Well. Yes. Her stock *is* pretty eclectic."

She stared at him. "Again I say, I beg your pardon? Kat Hathaway wouldn't cross the street with a fire extinguisher if I was in flames."

"Did you ever think the reason for that is that you *don't* buy your supplies from her?" He pushed off the counter and sat on the stool opposite Sylvia. "I've talked to her. She's got connections. Yeah, it might add an extra layer of middlepersons between you and the growers, but I bet it would still be cheaper than shipping everything in from New Jersey."

"I don't know." Sylvia gazed down at her cup, tilting it so that the tea ball tinkled against its sides. "Kat and I haven't seen eye to eye since my first days with Summer Kitchen. I doubt she'll be anxious to cooperate with me at this late date."

"I'll lay you odds I'll get Kat on board and connect with local growers to boot." He held out his hand, palm up. "Let me try anyway. Let me do it for you."

She studied him somberly for a moment before she took his hand. "Thank you, my dear. I'm more than happy for you to step into the breach." She let go of him and took another sip of her tea. "You know, Casey, in this world, there are *process* people and *product* people."

He raised his eyebrows. "Are we changing the subject now? Which one is better? Are you about to tell me I'm the worst kind?"

She shook her head, laughing. "There's no best and worst. It has more to do with what brings you satisfaction. Process people derive joy and fulfillment from the *making*. Product people from the *made*. For process people, the work, the project, the *process*, is where they want to stay. Often, it doesn't matter if they ever complete a particular task. If the joy of working on it fades?" She shrugged. "They'll leave it unfinished and move on. Product people are focused on results. To them, the point of starting anything is in getting *done*, usually in the most efficient manner. Consequently, process people can be a little flighty and leave a trail of unfinished tasks in their wake. Product people can cut corners in their haste to reach the finish line. It's the difference between *done is good* and *done is irrelevant as long as we enjoy the journey.*"

"Okaaay." He glanced sidelong at the half-wrapped duck.

"To produce the kind of food your father did, you have to be a process person. You have to enjoy the making, because these dishes are complex and time-consuming." She peered at him over her glasses. "Do you *enjoy* making these dishes?"

"N-no." Casey squirmed on the stool, making it wobble. "But only because I'm bad at it."

"I think it's the other way around. You're bad at it because you don't enjoy it. And my dear..." She reached out and gripped his wrist with her surprisingly callused hand.

"Spending your life doing something you don't enjoy is no way to live."

"But… but I enjoyed it when Dev and I made those tarts," he said, a little desperately.

"That's because you got to the result—your *product*—quickly and without a lot of fuss." She winked. "Or perhaps because of the company."

Casey's cheeks burned. "Uh…"

"Even a product person can enjoy the process if the journey is pleasant. And even a process person can anticipate the result when they know their work will be appreciated. You, Casey"— she saluted him with her cup—"are most definitely a product person. You absolutely lit up when you offered to intercede with Kat because of the result you want to attain."

"So you're saying I'll never be able to cook like my father?"

"I'm saying it will be unlikely to give you the same satisfaction it gave him. And perhaps you should consider that going forward."

Casey glanced at the recipe pinned to the corkboard on his fridge door. *Not a process I want to slog through again.* He checked the clock. Three fifteen. "Sylvia, do you mind if we cut out early today?"

"Actually, my dear, I would be most grateful." She set her cup down. "I feel in dire need of a meeting."

"Then if you'll excuse me?" Casey took off his apron and tossed it in the laundry basket next to the pantry. "I've got a product to achieve."

And Dev Harrison was going to face up to that *process* whether he liked it or not.

Chapter Sixteen

"We have to talk."

Dev's fingers smashed against the keyboard, and whatever he'd done caused the dreaded #REF! error to pop up all over the spreadsheet like a plague of demonic dandelions. "Fuck!"

"Sorry," Casey said, hovering in the doorway with his hands in the pockets of his jeans. "Didn't mean to startle you."

Dev slid down in the chair and clamped his elbows to his sides. *Why no, I'm not using the monitor as an electronic blanket fort. Why do you ask?* "Why aren't you in class?"

"I managed to fail today's lesson in record time, and after a little chat with Sylvia, she gave me a get out of jail free card." He stepped into the room, head tilted to one side. "Unless it's more of a hall pass. Whatever." He moved forward until his legs were pressed against the other side of the desk and craned his neck to meet Dev's gaze over the monitor. "Can we please talk?"

With his shoulders bunched nearly at his ears, Dev gestured to the screen. "Can't. No time. Got to prepare the financial forecast for the town for the Selectboard meeting."

"The meeting isn't for another two weeks." Casey folded his arms. "I checked with Kenny. Try another one."

"It's not just the town. The estate finances are tied up with it too. Accounting's not exactly my forte, so it takes me longer. A lot longer. Hours. Days." He poked at the ESC key. Nothing happened. Still #REF!s as far as the eye could see. "Sometimes weeks." He shook his head with a weak laugh. "Seems like I'm chained to the damn computer these days."

"Funny, because when I stopped by here after class the last couple of days, you haven't been here."

"Uh… That's because…" *Gah!* He used to be able to think on his feet. Why did Casey totally disconnect his brain?

Casey dropped into the chair next to the desk. "Give it up, Dev. You're here. I'm here. And we really need to talk."

Frowning, Dev huffed out a breath. "Fine. Talk."

"You know that thing we did in the kitchen?"

Dev raised an eyebrow and folded his own arms. "You mean bake?"

"No," Casey said between clenched teeth. "Why are you being so *difficult*? I mean the kiss. And…" He glanced away and flapped his hands. "And other things."

"That was a mistake."

Casey lifted his chin and met Dev's gaze squarely. "Why?"

Dev had a hard time reading the look in his eyes. Determination, maybe, but hurt lurked in those amber depths too, which either took a lot of nerve, borderline sociopathic tendencies, or exceptional acting talent. Hell, maybe all three.

"You know why."

"Because you didn't like it?" Casey covered his face with his hands. "Oh, god. I knew it. I'm a terrible kisser. You were revolted, weren't you? You only touched my dick to be nice."

Despite the anger that still simmered about Casey's subterfuge, Dev chuckled. "Calm down, Casey. Your kiss was fine."

"Fine?" he wailed, still hiding behind his hands. "*Fine* is worse than *terrible*. *Fine* is unremarkable. *Fine* is boring."

Fuck this. So Casey was a liar and a cheat. Didn't mean that Dev had to stoop to the same level. "If I'm honest? Your kiss was superlative. Outstanding. The best ever."

Casey peeked between his fingers. "Really? So you *did* like it? The dick-touching too?"

Dev's palms started to sweat. "The, er, dick-touching was... well, let's say I didn't do it just to be nice. I don't do things I don't like." Casey dropped his hands and stared pointedly at the monitor. "Okay, I don't do things I don't like that aren't *required*, as long as I've got all the facts."

"Then you didn't want it." He paled, making that spray of freckles stand out in a way that twisted Dev's guts. "I threw myself at you," he murmured, wide-eyed. "Practically tackled you to the ground without *asking*. That's the *worst* thing. Not *asking*. I'm so sorry. I—"

"Casey. Stop, okay? It was pretty clear I was into it, too, but that doesn't matter. Because you weren't free to give it."

His brows snapped down. "Give what?"

"Anything."

"What are you talking about?" Casey asked in a truly bewildered tone.

"Remember what I said about having all the facts? You left a damn big one out, and it put me in a fucking awkward position. You may be okay with cheating, but I'm not okay with being the means, especially when I wasn't informed."

"Wait." Casey's brow cleared. "You've been avoiding me because of *Bradley*?"

"What do you think?" Dev tore his gaze away from Casey's face and tried to figure out how to fix whatever his keyboard smash had done to the spreadsheet.

"See, that's why you need to *talk* to people, Dev, instead of being this big, stoic... *monument*." Casey reached over and switched off the monitor.

"Hey!" Dev protested. "I was working on that."

"It'll still be there when you turn the monitor on again. Look." He took a huge breath and blew it out. "That kiss was more than I've ever done with Bradley. For that matter, it was more than I've ever *wanted* to do with Bradley. This alleged engagement is all in his head. Well, his head and my uncle's."

"Did you ever tell them that?"

Casey rolled his eyes. "*So* many times. But *telling* somebody something doesn't do much good if they don't *listen*. And Uncle Walt and Bradley have this kind of... selective audio filter. If what you say doesn't align with their plans, then they just don't hear it."

"Mmmphmmm."

"Eloquent, Dev. Real eloquent. Although I suppose I should take it as a good sign that you haven't run away again like the last the last two days." He scooted his chair closer. "Granted, I *am* blocking you in your desk, but you're big enough that you could move me aside with no trouble."

"I would never touch you without your permission, Casey, and never in anger. If you believe nothing else about me, believe that."

"Okay, then, as long as we're talking about beliefs, let me be clear." He leaned forward, gaze fierce and intense. "I am not now nor have I ever been engaged to Bradley. I am not dating Bradley. I have *never* dated Bradley and I never would, because he's a total dickhead. Believe *that*."

"No argument there," Dev muttered.

"Furthermore, he is the *king* of entitlement, the emperor of condescension, and the grand freaking poobah of self-importance." Casey stuck his nose in the air. "And frankly, I'm a little insulted that you think I'd fall for *any* of that."

Dev's lips twitched. "You have to admit, I had reasons."

"Only Bradley's words." He jabbed a finger at Dev's chest. "Need I remind you that you bolted before you bothered to hear mine? Because if you'd stayed, you'd have heard me totally reading him the riot act." He heaved a heavy sigh. "Although, even if Bradley heard what I said, there's no telling whether he paid attention. Selective audio filter, remember?"

The back of Dev's neck burned like it always did when he was ashamed of himself. "That's fair. I'm sorry I ghosted you. I've been told I have... trust issues. And perhaps an occasional problem with self-worth."

"Apology accepted." Casey smiled tentatively. "So we're good now?"

"We're good."

Casey waggled his eyebrows. "Seal it with a kiss?"

Fuck, but I want to. However… "I don't think that would be such a great idea."

Casey's face fell. "So you *don't* want me."

"Whether I want you or not is not the issue." Dev punched the monitor's on switch, sending it flickering to life. "I've got duties. Responsibilities." *Burdens.* "Home is not just my home, it's my family's legacy. I can't fail the town just because I'm a lousy bookkeeper and suck at managing money." *And besides, you'll be leaving in two months.*

Casey's smile grew and gained an edge that made him look less like a rescue kitten and more like Randolph Scott on the trail of a particularly tasty mouse.

"You, Dev Harrison, are in luck. I may be culinarily clueless, but I've got seven-eighths of an MBA and I *aced* all my accounting and financial management classes. I don't have an ounce of my father's cooking talent, but I totally inherited my uncle's financial savvy. I bet I can get your books under control in no time."

The flutter in Dev's middle—was that hope or lust? Probably a little of both, because he'd totally get on his knees for a guy who knew how to vanquish this fucking budget—especially if that guy was Casey. "You'd do that?"

"In a heartbeat." His expression turned serious. "This isn't a quid pro quo, by the way. I'll take it on even if you don't want to kiss me again. I'll do it because it's something I'm good at and because you need the help. If you don't trust me with your financial data—"

"No! It's not that. I do trust you. It's just…" He scrubbed his hands across his close-cropped hair. "I ought to be able to handle this myself."

Casey regarded him for a moment, deadpan. Then he asked, "Why?"

"Because all the Harrisons before me have managed with no trouble."

"How do you know?"

Dev spread his arms, as though encompassing Harrison House and everything beyond. "Because Home is still here, and it's still the haven Persistence dreamed it would be."

"Yes, but that doesn't mean that your forebears found it *easy* or did it all alone. Come on, Dev. Let me help."

"I—" The landline on the desk jangled, which meant it was town business. Dev grimaced. "I've got to get that."

Casey flapped his hands. "Go ahead. I'm in no hurry. Not since I don't have to time my Dev ambush anymore."

Dev shook his head, grinning, and picked up the handset. "Dev Harrison."

"Dev, it's Pete. Got a little problem out at the Patel house. Could use your help."

"What kind of problem?"

"Some flatlander in a fancy car poking his nose where it don't belong. Acting like he owns the place."

Bradley. "I'll be right there." He hung up. "Sorry. Pete needs backup."

Should I tell him about Bradley's visit? No, not yet. After Casey untangled the books, he might discover that selling one or two properties might be the only answer, but until then, Dev preferred to keep Bradley's offer under wraps. Knowing Casey, he'd probably kick himself for bringing Home to Bradley's attention rather than placing the blame where it belonged: squarely on Dev's shoulders.

Casey rose and gestured for Dev to move so they could switch places. "Why don't I get started while you check in with Pete, then? I can give you my initial thoughts when you get back."

"I don't know how long it'll take," Dev warned.

"Doesn't matter." Casey smiled. "With Summer Kitchen not hanging over my head, I'm free as a bird for the rest of the day."

Dev held out the chair for Casey to sit, purposely keeping a safe distance, because Casey was really just a guest. Who was leaving. In two months. "The lock screen password is hometown, all one word, lower case, but use zeroes instead of Os. I'll give you a tour of the rest of the financial apps later."

Casey settled into the chair and scooted closer to the desk. "Works for me. Go on and do your thing with Pete. I'll be fine here."

Dev lifted an eyebrow. "Just *fine*?"

Casey smirked up at him. "No. I'll be *superlative*. Now shoo."

Dev strode for the door. Before he left the office, though, he glanced back at Casey, who was already studying the screen, his brows drawn together in adorable concentration, fingers already busy on the keyboard.

Leaving in two months, remember?

Dev ground his molars together and stalked down the hall and out the kitchen door. He sprinted across the field to his cottage and climbed into his elderly CR-V, all the while cataloging the reasons why it would be a bad idea to get involved with Casey.

He'd always been lousy at casual sex. It had taken him until he was in college to realize that he was demisexual, and that the initial spark of attraction wasn't enough for him. He needed the emotional attachment before true desire kicked in. His relationship with Nash was a cautionary tale on evaluating the *nature* of the emotional attachment, though. In the last eighteen months, he'd felt the loss of the attachment, of something to hang his life on, but not the loss of Nash per se.

Casey, though. The connection they'd been building before the Big Bradley Misunderstanding had been different. Warmer —bordering on *hot*, in fact, yet still effortless. Comforting *and* comfortable.

Pursuing it would be selfish, though, wouldn't it? What did it matter whether Dev had a boyfriend he could love and respect, and who felt the same about him, if it meant that Home and everyone who lived here suffered for it?

When he pulled up to the Patel house, a classic white-sided New England saltbox with forest green shutters and red brick chimney, Pete was roaring along the front lawn on his mower. Bradley's Lexus was nowhere in sight. Dev climbed out of the car and signaled Pete, who cut the motor but didn't climb off.

He tipped up the brim of his ball cap. "Afternoon, Dev."

"Where's the flatlander?"

Pete shrugged. "Told him you was on your way over and he had a sudden recollection of an appointment."

"He tell you his name?"

"Nawp." He resettled his cap on his grizzled hair. "Know who he is, though. Dropped Casey off at Harrison House his first day." He squinted up at Dev. "Not a friend of Casey's, is he? Doesn't seem the type."

"No. He's not."

"He left you this note." Pete pulled a crumpled piece of thick cream paper out of his overall pocket and smoothed the creases out against his belly. "Here."

Dev took the note, tempted to crush it in his fist. "If you see him around at any of the other properties? Give me a call right away."

"Ayup." He started the engine again and put the mower in gear.

Dev smiled wryly. Not a big talker, Pete. He unfolded the note and looked down at the forceful, jagged letters:

This deal won't last forever. Take it now, before I take it all.

He got back in the car, but rather than driving straight back to Harrison House the way his heart urged him to, he drove the circuit, passing each of the empty houses, his gut clenching tighter at each one.

They needed people to need *them*, to live in them, to love them. *And Home needs those people.*

Instead of heading to his cottage, he drove back to Harrison House and parked in front of the door—completely *on* the driveway, which was perfectly adequate, no matter what Bradley fucking Pillsbury said. He couldn't help the way his heart lifted as he banged through the front door and headed for the office. It gave an extra leap when Casey looked up at him over the monitor with a smile that crinkled the corners of his eyes.

He patted a neat stack of paper on the corner of the desk. "Got the budget for the antique fair sorted."

Dev blinked. "You did?"

"It wasn't too hard once I tracked down the missing formula. I had no idea Home did anything like this. It's pretty cool."

Dev fumbled with the papers, staring almost blindly at the neat rows of figures. The total was still red, but there weren't any more of those judgmental #REF! errors dotted all over the place. "It's really done? I was only gone for twenty minutes."

Casey shrugged. "Like I said, it wasn't hard once I traced the formulas." He widened his eyes, shaking his head. "Although, *wow*. Who knew Port-a-Potties cost so much?"

Dev gazed at him, heat growing in his belly. "Twenty minutes and you're done?"

"Um, sorry?" Casey bit his lip, that delectable blush throwing his freckles into relief. "I hope you don't take it as a slam on you. I mean, I can't cook. You've got an accounting weakness. So what? People have different abilities."

Dev set the papers down. "Twenty minutes and I've been wrestling with the fucking thing for days." He stalked around the desk until he was looming over Casey. "Twenty minutes and you're *done*?"

"Dev? Is that bad?"

Dev grabbed Casey's hand and pulled him up against his chest, claiming his mouth, *devouring* his moan as Casey laced his hands behind Dev's neck. Dev pulled back. "As much as I want to throw you across the desk right now—"

"Yes, please!"

"I'm not going to."

Casey pouted. "Why not?"

"Because"—he nipped behind Casey's ear—"I'm taking you on a date."

"A date?"

"Yes. A date. A real one. Wear something comfortable. Bring a light jacket." He dropped a kiss on that spray of freckles. "Be ready at five."

Chapter Seventeen

Naked except for the towel around his waist, his hair still damp from his shower, Casey glared at his wardrobe—if he could use that fancy a word for his motley collection of clothes, which didn't come close to filling the armoire.

"Dress comfortably," he groused. "What does that even mean? Sweats? Shorts? Jeans? A freaking caftan?" Not that he had one of those, but he preferred a more precise guideline for a mystery date than *dress comfortably.*

Randolph Scott, perched atop the armoire again, didn't deign to respond, since he was occupied by the serious business of grooming between his toes.

Casey huffed. "You're no help." Although expecting fashion advice from a cat was probably unreasonable.

He glanced back at his bed, currently strewn with half a dozen garments he'd already considered and discarded. Was he overthinking this? Probably. But he hadn't been on an actual date since his first year at business school. Remembering that series of one-and-dones made him want to curl up in a ball and hide under the bed.

The first guy who'd asked him out oh-so-casually suggested that the perfect place for their date would be Chez Donatien. Casey suggested a quiet coffee shop instead, someplace where they could get to know one another, someplace Casey wasn't completely incapable of eating because his stomach was perpetually tied in knots anytime he ventured into one of his dad's restaurants. The guy had grudgingly agreed—but then no-showed, leaving Casey sitting alone with a congealing latte for hours.

Alden, the second guy, had been low-key flirting with Casey all semester in their marketing class, and Casey had bitten the Chez Donatien bullet because Alden had claimed it was his birthday, and had seemed so sad that he was away from his family for the first time. Casey hadn't made the reservation himself, of course—despite what anyone thought, he had zero clout with his father and therefore with restaurant management. He'd asked Uncle Walt to intercede.

Once they were seated at the restaurant, Alden proceeded to order every appetizer on the menu—"To start," he'd said—and ordered the most expensive wine on the list. He'd been so occupied with the appetizer that the waiter had handed both IDs back to Casey, who—totally not intentionally—had spotted that Alden's address was in Westchester and his birthday was in July.

Casey hadn't said anything, pretended he hadn't seen. When the check came, Casey suggested they split the check in half, which he thought was more than fair considering he'd barely managed a bowl of soup and a sparkling water, while Alden had scarfed up all the appetizers, salad, entrée, dessert, *and* the wine.

Even before Alden had glared at Casey in astonishment and outrage, flounced off to the restroom and never returned, Casey had vowed there'd be no second date.

When the third guy tried the same line on him, Casey got the full picture, and was only mortified that he hadn't figured it out sooner: Nobody wanted *him*. Even Bradley didn't want *him*. Only the cachet of his name.

Dev, though… Dev seemed to want him, and that tied Casey's stomach up like tangled fishing line.

"I'm bound to screw this up, Randolph Scott." He looked up and met the cat's half-lidded gaze. "I have no *experience*. Dating is a *process*, right? How does a *product* person deal with that?"

Randolph Scott raised one leg and licked his butt. Casey planted his hands on his hips. "On the first date? No, absolutely not. You're worse at dating advice than you are at fashion."

Downstairs, the screen door slammed in its signature double bump. "Casey?" Dev called, his voice echoing in the stairwell. "You ready?"

As usual, Dev's deep voice sent phantom fingers walking up Casey's spine. Randolph Scott must have liked it too, because he leaped from the armoire to the desk to the floor and pawed open the door that Casey had left ajar.

"In a minute," Casey replied. Then he took advantage of Randolph Scott's doorman routine, crept onto the landing, and peeked over the banister, ready to jump back if Dev was looking up.

He wasn't, thank goodness. Instead, he was occupied greeting a very vocal Randolph Scott.

Hunh. Dev was wearing cargo shorts, a royal blue T-shirt that hugged his chest *very* nicely, canvas boat shoes with no socks, and was holding a navy hoodie bunched in one hand.

Casey scurried back into his room and more or less matched the outfit. His cargo shorts were olive, not khaki, and his T-shirt a vintage black number for a mid-80s production of *Tooth of Crime* at the Berkeley Repertory Theater. He scuffed his feet into his Vans, grabbed his Columbia hoodie, and trotted downstairs.

"Sorry to keep you waiting."

"No worries. I'm a little early."

With a last skritch of Randolph Scott's ears, Dev stood. The cat clearly disapproved, given the slit-eyed glare he favored both of them with before flicking his tail and stalking away.

As Dev gave Casey a once-over—or maybe twice-over, since his gaze flicked up and down two times—his smile took on an appreciative and distinctly predatory gleam. "Nice T-shirt."

"Th-thanks." *Enjoy the* process, *dammit.* "Yours is nice, too. Very... stylish."

"It's a plain blue T-shirt, Casey, not exactly a designer original."

"Maybe not." *Don't just* enjoy *the process*—embrace *it*. "But it displays what's inside it exceptionally well."

Dev blinked. "Uh... Okay then."

Casey winced. "Shit. Was that too smarmy? Should I tone it down? Keep the inappropriate comments to myself?"

Dev laughed. "No to all of the above. I appreciate the sentiment, trust me. It's been a while since anyone's expressed their approval."

"Hmmmph. You're *obviously* catwalk-ready." Casey flicked his fingers in Randolph Scott's direction as the cat continued walking. "We have it on the best authority. Perhaps you should invest in community vision testing for everyone in Home if they can't see what's right in front of them."

"Find me the funds in the town budget, and I might take you up on that." He held out his hand. "Let's go."

Casey's breath caught somewhere south of his throat. Dick-touching was one thing. He'd found that sometimes it was incredibly impersonal, since both parties were chasing their own orgasm and may or may not care that their partner got there too. Kissing was more intimate because it required face-to-face interaction, even with eyes clenched shut.

But hand-holding, especially hand-holding in public, represented something else entirely. It was a *declaration*. A declaration that you were happy—no, *proud*—to be connected with this person and didn't care who else knew it.

Casey laced his fingers with Dev's. "Wherever you want, I'm there."

Dev led Casey out the door, not bothering to lock it behind them, which Casey had learned was SOP in Home during the day. A dusty green CR-V with a dent in the rear passenger side door was parked in the drive. Dev opened the door for Casey, but then dropped his hand, uncertainty flickering over his face.

"I know this probably isn't the kind of transportation you're used to, but it's all I've got."

"Excuse me." Casey clambered in and grabbed the handle, glaring up at Dev. "You're correct in that it's not what I'm used to, because I grew up in Manhattan. My standard transportation is subway or bus. I don't have a car. Never even learned to drive one. And if you're comparing this extremely practical vehicle to Bradley's stupid Lexus, don't. Just hop in, Harrison. I believe you promised me a date."

Dev chuckled, saluting with three fingers. "Aye aye, captain." He closed the door and trotted around to take his place behind the wheel. As they exited the drive in a crunch of gravel, they both waved to Pete, who was tooling along Main Street on his mower.

"Does Pete mow all the lawns in Home?"

"Yup." Dev passed the Market and turned right onto the two-lane county road that led toward Merrilton. "The town contracts with him for maintenance on all the common spaces, and since everyone in town likes to toss everyone else business, all the residents pretty much hire him too. He does snow removal in the winter, tree pruning, garden mulching, you name it. Then there's his ride-share side hustle."

Casey bit his lip. "I may have stuck my foot in it a bit this morning. I noticed that Sylvia doesn't shop at the Market."

Dev grimaced. "Yeah. That's kinda been a bone of contention between her and Kat for the last fourteen years. I don't think it was intentional, originally. Sylvia was fresh off the show cancellation and newly in recovery. Figuring out alternate supply chains was one too many new things for her to deal with. But Kat took it into her head to be insulted and the rift never healed."

"Well…" Casey drew out the word. "I *may* have talked Sylvia into letting me take over ordering for the school. And *may* have mentioned partnering with Kat to source things locally and to act as intermediary."

Dev glanced at him, eyebrows raised. "She agreed?"

"Yeah. And I'm pretty sure Kat will go for it, too. We've already chatted about her local suppliers."

"Casey, my friend," Dev said, approval lacing his tone, which doubled down on the spine tingles, "we're *very* lucky you showed up in Home."

We? Casey turned away, throat thick. *Does he mean* he's *lucky too?* He reminded himself not to rush the process, not to barrel toward the product, and to keep the intrusive questions to a minimum. They passed the Home town limits, the sun casting dappled light on the road through the towering trees.

"I haven't been out of town since I arrived. Where are we going?"

"You'll see. Not far."

Casey turned back to Dev. "All this secrecy is not filling me with vast levels of confidence."

"Nothing nefarious, I promise. Check in the back."

Casey twisted around, craning his neck to scan the rear seat. An enormous basket covered with a blue gingham cloth rested behind him. He couldn't contain his grin and bounced in his seat. "A picnic? Where'd you get the food?"

"Some of it from Sylvia. Some of it from Kat." He winked. "You're not the only one who's trying to broker a truce between those two." He flicked on his turn signal and pulled off the road onto an unpaved path barely wide enough for the CR-V. He made another hard left and eased the car between the trunks of two sturdy maples, clearing the lane for other traffic. "Can you get out on that side?"

Casey eased his door open. "As long as your fancy car can handle a close encounter with some holly bushes."

"It can take it. But keep clear of those leaves in your shorts. Wouldn't want to start out the date with a dip into the First Aid kit. Could you grab the basket, please? I need to collect some things out of the back."

"Sure." Casey collected the picnic and joined Dev by the side-opening hatch door, where he was pulling an armful of folded... stuff out of the rear of the car. "What's all that?"

"Blanket. Inflatable camping cushion. Insect netting." He shut the door with a sharp bump of his hip. "I enjoy Mother Nature as much as the next guy, but I draw the line at rocks under my ass and wasps in my salad. Plus"—Dev's smile turned almost shy—"I'm hoping we'll be here for a while, and I don't want to fight the mosquitos for a taste of your skin."

Casey *may* have squeaked. Just a little. He swallowed twice and said, "Gotta love a man who thinks ahead."

This was a process he could both enjoy and embrace, because the product would be so worth it.

In fact, this time, *process* and *product* might be exactly the same thing.

Chapter Eighteen

As they stood on the rocks overlooking the quarry, Dev was mesmerized by the play of sunlight on Casey's hair, the way it brought out hidden glints of gold and copper amid the brown, like hidden treasure.

"Is this the quarry where the marble for the Home sidewalks came from?" Casey asked.

"Yep." Dev leaned closer, catching a whiff of citrus and vanilla, like a tender and perfect Summer Kitchen delicacy. *Casey on the menu. Mouthwatering.* "Stopped producing back in the Sixties when it started to fill with water. Now it's kind of the town swimming hole. The first chilly—and extremely brief—swim in spring is like a rite of passage for every kid in Home."

"Yeah?" Casey grinned up at him, eyes widening at how close Dev's face was to his. "You ever go skinny dipping up here?"

Dev leaned closer. "What do you think?"

The sun picked out more buried treasure in Casey's eyes. "I think I'd pay big money to see that."

"I'd give you the show, free of charge, except we've got a picnic awaiting us and by the time we're done eating, the mosquitos will be out in force. One day, though. When you're free in the middle of the day when the rocks are warm and the sun has dried up all the mosquito-spawning puddles."

"In the middle of the day?" Casey's tone was a nice blend of scandalized and thrilled.

Dev shrugged. "Everyone around here knows the quarry is clothing optional." He winked. "We'll both take the plunge."

"Damn it, Dev." Casey winced and shifted from foot to foot. "Now you've put that picture in my head, and these shorts are way too tight to accommodate a hard-on."

"I don't know." Dev glanced down at Casey's groin, which sported a substantial bulge behind his fly. "I'd say they're accommodating it very nicely indeed."

At the sight, Dev's cock naturally responded in kind. *Do we really need to eat?* But then he remembered: This is a date. A real date. And Casey deserved to have somebody care for him, not take the first opportunity to grope him.

He nodded at the spot under the biggest maple, in the shade, but with a clear view of the sunlit rocks and the water glinting below. "We'll set up over there for our picnic."

"You, Dev Harrison, are a cruel and unusual man."

Dev winked again. "You'll eat those words once you taste Sylvia's spanakopita." He leaned closer and murmured in Casey's ear. "And once you find out what I've got in mind for dessert."

Casey grabbed Dev's elbow. "What are you waiting for? Let's go."

Throughout the meal, Dev somehow kept from pouncing on Casey. Instead, he restricted himself to random touches and brushes of skin—no more than hand to hand, hand to knee, and once, as they were getting the insect netting hung from an overhead branch, hand to cheek when he'd brushed a mosquito away before it could land on Casey's face.

"That food was… *wow*." Casey lay back on the blanket and peered up at the leaves through the screen of white netting.

"Another strawberry?" Dev swiped the berry through Kat's chocolate sauce and dipped it in whipped cream. Then he rolled to his side, braced on one elbow, and dangled the fruit over Casey's mouth by its stem. "Come on. You know you want to."

Casey gave him a mock scowl. "We really need to discuss this compulsion you have about tempting me with fruit." He bit into the berry with his strong white teeth, a drop of juice escaping to glisten on his lower lip. "Mmmm."

"Just a minute. You've got a…" Dev leaned down, keeping his gaze fixed on Casey's, and darted his tongue out to capture the drop. "Mmmm is right."

"Dev."

The way Casey said his name, throaty and edged with need, snapped Dev's self control. Fuck strawberries. Fuck chocolate. Fuck whipped cream. He dove down and devoured Casey's mouth, the most delectable treat of all.

Casey met the onslaught, wrapping his arms around Dev's neck and pulling himself up to plaster their chests together, welcoming Dev's tongue with a stroke and slide of his own, his moan sending a spike straight down Dev's spine to land in his balls. The semi Dev had been sporting through the whole fucking meal sprang to full extension so fast he was dizzy.

Although maybe the dizziness was all because of Casey.

Casey pulled out of the kiss with a gasp. "Will we get arrested for public indecency if you fuck me here?" He nibbled delicately on Dev's collarbone. "Because I really want to get on my hands and knees for you right now."

Dev groaned, his dick throbbing. "Christ, Casey." He buried his face in Casey's neck and inhaled. "Don't tempt me."

"Why not?" Casey nipped his way up Dev's throat, but before he reached Dev's mouth, he stopped and pulled back. "Oh. I forgot. It would probably be pretty embarrassing for the town manager to get caught dick deep in some guy in public, huh?"

Dev cradled Casey's cheek in one palm. "For one thing, if I get ousted from office, I won't cry a single tear. But you're not just *some guy*. You're important. You matter. And I would never expose *you* to that kind of embarrassment."

"I don't mind a little… exposure." Casey let go of Dev's neck and grabbed the hem of his *Tooth of Crime* T-shirt, stripping it off and tossing it aside to land on top of the picnic basket. "Now you."

Dev frowned down at him. "Are you sure?"

"Exactly how much traffic does this spot get?"

"Not much, to be honest, especially not at this time of day."

"Then do it." Casey snapped his fingers. "Come on. I've been dreaming about your naked chest since I saw it that first time."

Dev grinned. "Really? Is dreaming *all* that you do?"

"If you're asking whether I wank off at the memory, I plead the Fifth."

"That's good enough for me." Dev reached behind his head to grab the neck of his T-shirt and yanked, sending it after Casey's once he'd freed his arms.

"Oh," Casey breathed, his hands hovering over Dev's pecs. "May I?"

"If you don't, I might spontaneously combust."

Then Casey's hands, so soft, so gentle, were on Dev's skin, tracing a path from the hollow in his throat to his navel, tracking each rib from spine to belly, circling his nipples with tortuous gentleness.

"I'm not made of glass," Dev said through clenched teeth. "You can be a little more forceful."

Casey shifted his gaze from Dev's chest to his face, eyes glinting and lips quirked. "You want that, do you?"

"With you?" Dev met that gaze, although his own was probably full of naked longing, not mischief. "I want everything."

"Oh, god." Casey clenched his eyes shut. "I may come in my shorts."

"I know how to fix that." Dev ran his hand down Casey's side and slid his finger under his waistband. He popped the fly button. "Take 'em off."

"God, yes." Casey unzipped and wriggled out of his shorts and briefs, wincing a little as he shoved them lower and kicked them off.

"Something wrong?"

"There's a rock poking my ass."

"Can't have that." Dev slipped his hands under Casey and rolled so he was on the bottom and Casey was straddling his hips. "Nothing can poke your ass except me." To suit actions to words, he trailed a finger down Casey's crease to tease his hole.

"*Ungh.*" Casey canted his hips up, chasing more pressure, but Dev lifted his hand.

"No. Not without lube. I know it's been a long time for you, and I won't hurt you."

Casey glared at him. "Sadist." He sat up, resting on Dev's thighs, studying him speculatively, head to one side. "Want to risk getting caught with your pants down?"

In answer, Dev unbuckled his belt, unzipped his own fly, and raised his hips. Casey grinned and tucked his hands inside Dev's briefs. He didn't strip Dev's shorts all the way off, though. Instead, he pulled them low enough to let Dev's cock spring free.

"Oh my goodness." Casey licked his lips. "You can bring *that* on a picnic with me anytime." He leaned down and teased the slit with the tip of his tongue.

"Now who's a sadist?" Dev growled. "Get my damn pants off, Casey. I want to feel you on top of me."

Casey didn't comply immediately—he licked a broad stripe up Dev's length with the flat of his tongue first—but at last they were both naked. Dev opened his arms and Casey settled against him in the cradle of Dev's legs, chest to chest, their cocks snugged next to each other between their hips.

With Casey gazing down into his eyes, his expression soft, his full lips parted, Dev couldn't breathe. Had anyone ever fit so well against him? Had anyone ever felt this perfect? Had anyone ever *looked* at him with that much warmth, as though he was the only thing that mattered?

The answer, of course, was no. To all of the above.

And if Casey hadn't undulated his hips, sliding his cock against Dev's in delicious friction, that answer would have sent Dev screaming straight off the rocks and into the water. Because if he said *yes* to Casey, to whatever this was that was between them—*gah! Other than their cocks*—then he'd be saying no to his family, his responsibilities, his home.

Because Casey would be leaving. And if Dev wanted to say *yes*, he'd have to follow.

Casey's thrusts grew more frantic. "Dev. I'm close," he panted.

Despite his doubts, Dev couldn't help responding, flexing his own hips in time with Casey's, heat growing, building, throbbing, until with Casey's strangled cry and the burst of wet heat between their bellies, the spark ignited and Dev roared his release, the sound echoing across the quarry and startling a jay out of the tree above them with an indignant squawk.

Casey uttered a contented little chirrup that arrowed straight to Dev's heart and lodged there, feathers quivering, until it dissipated in warmth that spread from his middle to the tips of his fingers and toes. *Somehow, we can make it work.* Because this—this feeling, this moment, this man? Dev refused to give any of this up.

"Casey?"

"Hmmm?" Casey nestled closer, tucking his face against Dev's neck.

"Do you think—" An insistent buzz from Dev's discarded shorts made him wince. "Shit. That's the high priority town business email notification. I have to check it."

Casey raised up on his elbows and stroked Dev's cheek. "I understand. You've got duties."

"Hey." He captured Casey's hand before he could pull away. "That doesn't mean our date is over. If you're game, I'd like to continue it. Tonight. At my place." He kissed Casey with a tease of tongue. "In my bed. Maybe we can explore that hands and knees scenario."

Casey brightened. "Really?"

"Absolutely." He sat up, keeping Casey cradled in his lap. "There are wet wipes in the picnic basket, although I expect Kat thought they'd be for our hands, post dinner."

"Hello, have you *met* Kat? I'm pretty sure she had a good idea how we'd be using them." Nevertheless, Casey scrambled off Dev's lap to dig in the basket.

Dev took a moment to admire the perfect pale globes of Casey's ass before he snagged his shorts and retrieved his phone. He frowned at the message header, recognizing the sender as one of the regular antique fair vendors. After he read the email, he let his hand fall to his lap.

"Here's one for you." Casey held out a wipe with a grin, but his smile faded when he caught Dev's expression. "Dev? Is something wrong?"

Dev set the phone aside and accepted the wipe. "It's nothing. One of the vendors had to pull out of the fair, that's all." As he cleaned himself up, though, ice crept up Dev's spine.

The timing was probably a coincidence, but he couldn't help imagining that the gods of karma had fired a warning shot over his head because he'd committed the unforgiveable sin.

He'd seriously considered leaving Home.

Chapter Nineteen

Casey's blood thrummed all the way back to Harrison House. *I'm spending the night with Dev!* He hadn't dared dream their date might go this far. Okay, so he'd dreamed, but he hadn't been confident enough to hope for it or arrogant enough to plan for it.

Granted, Dev seemed a little distracted as they drove. Every time Casey shot a glance at him, that tiny frown was pleating Dev's forehead between his eyebrows. As much as Casey would have liked to believe it was because he was concentrating on the road, he couldn't really chalk it up to that. Yes, the two-lane road was winding, but traffic was nonexistent.

By the time Dev pulled up in front of Harrison House, Casey's excitement had dimmed but hadn't vanished entirely. Although, if Dev was sincere about extending their date, wouldn't they have gone straight back to his cottage?

Dev turned to him, his face serious in the twilight. "I need to follow up on something quickly before we go, so if you'd like to grab a quick shower?" He grinned, and it was *almost* as bright as normal. "I don't imagine those wet wipes did an impeccable job. I know I'll be showering myself once we get to my place, so we can start with a clean slate, so to speak."

"Works for me." Casey scrambled out of the car and waited for Dev to join him by the steps. He laced their fingers together and counted it as a good sign when Dev didn't pull away.

Inside the vestibule, Dev gestured toward the stairs. "Grab whatever you need for tonight and tomorrow morning." He bent and kissed Casey softly. "I'll meet you here in fifteen?"

Casey caught him behind the neck and pulled him into a second kiss. "Make it ten."

Laughing, Dev squeezed his hand once, and then strode off in the direction of his office.

He really wants me. Maybe not as much as Casey wanted *him*, but heck, that was impossible. Casey took a moment to enjoy the view before Dev vanished around the corner and released his excitement from its self-doubt straitjacket.

Randolph Scott leaped from the top of the grandfather clock in the curve of the stairwell and gazed up at Casey, his ears flattened. Casey planted his hands on his hips and glared back.

"Don't judge. You've got to admit that Dev from the rear is a truly inspiring sight." He sighed. "Although from the front he's pretty damn inspiring, too."

Casey left Randolph Scott nosing the picnic basket and raced up the stairs. Ten minutes. He could get ready in ten minutes. Hell, if more sex with Dev was at the finish line, he could make it in five. He bounded into his room and stripped off his T-shirt. But as he was about to launch it onto the bed, he froze.

The clothes he'd discarded after dressing for the picnic were still scattered across the foot of the bed.

However, they weren't alone.

Shirt clutched in his hand, he crept closer, belly jittering like his failed crème pâtissière, and stopped well short of his pillows.

Because there, set precisely in the middle of each one, was a dead mouse.

"Randolph Scott," Casey bellowed. "What the actual *fuck*?"

"Casey?"

Casey turned with a squeak, clutching his shirt to his bare chest, which was… way too princessy for his own self-respect. "Oh. Kenny. Hi. Didn't, um… Was I expecting you?"

Kenny shook his head. "Not really. I spotted a Shaker-style end table at an estate sale that I thought would work in the living room, so I brought it by. I didn't realize you'd be here." He smirked, his glasses glinting orange in the last sunlight slanting in through the window. "Kat said you and Dev would be out tonight."

"Yeah, well, that's a work in progress." He pointed to his pillows and their unwelcome occupants. "But in the meantime, Randolph Scott is punking me."

Kenny moved closer, shoving his glasses up with one knuckle. "That's not punking, Casey. It's a statement of affection."

"Affection?" Casey's voice may have risen an octave or two on the word. "How are deceased rodents statements of *affection*?"

"He's sharing resources with you. He had two dead mice—" Kenny leaned closer and peered at something Casey had taken for a dark thread. "Make that three."

Casey pressed his fist to his mouth, willing his stomach contents to stay put. He closed his eyes and took a deep breath. *I will not throw up. I will not.* "Please," he said faintly, eyes still shut, "please don't tell me that's a mouse tail."

"You want me to lie to you?"

Casey started to sink down on the desk chair but then bolted upright, eyes flying open. He squinted at the seat to make sure it didn't contain any other mouse parts, and then plopped down with a sigh as Randolph Scott trotted into the room and jumped onto the bed. He patted one of the mice with a big front paw, and then minced across Casey's scattered clothes—*god, I'm going to have to wash* all *of them!*—to sit, tail curled around his paws, regarding Casey with a distinctly smug expression.

"If you're waiting for a thank you," Casey said with a scowl, "you'll keep waiting."

"Aw, Casey. He only did it because he loves you." Kenny gestured to the pillows and the—*eww!*—tail. "It's all about the math. He's saying, *Look, I had three dead mice, and I gave two of them to you.* You got the lion's share."

"Yeah, well, I don't think much of his luxury turndown service," Casey grumbled. "Now I need to get new pillows." He glanced at Randolph Scott, who was calmly washing the same paw he'd tapped the mouse with. "And possibly a new wardrobe."

"Don't be such a spoilsport. Just keep your door closed from now on."

"I do keep it closed!" Casey pointed at Randolph Scott. "But he can open those paddle door handles. I've watched him do it."

"Well, don't worry about it tonight." Kenny grabbed a couple of tissues from the box on the bedside table. "I'll take care of these for you. I expect Dev has some extra pillows somewhere, although"—Kenny waggled his eyebrows—"if you were to sleep *elsewhere* tonight, I can have Pete bring in some new ones from Merrilton tomorrow."

The excitement that had waned in the face of multiple mouse carcasses returned. Except…

"I don't want Dev to think I'm only going with him because my pillows were defiled."

Kenny picked up the mice with the tissues, much to Randolph Scott's wide-eyed alarm. "I'm pretty sure Dev knows you're not only after him for his bedding." He smiled as Randolph Scott jumped off the bed and danced around his feet, mewing in distress. "He knows you're a good guy. All of us do." He saluted with the mouse-filled tissues. "Enjoy the rest of your evening." He left, Randolph Scott at his heels.

Casey stood and pivoted slowly. Could there be other *surprises* lurking elsewhere? He shuddered. *Note to self: leave nothing open.* Luckily, his Dopp kit was in the bathroom, safely shut inside the old-fashioned vanity cabinet above the toilet. The linen closet had Shaker knob handles, as did his bedside table and armoire. Those, at least, were safe from feline incursions.

He hoped.

But Randolph Scott was a very resourceful cat. Maybe Casey could talk Dev into installing childproof latches, at least in his room? That was a conversation for later, though. Tonight, he didn't even have to mention the mice because he and Dev were already planning to spend the night elsewhere. Dead mice, childproof locks, and pillow replacement could wait until tomorrow.

He glanced at the retro brass alarm clock on his nightstand. *Shit!* He'd already been up here for more than ten minutes.

Casey grabbed clean shorts, T-shirt, and briefs from the armoire drawers—making doubly sure to close everything up tightly—and raced for the bathroom. A glance over the banister assured him that Dev wasn't already in the vestibule, tapping his foot with impatience.

He'd never do that, anyway. Dev wasn't Donald, or Bradley, or any of the guys Casey had almost dated. He'd wait. But that didn't mean he should have to. Casey refused to be one more person whose needs Dev had to cater to at the expense of his own. So, although he was *thorough* with his shower, he was also quick.

Since his scruff hadn't reached Neanderthal chic levels yet, he didn't bother to trim it. His hair could air dry on the way, and if it was still damp when his head hit Dev's mercifully mouse-free pillows and Casey looked like a clown college drop-out in the morning? That was a tomorrow-Casey problem, along with childproof locks, et cetera.

Only two minutes past the initial fifteen target, Casey trotted downstairs, smoothing his Hunter's Moon T-shirt, and hoped his smile wasn't too lascivious. "Sorry I took longer than I..." His steps slowed as he peered around the empty vestibule. "Dev?"

He peeked into the living room. Also empty, as was the dining room, the butler's pantry, and the kitchen. The picnic basket was still by the front door, its gingham covering slightly askew from Randolph Scott's inspection. Casey shuddered. *As long as he was taking something out and not putting something in.*

Clearly, Dev had gotten caught up with something in the office, and Casey couldn't get bent out of shape about that. He'd known going into this that Dev was an important guy, but there should be limits for Dev's own sake, dammit.

As he headed down the hallway toward where the glow of the office light spilled out onto the gleaming wood floor, Casey couldn't hear Dev's voice, so maybe he wouldn't have to give some thoughtless Home resident a piece of his mind about Dev deserving a little time off from being everybody's go-to guy.

He pressed a hand to his middle to calm the butterflies doing loop-the-loops there. *Soon. This is happening soon.*

When he stepped inside, though, Dev wasn't on the phone or busy on the computer or rifling through the neat stack of financial statements Casey had left for him. Instead, he was simply sitting in the chair, staring at nothing, his jaw tight.

"Dev?" Casey moved farther into the office so he could see over the monitors. Dev's hands were clenched on his chair's arms. "What is it?" Casey's belly dropped. "Oh god. It's not Ty, is it? Sylvia? Kat?"

He knew nothing had happened to Kenny, but Dev's notion of family didn't stop with his inner circle of friends. Casey hurried around the desk and crouched next to the chair, laying a hand on Dev's forearm. *Jeez, he might have been carved from quarry marble.* "What can I do to help?"

Dev shook his head, muscles bunching in his jaw, but didn't speak.

"You're scaring me, sweetheart." Casey ran his hand up Dev's arm to rest on his shoulder. "Please. Tell me what's wrong."

"It's over." Dev's voice was barely audible.

Casey sucked in a sharp breath, fingers going numb. *Over? It never started.* "I understand. I'll go—"

"No!" Dev grabbed Casey's hand, his grip nearly painful, his eyes wide and horror-stricken. "Not us. I don't mean us. Never us."

Relief washed through Casey so fast his knees wobbled. "Okay. Good. In that case, tell me about it. Whatever it is, we'll figure it out."

"Casey. This isn't your problem."

Casey rose, wrapped an arm across Dev's shoulders and kissed the top of his head. "That's where you're wrong. If it's your problem, then it's mine. And one thing I've discovered about myself is that while I'm not great at long and involved processes, if I've got a goal in my sights, I can totally get results. Now." He nudged Dev's knees apart enough that he could sit on one muscled thigh—not to start anything, but so they could share the single chair. "Tell me all about it."

Chapter Twenty

Funny, but Casey's weight in Dev's lap, Casey's arm across his shoulders, Casey's warmth against his chest wasn't the least suggestive or sexual. Dev could read the intent behind Casey's actions as though Casey had announced each one: *Here, I'm putting my arm around you to hold you up. I'm sitting down with you so we can face this together. I'm leaning against you so you're not alone.*

As bleak as Dev's outlook was at the moment, a little bud of joy sprouted under his heart. He buried his face in Casey's neck and took a shuddering breath. Nash would never have offered unasked support like this, any more than Dev would have taken it. Their relationship had been one endless tug of war, a seesaw where one was always down so the other could be up. A zero-sum game in which there wasn't enough praise or admiration or space for both of them to be happy at once. And forget being vulnerable. That would have been the kiss of death.

With Casey, Dev could admit he needed help without worrying it would be kicked back in his face later as weakness, incompetence, inadequacy.

"Please tell me nothing's happened to Ty," Casey murmured, his breath ghosting against Dev's temple.

"Ty's fine. Everybody's fine." He pulled back so he could look up into Casey's eyes. "But Home…" He swallowed thickly. "Home is dead."

Casey's eyebrows bunched. "What do you mean, Home is dead?"

"I mean that we're broke. Bankrupt. Shit out of money."

"That can't be." Casey shifted on Dev's knee and scrabbled the stack of financial statements closer. "I saw the numbers. It'll be tight for a bit, but once the vendor registration fees roll in next week, and with the commissions after the antique fair, cash flow will ease up."

"That's what *should* have happened. But remember I told you up at the quarry that a vendor had dropped out?" Dev nudged the mouse, waking the monitor and displaying the three emails splashed across its screen. "Look at those."

Casey peered at the screen, squinting at the tiny font. He reached for the mouse, but for some reason, shuddered and just leaned closer. "Three more vendors leaving?" He huffed, clearly more annoyed than gutted. "The least they could do is give a reason."

"They don't have to. Until Friday, registrations can be canceled with no questions asked. They'll lose their deposit, but that's a minor amount. In fact, the registration fees aren't that big either because the real money comes from those commissions. It's always been that way. Vendors only have to pay a percentage of their sales after the fair, so if they have a bad day, they're not crippled by it."

Casey gazed at him with fond exasperation. "That is so on-brand for Home, but I've gotta say, completely out of step with modern business practices. Most events like this demand full payment upfront and it's the vendor's business to, well, drum up enough business to make a profit."

"I know. But it's our major draw. Vendors always called it the Fair Fair, because they know we only make money if they make money."

"Admirable, but that doesn't mean they get to leave us in the dark about their reasons this time. One cancellation is an anomaly. Two a coincidence. Three is a pattern, and four?" His lips thinned. "Four means something fishy is going on and unless we know why it's happening, we can't fix it."

That little bud unfurled another petal. *He said we.* Nevertheless... "This isn't your problem, Casey. You've got enough on your plate already, so you shouldn't let this worry you."

"Does it worry *you*?"

"Of course it does, which is why I have to deal with it. But this isn't the evening you signed on for."

"Newsflash, Dev." Casey framed Dev's face with his hands. "More sex would have been nice, and I'm not ruling it out in the future, but I'm not gonna whine and stamp my feet because you've got big problems hanging over your head."

"You'd be the first," Dev muttered, remembering Nash's meltdown tantrum when he'd announced he was leaving the band to take over his family's legacy. He hadn't even hugged Dev or offered him any comfort over Garlan and Grandfather's deaths, and he'd *met* both men.

"I know some people think sex is the reason for a relationship," Casey said, "but to me, it's more the result."

"Are you saying we're in a relationship?"

Casey mock-glared at him. "Everybody who isn't a complete stranger is in some kind of relationship with you. I mean, Bradley is in a relationship with me, but it's a really annoying one, built on his complete refusal to consider anyone's perspective but his own and my continuing efforts to make him go away. I hope that the relationship we're building—that we've already built—has a different profile and nobody gets to decide what it looks like except us." His lips quirked. "I mean, I've already gotten more action today than I've had in years. Make that *ever*. So I'm perfectly happy to let this unfold. To let *us* unfold." He gnawed on his lower lip, uncertainty flickering over his face. "That is, if you want to."

Dev leaned his forehead against Casey's and closed his eyes. "God. So much."

"Good." Dev didn't have to see Casey's face to know he was smiling. He could hear it in his voice.

"I wish I could tell you things will get better. But Home has been sliding for years now, even before my brother died. I may not be the best relationship bet."

Casey drew back enough to drop a kiss on Dev's forehead. "I'd say relationships are more give and take, but that implies that somebody is *taking*, which isn't always a positive thing. I prefer to think of it as share and share alike—good times and bad, successes and failures." He pointed at the screen. "Problems and solutions. So let's tackle this one, shall we?"

Dev gazed at Casey's determined expression and laughed helplessly. "This isn't something that's an easy fix. Maybe it would be better if you just left it to me."

Casey swiveled his gaze from the monitor and fixed it on Dev, eyes narrowing. "Now, I can imagine several reasons why you might say something like that." He held up his index finger. "One, you're executing the standard Dev Harrison maneuver of taking on all responsibilities, whether they're yours or not."

"I don't—"

"Two." He added his middle finger, which might or might not have been a statement. "You're afraid that if I see the scope of the problem, it might scare me away, which is a little arrogant on my part because that assumes that you *want* me to stick around."

"I do. But that doesn't mean—"

"Or three." He added his ring finger and waggled all three. "You don't think I can do it."

Dev blinked. "Uh…"

"Aha!" Casey nudged Dev's shoulder with all three fingers. "If we intend to make this *relationship* work, Devondre, you'll need to stop judging me by my kitchen ineptitude. I *can* do other things." He tapped the financial statements. "Remember?"

Dev bowed his head. "Please accept my abject apology."

"Oh, don't be abject. It doesn't suit you at all. But nevertheless, apology accepted. Thank you."

"All right." Dev snaked his arm around Casey's waist. "What's the plan?"

"The first step is to find out what's going on." Casey peered at the screen. "Good. This one has a phone number." He held out his palm and waggled his fingers. "Give me your phone. They're more likely to answer if the call isn't from a stranger."

Dev handed it over and Casey keyed in the number.

"Hello?" a woman's voice said tentatively.

"Hello, Leslie. My name is Casey Friel and I'm calling you on behalf of Antiques at Home."

"Oh." Leslie uttered a squawk of nervous laughter.

"You're on speaker with me and Dev Harrison." Casey kept his voice soothing and upbeat. "Since you've been a regular at our event for so long, we were hoping you could share your reasons for cancelling your booth this year. We sincerely hope nothing bad has happened to you or your business."

Her sigh was audible. "Oh, no. I'm so, so sorry. I feel really bad about pulling out at the last minute, but the fellow at Green Mountain Shadows made the offer too tempting to refuse."

"Green Mountain Shadows?" Casey shared a glance with Dev. "The resort in Merrilton?"

"Yes. Because it's a new thing this year, and a decision they made so last minute, they offered us a free spot at their fair both this year and next year. The Fair Fair—I mean, Antiques at Home—has always been good to us, and its rates are completely reasonable, but, you know, they're not *free*. Plus, the foot traffic in Home has decreased over the last couple of fairs. The resort's new event offers more potential traffic and an annual event rather than biennial. I couldn't afford *not* to take the offer."

Dev's grip tightened around Casey's waist, the only thing that was keeping him from drowning in *what the ever-loving fuck*. Casey patted his hand. "We understand. Thank you so much for sharing with us, and I hope the event is successful for you."

"You're being super gracious. I truly appreciate it. And if the resort's event isn't what they promise, I hope you know I'll be the first to sign up for your next fair. Thank you so much."

Casey disconnected the call and set Dev's phone down with what seemed deliberate gentleness. "Did you have any idea that the resort was planning a rival event?"

"No. And it's not like we're competitors. Home doesn't even have an inn anymore. The concierge *recommended* our fair to guests looking for activities in the area."

Casey *hmmm*ed softly. "I suppose they might have decided a competing event was a way to capitalize on their in-house revenue, but if they're offering vendors spots for free, that doesn't really track. Unless they're counting on higher occupancy to compensate."

The computer pinged with an incoming email. Dev dropped his head against the chair back. "Don't tell me. More vendors dropping out?"

Casey leaned toward the screen. "Wish I could say it wasn't, but I'm guessing we can count on everyone dropping out. Leslie was right. Margins for antique dealers aren't so great that they can turn down a chance to increase them like this."

"Fuck, Casey. We've already lost the Inn and the dance studio. Without the fair, without the tourists it brings to town, the other local businesses'll feel the pinch—Kat, Kenny, the Knit Shop, Curiosity, Mountain Laurel, Artists United, hell, even the historical society. This could gut them." He clutched his hair. "And what the *hell* am I going to do with all those Port-a-Potties?"

Casey gently freed Dev's fingers from his death grip on his hair. "Don't worry about the Port-a-Potties. I bet I can work something out with the rental agency. If nothing else, the resort will need them for their event."

Dev rubbed the bridge of his nose. "I might have to sell to your fucking fiancé after all."

"If you mean Bradley"—Casey poked Dev's shoulder again—"first of all, *not my fiancé*. Second, what do you mean sell to him? Sell what?"

"He offered to buy Harrison House."

Casey stared at him for a good ten seconds, apparently speechless.

"Casey?"

"No. Just no."

"Of course not. I'd never sell—"

"That's not what I mean. I know you'd never sell Harrison House. When was he here? And why didn't you tell me?"

"He, um, came back. A couple of days after he showed up in the summer kitchen."

Casey took a deep breath and let it out slowly. "Okay. First rule of relationships? No hiding stuff like this."

"To be fair, we didn't exactly have a relationship at the time."

"Remember what I said? *Everything* is a relationship. It's simply a question about quality. Now, I know we've both got a lot to think about, but I believe you invited me back to your place tonight?"

"I did. I'm not sure I'm up for—"

Casey laid a finger across Dev's lips. "Shush. I'm not going to importune you for sex. But you've had a blow tonight. If it's okay with you, could I just sleep with you? Hold you?"

"You don't have to do that."

"That wasn't the question, Dev."

Dev closed his eyes, took a breath, let it out slowly. *Remember. It's okay to let* Casey *know you need help.* "Yes. I would like that very much."

Casey nodded decisively. "Good." He grinned. "Although I confess I might have an ulterior motive for avoiding my own bed." He wrinkled his nose. "Randolph Scott left a dead mouse on each of my pillows."

Def lifted an eyebrow. "He left you two dead mice?"

"And a tail."

The other eyebrow joined the first and Dev whistled. "Damn. He must really like you."

Casey traced Dev's lower lip with a fingertip. "As long as *you* like me, that's what matters."

"I do." Dev kissed Casey's fingers. "Now let's go to bed. Because you're right. I really want to be held tonight."

Chapter Twenty-One

Casey had always had an uncanny ability to wake up at whatever time he wanted, probably because he'd learned to keep out of his father's way in the mornings, when Donald was fresh from the farmers' markets and already barking at his sous chef over the phone.

Since he knew when Dev took his morning run, he'd set his internal clock to wake up an hour before that, just as the wan dawn light filtered through the Roman blinds in Dev's bedroom, casting a soft glow over the butter-yellow walls with their white wainscoting, over the gleaming wood floors littered with discarded clothing, over the rumpled patchwork quilt and white sheets, and of course, over Dev himself.

Apparently, Dev's worry followed him into sleep, because there was a little divot between his eyebrows. Casey was tempted to kiss it, but he didn't want to wake the man. He suspected Dev hadn't been sleeping well lately—maybe not for the last year and a half, since his brother and grandfather had died and the care and feeding of Home landed squarely on Dev's shoulders.

And what shoulders. With the sheets pooled around his waist, Dev's admirable upper body was on full display, but Casey wasn't tempted—okay, he was a *little* tempted, because *damn*—but he wouldn't, because he recollected the surprise and wonder on Dev's face when Casey had made it clear that he'd meant it when he said he didn't expect sex.

Casey chuckled softly. He'd bet his last nickel that Dev had never been the little spoon before in his life.

He climbed out of bed, careful not to jostle the mattress. After he excavated his clothes from the random piles and got dressed, he eased Dev's phone off the nightstand and took it out into the living room of the charming little cottage—not because he wanted to snoop, but because he didn't want Dev to wake with the ping or vibration of a message.

Casey pulled out his own phone and typed a text:

CF: Didn't want to wake you. Got an errand to run. CU later this morning.

He gazed down at the screen for a moment, teeth sunk into his lower lip. *Oh, what the hell.* He added a heart emoji and hit *send.*

When he crept back into the bedroom to return the phone, Dev was still asleep, his face nestled into Casey's pillow, and Casey nearly abandoned his plan and climbed back into bed. But if what he suspected was true, he didn't have any time to waste.

He slipped out of the cottage, softly closing the door behind himself, and trotted across the field. He hesitated between the Uber or Lyft apps, but then just called Pete directly.

"Ayup?"

"Pete, it's Casey. I need you to put on your ride share hat, whichever one you like. I need a lift to the resort and I want to leave before Dev gets up."

"Mmmphmmm."

Casey caught the edge of judgment in the multipurpose Home grunt and hurried to say, "I'm not bailing, if that's what you're thinking. But I'm pretty sure I'm the only one who can fix this particular problem, and it can't really wait. Pick me up in front of Harrison House?"

"Three minutes." Pete disconnected, and Casey had to laugh. *Never one for idle chitchat, our Pete.*

Casey debated whether to run upstairs and change clothes, but given that his room was still tainted with the ghosts of mice past, he abandoned the idea. He might be rumpled from tossing his clothes on the floor in his hurry to comfort Dev last night, but at least he didn't smell like sex.

He lifted the hem of his shirt, pressed it to his nose, and inhaled. *No. I smell like Dev.* And *that* was more empowering than Excalibur, Mjolnir, and the Lasso of Hestia combined.

Pete rolled up in his pickup rather than the hybrid Escape he used for his ride share gigs. Casey climbed in.

"Which app should I fire up?"

"Neither." He pulled out of the drive in a crunch of gravel and headed up Main Street.

He didn't say another word on the way to town, and Casey, gnawing his lip until it was probably raw, didn't attempt to break the silence. But when Pete pulled under the porte-cochere in front of the resort's enormous main doors, Casey turned to him.

"I'm not sure how long this will take. You don't need to wait."

"Need a ride home when you're done?"

"Well. Yes."

"Mmmphmmm."

This time, the grunt held definite approval. Casey waited a moment, but no additional words were forthcoming, so he climbed out of the truck. Pete pulled into a guest parking slot right next to the doors.

You've got more faith in me than I do, my friend.

The sun had cleared the treetops, its amber rays sending Casey's shadow stretching out in front of him as he marched toward the club wing. He knew which room to aim for—Bradley had texted him the number, announcing it was one of the top suites, when he'd ordered Casey to meet him the day he'd barged into the summer kitchen. Naturally, Casey had ignored the text.

But as he stood in front of the door, belly in knots, he remembered Bradley offering to buy Harrison House, Bradley cruising past the vet clinic like a creeper, Bradley refusing to take no for an answer every time ever, and hoped like hell that *he* wasn't the catalyst for Bradley's decision to take aim at Home.

Rather than knock—it was early, and the other guests didn't deserve to be awakened—Casey pulled out his phone and called Bradley's number, something he'd never done before, and frankly had never expected to do ever.

Bradley answered after the second ring, so either he was already awake or a light sleeper. "Casey. While I trust this means you're ready to behave like an adult, I have a conference call in five minutes that—"

"I'm at your door."

Bradley didn't respond, but Casey heard his footsteps in stereo from the phone and from inside the suite. When the door opened to reveal Bradley in his normal pressed-chinoed, Lauren-button-downed, hair-producted take on casual morning wear, Casey disconnected the call and tucked his phone away. "We need to talk."

"I've been saying the same thing for days, but you've picked a highly inconvenient time. Call down for room service and have breakfast sent up. After my meeting—"

"I'm not here for breakfast."

Bradley frowned. "Then why the devil are you here at this hour? Really, Casey. I thought you'd finally come to your senses and were ready to—"

"Are you behind all the vendors pulling out of Home's antique fair?" If Casey had expected Bradley to look guilty or even self-conscious, he was wide of the mark. If anything, the expression on Bradley's face was smug satisfaction. "I *knew* it. You *are*." He barged past Bradley into the middle of the suite's living area and whirled. "Why the hell would you do something like that? Home is nothing to you."

"Precisely. *Home*"—Bradley sounded as though he'd unexpectedly taken a swig of curdled milk— "is nothing. But it *could* be something with the proper upgrades, positioning, and rebranding."

"The people who live there don't want to be rebranded. They like the way things are now."

Bradley scoffed. "They couldn't possibly. No one could. No accommodations for overnight guests. No restaurants. No liquor license within twenty miles. Southern Vermont is a prime target for leaf-peepers and hard-core skiers, but *Home*"—there was that sour-milk tone again—"isn't equipped to handle the tourist trade even if they could attract it."

"Maybe they don't want their town overrun at all seasons. Ever think of that? They like its quieter pace. They like having it to themselves most of the year. That's why the antique fair is biennial. It suits them and their needs."

Bradley shook his head sadly. "I'm not sure what they taught you in that business school of yours—"

"You mean Columbia? *That* business school?"

"—but the economy of every town in or near a tourist destination depends on tourist dollars. Since the people in charge aren't fulfilling their mandate to capitalize on opportunities that should be obvious to anyone with a modicum of insight, new management is clearly needed to bring the town up to its full potential."

Casey frowned. "You make it sound as if Home is nothing more than a commodity."

Bradley lifted his eyebrows. "Isn't it?"

"No. Not entirely. Home is its people. It always has been. Tell me, Bradley. The Market, Make It Do, Mountain Laurel nursery, the vet clinic, all the other Home businesses. Where do they fit in your rebranding plan?"

"I'm sure the investors will have some input, but any business that wishes to remain will obviously be expected to conform to the upgraded town model."

"What if they don't want to change?"

"Then I'm sure the corporation will offer them reasonable terms to relocate."

"Corporation? You're going to *incorporate* Home?"

"It's the most efficient business entity for what we expect to accomplish."

Casey ran his fingers through his hair. "But why? There are other places, other targets, other projects you can add to your portfolio. Why Home?"

Bradley's gaze tracked Casey's fingers and his tongue darted out to moisten his bottom lip. "Because it's ripe for the picking. Unspoiled. Pure potential."

Casey froze at the avaricious glint in Bradley's eyes. "Are we still talking about Home?"

He took a step toward Casey. "If I were to be offered something of equal value, something that would fit perfectly with my own brand, I might be willing to... negotiate."

Casey took a step back. "What kind of *something*?"

"Casey." Bradley's caressing tone sent a spike of alarm down Casey's spine. "Don't you think it's time to accept the inevitable? I've arranged a private tutor for you back in Manhattan. You'll come back with me today. Move into my penthouse while you perfect your kitchen skills. Then, we'll christen Chez Donatien's grand reopening with our wedding reception. After that, you can transition into executive chef and we'll promote the sous chef."

"So all of this—scuppering the antique fair, trying to buy Dev out—it was all just maneuvering to get me back in line?"

He shrugged. "I want Chez Donatien to succeed. And I always get what I want."

Okay, *that* tone wouldn't be out of place in a serial killer. "So I was right. You only want me for the optics. For the hype."

"Is that what you think?" Bradley reached out and twined a finger in one of Casey's curls. "Ripe for the picking," he murmured. "Unspoiled. Pure potential. How could I resist?"

Casey grabbed Bradley's wrist and squeezed until Bradley's fingers twitched and he released Casey's hair. He let go and wiped his palm on his shorts. "So if I go back with you, you'll let Home be?"

"If I must. I'll even cancel the replacement antique fair." He shrugged. "It might cause me some minor inconvenience, but nothing I can't absorb."

"But what about the vendors? You promised them a free venue."

"They ought to know better. Nothing is ever free. Maybe *Home* can lure them back, although if I were the town manager, I'd refuse to take them. Disloyalty must be punished." He swept Casey with the same proprietary gaze he used on his Lexus. "Something you'll have to learn."

"But then the vendors lose sales, and Home is out a revenue stream. That doesn't benefit anyone."

"On the contrary. It benefits me." Another up and down sweep of his cold blue eyes. "And once I've schooled you, you'll be begging me to close the deal. Among other things." He ran a finger back and forth along his leather belt. "It's time, Casey. Time to face reality. Compared to what I can offer, there's nothing for you here." He tongue darted out to lick his lower lip. "And if you don't fall in line, I'll make sure there's nothing here for anybody else either."

Casey swallowed thickly. "Fuck you, Bradley." He brushed past Bradley and flung open the door. "There's *everything* for me here, and I refuse to let you destroy it."

Bradley laughed. "That's so... precious." *Ugh, he sounds worse than Gollum.* "You actually believe you can stop me. You're even more naive than I thought."

"Maybe I am. But you've forgotten one important thing."

"Is that so? What might that be?"

Casey forced a smile. "I'm not alone."

Chapter Twenty-Two

Dev checked his phone for the tenth time since he'd awoken to an empty bed. Casey's text—especially the promise that he'd see Dev later and the heart emoji—had eased Dev's disappointment a little. Still, he had to admit this morning was the first time he'd woken refreshed since the accident.

Therapeutic cuddling for the win.

When he'd gotten to his office, though, his mood had crashed and burned spectacularly. Every single vendor had canceled except Curiosity, Home's own antique store, but they were never charged registration or commission fees anyway because they were part of the town. Now Dev would be put in the position of telling Fabiola that one of her regular income streams had completely dried up. That would definitely be a hardship for her. Would it be bad enough for the business to fold? For yet another longtime resident of Home to move away because what was once a haven was now a financial sinkhole?

The longer Dev looked at the numbers, the lower his heart sank. He'd have no choice but to sell to that Pillsbury prick unless he could pull a rabbit out of his ass in the next six weeks to cover the negative cash flow.

"Fuck," he muttered, dropping his head into his hands. "Maybe I'll set the Port-a-Potties in the front yard and call it an art installation."

"Let's not go quite that far."

At the sound of that voice, its tone fond, Dev shot upright, a smile cracking his face. "Casey."

Casey walked around the desk and stood behind Dev's chair, wrapped his arms around Dev's neck, and planted a kiss under Dev's ear. "Hello, there."

"Mmmm," Dev hummed. "I missed you this morning."

Casey let go and spun the chair. He cradled Dev's face between his hands. "You saw my text, didn't you? You didn't think I'd just run out on you?"

"Yes, I saw it. I wouldn't have thought the worst of you, but I appreciate that you took the time to let me know why you'd gone." He drew Casey down into his lap, sighing contentedly when Casey nestled closer, tucking his head under Dev's chin. *More therapeutic cuddling. I could get used to this.*

Dev reached toward the monitor. He didn't want the bad news staring him in the face, not with Casey in his arms. But Casey caught his wrist gently.

"You were stressing about finances again, weren't you?"

"How could you tell?"

"For one thing, when I walked in, you were muttering about Port-a-Potties. For another, your monitor is littered with cancellation emails."

Dev rested his cheek against Casey's soft curls. "It's done, Casey. Our major town fundraiser is dead in the water."

"I'm so sorry, Dev." He pulled back. "This is all my fault."

Dev drew him back against his chest again. "Since you've only been here since the end of May and Home's finances have been teetering on the brink ever since I got back to town, this isn't on you. If anyone's at fault, it's me, for not staying more engaged with things. I was so caught up with the band, with music, that I left everything to Garlan and Grandfather. If I'd come back to Home more regularly, responded to their invitations more often, maybe I wouldn't be so fucking clueless."

Casey planted his palms against Dev's chest and pushed far enough away to glare. "Stop that. Stop that right this instant. You aren't the only Harrison in Home." When Dev opened his mouth to protest, Casey held up an admonitory finger. "Ah! Nope. I don't want to hear about how Ty isn't in the line of succession, or whatever stupidly archaic patriarchal tradition you've got bouncing around in your head. Saving Home is *not* solely your responsibility." He sighed and laid his head on Dev's shoulder. "However, the issue with the antique fair is really and truly my fault."

"How do you figure?"

"Bradley," Casey said darkly. "He's a controlling, manipulative, vindictive shithead. He's the one who arranged the rival fair at the resort expressly to get me to toe the line and come back to Manhattan and marry him." Casey shuddered. "Ugh. I wouldn't put it past him to have a BDSM dungeon in his penthouse, and that is *not* my scene." His brow wrinkled in thought. "If it's on the top floor of a thirty-seven-story building, would it qualify as a dungeon?"

Heat pulsed behind Dev's eyes. "Did he *threaten* you?"

Casey's expression softened. "No, dearheart. He threatened *you*. He threatened Home. Even if he'd stood a ghost of a chance with me before—which he didn't—the little chat I had with him this morning would have ensured that I booted him to the curb."

"He told me he always gets what he wants."

"Yeah, he told me that too." Casey grinned. "Guess he'll have to drown his sorrows in Evian, because he's not getting his way this time." He scrambled out of Dev's lap. "Come on."

Dev took Casey's offered hand and stood. "Where?"

"Not far. Just outside."

Dev let Casey lead him out of the office. The picnic basket still sat on the vestibule floor, but it contained more than the remains of their meal. Randolph Scott was parked on top of the gingham cloth, his paws tucked under him and his eyes closed.

Casey paused, looking down at the cat. "Did you let him in?"

"No."

"Then how does he get *in* here?"

Dev shrugged. "Randolph Scott writes his own rules. I'm sure even if I found his means of egress and blocked it, he'd find another way in."

"Remind me to chat with you later about childproof locks on everything in my bedroom." He pushed open the screen door and dragged Dev across the porch, down the steps, and across the driveway onto the lawn. He dropped Dev's hand and spread his arms, turning in a circle. "Look around, Dev. What do you see?"

Dev frowned. "Same stuff I always see. A house that needs a coat of paint. Oaks that are gonna drop a shit-ton of leaves in a few months. Lilacs in dire need of a trim."

"No, silly. You're seeing the *trees*. Maybe even the bark and the leaves. Look at the *forest*."

"Casey, I have no idea what you're talking about."

He planted his hands on his hips and gazed up at Dev, his expression fond but exasperated. "They say familiarity breeds contempt, but *really*, Dev. You've let saving Home blind you to the reasons it deserves saving."

"Are you kidding? I know why it needs saving. The people. The legacy. The community."

"Yes, all those things. But you're missing something that it has in abundance. *Charm*. It's a completely charming, quirky little New England town that doesn't have a strip mall or billboard anywhere in sight."

"Billboards are illegal in Vermont, anyway."

Casey glared at him. "Good to know, but will you please *listen*? You're so used to Home that you don't see how truly remarkable it is anymore, but I guarantee you Bradley didn't miss it. That's what he wants to exploit." His expression darkened. "And if we let that happen, he'll destroy the whole reason he wanted it in the first place, because Bradley may have a kinky side that he keeps hidden behind his preppy blazers, but it's like his life's goal is to mash down anything odd or different or *interesting*. Homogenize it until each item in his portfolio looks exactly like all the others, decked out in high-end Pillsbury *sameness*."

Dev nodded slowly. "You know, when he was talking about buying Harrison House, he harped on things that had to change."

Casey tapped his fingers on Dev's chest. "Exactly. And what makes Home so lovely is that it *celebrates* differences. Nobody who lives here is expected to change to meet some arbitrary yardstick of acceptability." He smiled up at Dev. "Only to be their own unique selves. Only to be happy. Only to *belong*."

"Okay, I get that. But what has that got to do with—"

"I know how to solve the Port-a-Potty problem," Casey blurted.

A tiny sprout of hope poked through Dev's misery. "You got the company to cancel the order?"

"Are you kidding? I'd be tempted to hold on to them and follow up on your art installation idea just so Bradley will have to hire them from Paramus or somewhere"—his grin turned mischievous—"because if it worked for the world's biggest ball of twine or biggest prairie dog, why not? But no. My thought is to put them to their original use. In fact, we might actually need more."

"By turning Home into a temporary rest stop between Hartford and Burlington? We're not exactly on the main route."

He shook his head, eyes sparkling. "By holding another event."

Dev's hope died like he'd spritzed it with weed killer. "How? The resort's cornered the market on antique vendors, and Curiosity will hardly draw enough tourist traffic to justify one Port-a-Potty, let alone two dozen."

Casey waved Dev's words away. "Not another antique fair. Not an *instead-of* event, because we don't want to punish the vendors. They're our friends and they're just trying to make a living, the same as we are."

Again, Casey's use of *we* sent a spike of joy coupled with despair spiraling through Dev's middle. He cleared his throat to dislodge its lump. "Then what?"

"An *addition-to* event, a draw for the antique crowd *plus*. A crossover event that'll benefit Home *and* the resort. Make us partners, not adversaries."

Hope, that herbicide-resistant bastard, sprouted once more. "What did you have in mind?"

Casey clasped his hands under his chin. "A food and music festival."

Dev blinked. "Wait a sec. You *want* to cook for people?"

Casey rolled his eyes. "Of course not. We don't want to turn Home into the murder capital of Vermont. But think about it. I may not be a chef myself, but over the years, I've met dozens of people in the restaurant industry. Sylvia's got connections, too, and Kat's network of local growers and suppliers is intense. One of my friends from business school got into food trucks, and I'll bet I can tap her resources."

Dev could almost see it in his mind's eye. "That... might actually work."

"Of course it will. You were in a band, right?" Casey wrapped his arms around Dev's waist. "Did you keep up any of your connections?"

"Some," Dev said cautiously. The only bridges he'd actually burned were with Nash and POV.

"Fantastic! At this late date, we'd probably need to focus on the local music scene, but that's all to the good, right? We can call it Home Grown Tastes and Tunes."

That does it. Game over.

Dev toppled straight off the cliff and into full immersion love. He picked Casey up and planned a kiss on his mouth.

"You may never be a chef, Casey, but you're brilliant. I'm all in. What do we do next?"

Before Casey could answer, Randolph Scott uttered a muffled mew. The two of them looked down in time to see him drop a dead mouse next to Dev's foot.

Casey let his forehead fall onto Dev's shoulder. "I don't suppose we can prevent him from killing rodents for the festival?"

"Don't press your luck, babe. One miracle per summer is the best we can hope for, and if we pull off the festival, that'll fill our quota."

Chapter Twenty-Three

Casey peered around the newel post and through the archway into the living room. Kat Hathaway sat in the Kennedy rocker next to the fireplace, right below Home's framed town charter, staring fixedly out the window. Sylvia was about as far away from her as possible, sitting bolt upright on the threadbare Victorian loveseat, a magazine in her lap. She was not turning the pages.

The pitcher of iced tea on its enamel tray was untouched on the coffee table, its attendant tumblers empty. He'd hoped for a little mutual beverage interaction, but that clearly hadn't happened.

He sighed, wishing Dev were here for moral support, but he'd retired to his cottage to start working his music contacts. As the person in charge of the food half of the festival, Casey really needed to get Kat and Sylvia behaving like allies, not adversaries, and their… competitive inattention didn't bode well for his plan.

He scuttled backward before either one of them spotted him and took a moment, standing next to the console table by the staircase where he'd left the tray of canapes—puff pastry topped with goat cheese, thinly sliced radishes, and microgreens.

He'd asked Sylvia to make them this morning to demonstrate them for him. She'd been mystified but had complied. Of course, he hadn't divulged where precisely he'd procured the goat cheese, microgreens, *and* the radishes, even when she'd expressed her awe and delight over the quality and freshness. She'd assumed he'd called in a favor from one of his father's suppliers.

He'd quickly changed the subject. Maybe he'd felt a tad guilty about misleading by redirection, but all in a good cause.

He picked up the tray and marched into the living room. "Good afternoon," he said brightly. "Thank you both so much for agreeing to meet with me." He approached Kat and held out the tray. "Would you like a canape? Goat cheese, radishes, and microgreens on puff pastry."

She took one, its parchment liner crinkling in her fingers. "Don't mind if I do."

He slid the tray on the table in front of Sylvia, who set her magazine aside and took a canape with a smile directed expressly at Casey. He poured three glasses of tea and handed them around.

"All set? Excellent. Now." He sat down next to Sylvia and schooled his expression into seriousness, not hard to do considering he didn't need air conditioning with the chill the two of them were blasting. "I've got some bad news to share with you both."

"Bad news?" Kat set her tea on the marble coaster on the table at her elbow. "It's not Dev, is it?"

"No. He's fine. But I'm afraid there's a threat to our town. A big one." His palms were sweating, so he laced his fingers together and clamped his folded hands between his knees. "The Fair Fair is a no-go."

Sylvia jerked, ice tinkling in her glass. "What?"

"How?" Kat's expression was thunderous. "And what the hell is Dev gonna do with all those Port-a-Potties?"

"As to what and how, the reasons aren't important. Casting blame is irrelevant and unproductive." He flicked his gaze between both women. "At some point, we just have to buckle down and solve the problem. Which brings me to why I invited you both here together. I've got a solution to the excess of Port-a-Potties, but it's going to require the two of you to cooperate closely, because we don't have much time if we expect to save Home."

Kat's scowl deepened, which Casey didn't think was possible. "Then why ask her? She doesn't care about Home. She doesn't live here. She doesn't even shop here."

Sylvia turned pointedly to Casey. "I don't shop here because every time I come into the Market, she practically chases me out with a broom. That she's riding on."

"Ha!" Kat took a vicious bite from her canape. "I don't need her looking down her snooty nose at my shop because it doesn't measure up to your big city places."

"As it happens," Sylvia said to Casey, "when I lived in the city, I did most of my personal shopping at the corner bodega."

"Bodega, shmodega. She—"

Casey stuck his fingers in his mouth and whistled loud enough to cause both women to flinch. "Time out. In the first place, both of you are here in this room and you need to *talk to each other*, not triangulate the conversation through me. Secondly, as I understand it, this feud has been going on for almost fifteen years. It's time for it to stop."

"She started it," Sylvia muttered.

"Like fun I did," Kat growled.

"What did I just say?" Casey narrowed his eyes. "Blame is immaterial. We're focusing on solutions here. Also—" He jerked his thumb at the framed cross-stitch over his head: *Welcome Home. Don't be a dick.*

Both of them huffed, nearly identically, and turned away. Casey set his jaw and plowed on.

"Kat, I spoke to Sylvia about why she didn't use you to source the supplies for Summer Kitchen. The reason had nothing to do with disapproval of the Market. She was new to the area and had other stressors in her life, so she fell back on suppliers she knew, even though they were more expensive and difficult to manage from a distance."

"She could have asked," Kat said.

"From what I understand, once you found out about where she ordered the Summer Kitchen supplies, you were hardly approachable."

"So if she doesn't look down on us here in Home, why does she live in Merrilton? I know Dev's offered to rent one of the empty Harrison properties to her."

Sylvia gripped her glass with both hands. "Since I only run classes in the summer, Casey, and since enrollment has dropped off, there's no reason for me to be here most of the year. And there are no meetings in Home."

Kat blinked, looking *at* Sylvia for the first time since Casey had entered the room. "Meetings?"

Sylvia met her gaze for an instant before focusing on her lap. "Yes. Meetings. Merrilton has several, in the library, the town hall, and the Oddfellows lodge, so it's more convenient for me to live nearby."

"I… forgot," Kat said quietly. "That you'd need those. I'm sorry."

Sylvia shrugged one shoulder. "It is what it is. I probably should have made more of an effort once I'd been around for a while. But change is hard, you know?"

"Yeah." Kat rose and scooted her rocker closer so she was within reach of the canapes. She snagged another one. "I get it. And I could have been nicer. Pete tells me rabid badgers would be better at customer service than me." She snorted. "Like he's got room to talk."

"Great." Casey clapped his hands. "Now. Kat, Sylvia's agreed to let me order all the supplies for Summer Kitchen, and I want to use you as you as my source."

"Really?" Kat asked, a canape stalled halfway to her mouth. "You'd do that?"

"I agreed to let him *try*," Sylvia said.

Casey could detect a chill creeping back in, so he grabbed a canape and held it in his palm. "Sylvia made these this morning."

Kat looked at the pastry in her hand. "I thought you made them, Casey."

"Are you kidding? If I wasn't the only Summer Kitchen student, Sylvia would probably have expelled me by now for gross incompetence and reckless endangerment. And Sylvia? Kat sourced the goat cheese, the microgreens, *and* the radishes from local farmers."

Sylvia looked from the empty canape tray to Kat. "That chevre is *amazing*. It's really local?"

Kat nodded. "The produce too."

"See?" Casey leaned forward, projecting *earnest entreaty* for all he was worth. "Cooperation. That's what we need. What I need. What *Home* needs, from you both."

Kat's gaze flicked to the cross-stitch and then to Sylvia. "All right." She gripped her knees and nodded decisively. "I'm in."

Sylvia blinked at her. "Really?"

Pink infused Kat's narrow face. "Well, it's possible I might have jumped to conclusions. But I like to think I can admit when I'm wrong."

"If anybody can appreciate starting over, it's me." Sylvia held out her hands. Casey grasped one immediately and Kat only hesitated a second before she did the same. Sylvia squeezed once and then let go, expression turning businesslike. "What's your plan, Casey?"

"I'm putting my lessons on hold for the foreseeable"—*thank goodness for an excuse*—"so I can focus on organizing a new event for Home. A food and music festival to take place the same weekend as the antique fair. Which, by the way, is occurring, but in Merrilton in conjunction with the resort." When both women opened their mouths, Casey held up both hands. "Don't ask. Once again, not important. We've only got five weeks to pull this together. Dev's handling the music side.

But"—he clasped his hands under his chin—"please, please, *please* can I count on the two of you to co-chair the food options?"

"Just tell us what you need." Kat shared a tight smile with Sylvia. "We'll make it happen."

"Absolutely," Sylvia said.

"*Thank* you." He faced Sylvia. "You've still got connections in the restaurant business, right? And not just in Manhattan. All over the Northeast?"

She nodded slowly. "Yeeesss. But the higher profile chefs won't have much to do with me."

"Good." When she raised her eyebrows, he grimaced. "Sorry. I don't mean it's good that they won't speak to you. I mean we're not looking for high-end people. Home isn't a high-end place. It's comfortable. Charming. *Homey.* We want vendors who fit that profile."

"Okay," she said, a tiny frown pinching her brows and her mind clearly sorting through her mental Rolodex.

"Furthermore, we want vendors who'll work with local ingredients, local suppliers." Casey turned to Kat. "That's where you come in, Kat. I don't want us to focus only on prepared foods. I'd like the ingredients around too. A farmers' market feel. Maybe collaborations between some of the growers and some of the chefs. Like... buy your bread from the baker's stand, your veggies from the grower's stand, and your cold cuts from the sausage maker, then have it all put together by a chef who can put a spin on the sandwich with sides and sauces. Maybe make it a competition—who can make the best sandwich. I don't know. But I'm betting you two can come up with a dynamite formula."

As Sylvia and Kat gazed at each other, Kat drumming her fingers on her knees and Sylvia gnawing the inside of her cheek, Casey held his breath. He nearly passed out before they grinned at one another.

"Hell, yeah." Kat held out her hand this time. "Partners?"

Sylvia shook it. "Partners."

Casey let his breath out in a whoosh. "Oh, thank heavens. By the way, I'll give you the contact info for one of my business school friends. They've got a line on at least half a dozen food trucks who might want in on the fun." He stood up. "I've got to go talk to Kenny about building the stage and the booths for us now. Can I leave everything in your hands?"

"Sure thing," Kat said.

"You can ping me any time you want, and we'll have regular meetings with the whole group, but I trust you both to bring it all together."

As he left, Kat was pouring them both more iced tea and Sylvia had pulled a notepad out of her handbag. Casey practically skipped out the front door, mentally patting himself on the back. Randolph Scott joined him on the porch, thankfully dead rodent free.

"Come on, cat. Let's go see Kenny." Casey headed down the sidewalk toward Kenny's shop, Randolph Scott trotting along beside him, tail up. He looked down at the cat. "Participation. That's the key. But if we keep the barrier to entry as low as possible, we ought to be able to attract—"

His cell phone buzzed with an incoming call, and he frowned. Had Kat and Sylvia reached an impasse already? But when he pulled the phone out of his pocket, the number was flagged as Unknown. *At least it's not Bradley.* Casey didn't think Bradley was inventive enough—and certainly way too arrogant —to try to disguise his number.

"Casey Friel," he said.

"Casey. Is that who... Oh, yeah." The man's rough, staccato voice was unfamiliar. "Joe Rintoul here. I understand you're in charge of this event... What is it? Where's the fucking..." Paper rustled on the other end of the line. "Oh. Here it is. Home Grown Tastes and Tunes?"

Casey shared a wide-eyed gaze with Randolph Scott. *That was quick.* It hadn't even been forty-eight hours since he'd proposed the event to Dev. "Yes, that's correct. Are you a chef?"

"What?" He barked a laugh. "Not me. No, I'm a manager. I represent Persistence of Vision, and they're interested in performing at your little shindig."

Casey sucked in a breath. "POV?" he squeaked. "Really?" Having a name act like POV would certainly put them on the map, but... "Does the band understand that this will be a very small event at an outdoor venue? We can't possibly hope to compete with their usual engagements." He grimaced. "And I know we can't afford their booking fee."

"Trust me, I pointed that out to them. But for some reason, they want to do it. And they'll settle for room and board, a modest upfront fee"—he named a figure, which was actually less than Casey and Dev had discussed for all the acts—"and ten percent of the take."

"Two," Casey said. "This event is a fundraiser for the town. The acts are here for exposure, not a big payday."

From the muffled conversation, Joe must have put his hand over his phone. Casey held his breath again. If he kept this up, he'd need to start packing his own oxygen tank. But if they said yes...

Before Casey could pass out from oxygen deprivation, Joe was back on the line. "Listen, I'll get back to you. Gimme your email."

"O-okay." Casey was a little leery of stepping out of his food lane and into Dev's music bailiwick, but POV! Surely Dev would be happy about it, and with all the empty properties on the Harrison roster, the room and board shouldn't be a problem either.

After Joe disconnected the call, Casey practically skipped down the sidewalk, Randolph Scott prancing along at his side. He wouldn't mention it to Dev yet, not until he heard back from Rintoul, because he seriously doubted the band would go for it, and he didn't want to get Dev's hopes up. But the fact that they'd *heard* about Home Grown? That they'd expressed initial interest?

He grinned down at the cat. "You know what, Randolph Scott? I think this is actually going to work."

Chapter Twenty-Four

Three weeks ago, on possibly the worst day of his life, Dev would never have imagined things could turn around so quickly. Home Grown Tastes and Tunes was coming together so seamlessly, he wondered why they'd never thought of it before.

Of course, he hadn't thought of it now, had he? That had been Casey. All Casey. Casey, who now spent his nights in Dev's bed, although with their crazy out-of-sync schedules—Casey dashing from before dawn and Dev working his contacts well past midnight—when they were actually both between the sheets and awake at the same time, they were usually too exhausted to do more than kiss.

Whistling, he strolled out the front door of his cottage a little before noon. His good mood probably had as much to do with setting his alarm this morning so he could ambush Casey with a morning blowjob before he could rush out the door as it did with the way the whole town was rallying behind the event.

Casey had put Pete in charge of logistics—sourcing the generators to run power for the stage and all the food stands, making sure there was enough parking, planning the layout of the food stands and food trucks—and Pete had stepped up with nothing more than a tip of his ball cap.

With the help of kids from the woodshop class he taught at the regional high school, Kenny had designed and built three dozen modular vendor stands that could be broken down and stored. "For next year's festival," he'd told Dev with a wink.

The artists at the co-op—who were usually more Artists Contentious than Artist United—had, with cajoling from Casey, designed the festival logo and graphics and produced all the signage.

And after fifteen years of animosity, Kat and Sylvia were suddenly best friends, either chatting over lattes at the Market or huddled together in the summer kitchen, sampling offerings from the food vendors who were clamoring for a spot.

Casey had been right. Home—its charm, its setting, its accepting community—had been exactly the draw that he'd promised Dev they'd be. And Casey had managed it all, including guilting Green Mountain Shadows' manager into funding a massive cross-promotion campaign that was so successful in terms of resort occupancy that now she was more enthusiastic than Casey, even though she'd had to foot the bill.

Dev himself had been surprised and gratified that so many of the local musicians had remembered him and been happy to appear for the modest fee they were offering. He had enough acts now that he could finalize the roster tomorrow and add it to Casey's marketing push.

When he slipped into the summer kitchen, Casey was leaning with his elbows propped on Peach's counter, his hair flopping over his forehead as he gazed at Sylvia, who was shaking her head. Anyone unaware of Casey's unexpected steely core might mistake that wide-eyed look for pleading, but Dev knew better by now.

Casey, determined to get his way, was about to move in for the kill.

Dev took a moment to admire the way Casey's shorts hugged the curve of his ass before keying in to their conversation.

"Please? Come on, Sylvia, it'd be great PR for Summer Kitchen."

"This festival isn't about promoting myself, Casey." She crossed her arms. "Can you imagine what Kat would say if I suddenly made it all about me?"

"But it's not, don't you see? More students at Summer Kitchen—and by the way, why not Fall and Spring Kitchen too?—means more people staying in Home. More people shopping at the Market. More people stopping in at Mountain Laurel or Artists United or Curiosity. It's been literally two decades since anybody outside the school has tasted your food."

"Kat has. So has Ty."

"They don't count." Casey caught sight of Dev hovering in the doorway and his smile bloomed. "Dev!" He pushed himself off the counter and hurried over, although the kiss he pressed to Dev's mouth was anything but quick. "Come here and help me convince this stubborn woman that she needs to have a spot at the festival, too."

Dev slung his arm over Casey's shoulder. "You need to have a spot at the festival, too."

Casey nudged him with an elbow. "Maybe make a little more effort? Just repeating what I say isn't the best argument."

Dev chuckled and dropped a kiss on Casey's curls. "You forget, Sylvia. I've eaten your food too. Just recently, remember? That picnic basket you put together for us was—" He brought his fingers to his mouth in a chef's kiss. "Well, let's just say perfection is an understatement."

"That's it!" Casey bounced under Dev's arm. "Picnic baskets!" He looked up at Dev. "Where did you get that basket?"

"There's an artist who works out of Simple Gifts, the Shaker immersion place across the Massachusetts border, near Devon. In fact, I think Kat buys a lot of produce from their farm." He glanced at Sylvia. "What's the owner's name?"

"Tim, the Vegetable Guy," Sylvia said. "He's already booked a stand for the festival, as have some of the other artisans who work there. The gingham cover and napkins in your basket? Those were handwoven at their weaving studio."

Casey's eyes widened. "That cloth was *handwoven*? And I let Randolph Scott *sit* on it?"

Sylvia chuckled. "The folks at Simple Gifts pride themselves on practicality, just like the Shakers did. If the cloth can't stand up to one little cat—"

"Bite your tongue," Casey said in mock outrage. "Randolph Scott would be mortified to hear you call him *little*."

Dev reeled Casey back in. "Don't worry. The cloth will survive, as will Randolph Scott."

Casey gave him the side-eye. "If you say so. But never mind. What if we partnered with the artisans and offered premium picnic baskets? People could eat out on the lawn in front of the stage while they watch the performances. They'd enjoy your delicious food, Sylvia, and go away with an outstanding memento of the day."

"But what if nobody wants them?" Sylvia fidgeted with her tea mug, rotating it in precise quarter turns, and didn't meet their eyes. "As lovely as the baskets are, we don't really need to be stuck with dozens of them, let alone quarts of langoustine ceviche spoiling in the heat."

"Sylvia," Casey said severely, "you're not trying to replicate your restaurant menu. You're creating *picnics*. Like the one you put together for Dev and me. Food appropriate to the day." He looked up at Dev with a wicked grin. "Maybe some rustic tarts."

"Casey's right, Sylvia," Dev said. "This is a fabulous idea. Other people deserve to taste your food again."

"But the *waste*," she wailed.

"If you're worried about how to plan for it, don't give it a thought," Casey said. "You and Kat can come up with some menu options. No more than three or four, though. Give people too many choices and they can't decide squat. Once you've got it figured out, I'll put a pre-order form online on the festival website, with the warning that we'll have very few available on the day. I bet we'll sell out both options. In fact?" He crossed his arms and jerked his chin down in a decisive nod. "I *guarantee* it."

Sylvia's worried frown softened into an expression of wistful, almost childlike hope that caught Dev right under the heart. "You really think so?"

"Positive." The door opened, and Casey glanced over his shoulder. "Oh look. Here's Kat now."

"Morning." Kat handed Sylvia a latte. "Did I miss something?"

"No, you're just in time." Casey left Dev's side to lean on the counter again and give Sylvia the full puppy-dog eye treatment that he'd probably perfected volunteering at Ty's shelter. "Fill her in, Sylvia? About the baskets, the artisans, everything? I know the two of you can handle it beautifully, but if you need me, just text and I'll be here."

As Kat settled on a stool next to Sylvia, Casey backed up a step with a satisfied grin. Gazing at his sparkling eyes, Dev's chest felt as though it was three times its normal size—and points further south were threatening growth as well.

Dev surreptitiously tugged on his shorts. "Casey?" His voice broke, so he cleared his throat. "Can I, uh, speak with you for a moment? Outside?"

Casey blinked at Dev's tone. "Sure?"

"Later, ladies." Dev looped an arm around Casey's waist and hustled him out the door.

"Dev." Casey laughed as Dev propelled him across the field toward the willow tree that stood opposite the stage that Kenny and his shop kids were in the process of finishing. "What's so urgent?"

Dev pushed aside the willow fronds and drew Casey inside their leafy curtain. "This."

He lifted Casey off his feet so they were face to face and kissed him, hot and wet and slick.

Casey moaned and wrapped his legs around Dev's waist, his arms around Dev's neck, returning the kiss with enthusiasm. At his angle, Dev's aching cock lined up perfectly with Casey's erection. He cradled Casey's ass in his hands and thrust against him, the friction almost enough to distract him from the heat of Casey's mouth, the slide of Casey's tongue against his.

A clatter from the stage made Casey gasp and pull away. He glanced over his shoulder. "Can they see us in here?"

Dev nibbled on the spot below Casey's ear. "Don't care if they do."

"Dev." Casey's chuckle cut off when Dev nosed aside the neck of his T-shirt and sucked on the curve of his shoulder. "Do you have an outdoor sex kink you want to tell me about?"

"No. I have a Casey sex kink." He kissed his way up Casey's throat and captured his mouth again. "And other than that way too brief blowjob this morning, I haven't had a chance to indulge it since we launched this goddamn time-suck."

The worry wrinkle appeared between Casey's brows. He laid a gentle hand against Dev's cheek. "Do you wish we hadn't done it?"

"Fuck no." Dev kissed the little wrinkle until it smoothed away. "What you've done for the town, for its people, for me? Casey…" Dev took a huge breath. "I don't even have the words. On the one hand, I'm so grateful I want to drop to my knees right now and blow you for the second time today."

Casey's pupils dilated. "Just so you know, I'd be onboard with that."

"On the other hand, I want to wrap you in my arms and never let go because thanks to you, I've also discovered the joys of therapeutic cuddling. And you're right. Sex isn't the only reason for a relationship. Not the kind I want." He gazed into Casey's eyes, the willow leaves turning their hazel green and secret. "There's something I need to tell you. I—"

"Oh my god!"

Casey was gazing beyond Dev's shoulder in horror, and Randolph Scott's muffled mew was a big fucking clue why.

"Don't tell me." Dev laid his forehead against Casey's. "Another dead mouse?"

"It's, um, bigger. I think it's a rat. God, Dev, what if he does this during the festival?"

Dev angled his stance to block Casey's view. "I think the guests will be safe. The only person he's presented with rodent corpses lately has been you." Dev glanced down at the cat, who was washing one hind leg in complete unconcern. "Cockblocker."

"I'm sorry we haven't had time for, you know, *more*. I promise I'll try to stay awake tonight long enough to do *something*."

Dev smiled fondly. "Don't feel guilty. If we feel up to it, we'll fool around, but sex should never feel like a chore, and I've been just as beat as you." He kissed Casey's forehead and set him on his feet again, enjoying the slide of him along Dev's front. "I've forgotten how *exhausting* musicians can be."

"Oh!" Casey pulled his phone out of his back pocket. "I almost forgot. There's another act who wants a spot." He grinned up at Dev. "You'll never guess who."

Dev frowned. "I thought I'd hit up all the local acts. Everyone as far away as New Haven."

"This band isn't local." Casey bounced a little on his toes. "They're *international*."

"Casey, we can't afford an international act."

"I know, but they're performing for a small honorarium, room and board, and 5% of the concert take." He gazed up at Dev, his worry wrinkle back. "I didn't think you'd mind, given the increased visibility. I mean, you've got those empty houses, but we've got room to put them up at Harrison House, so that's an option too, and I bet Sylvia would agree to prepare their meals. To be honest, I thought they'd changed their minds. After their manager called the first time, I never heard back, so I kind of spaced it. But then he followed up this morning to confirm." He flashed the screen at Dev. "Persistence of Vision! Can you believe it?"

The mental gut punch must have shown in his face because Casey's worry frown deepened. "Dev? I'm sorry. I know I should have referred them to you, but—"

"Hey." He kissed the top of Casey's head. "I'm not mad at you." He forced a smile. "But POV? It's my old band. The one I left after the accident."

Casey goggled at him. "Holy shit," he breathed. "No *wonder* their music lately has sucked."

Chapter Twenty-Five

One day more.

As Casey strode from the old dance studio that would be acting as the festival's registration area, the lyrics from *Les Miz*'s anthem were playing on repeat in his head, because tomorrow was the day. The opening of Home Grown Tastes and Tunes, and no matter how confident Casey was that the event would be a success—vendor spots were sold out, the music roster was full, they'd had to cut off orders for Sylvia's picnics because the basket weaver said she was out of stock—he still worried that somehow Bradley would find a way to scupper the whole thing.

He hadn't heard a peep from Bradley since their confrontation at the resort, but as Casey had been promoting Home Grown, he kept running into Bradley's marketing for the antique fair, which had appeared as far away as Atlantic City.

Casey suspected that Bradley was blanketing the northeast with his publicity as a not-so-subtle dig: *See what I can accomplish with my name and network?* But as far as Casey was concerned, Bradley's OTT campaign just meant Casey didn't have to spend as much on his own efforts. He was perfectly willing to coast along in the wake, because more visitors to Merrilton meant more potential visitors to Home.

The resort manager had told Casey their occupancy was maxed out, as were most of the other inns and B&Bs in Merrilton. She and her staff were already pimping Home Grown to their guests, although she'd confided that a lot of them were here specifically *for* Home Grown, and had been disappointed that Home had no onsite accommodations.

We really need the inn to reopen. And maybe explore turning Harrison House into a B&B or some kind of retreat rental.

Because next year, Home Grown is going to be even bigger.

Casey slowed as he crunched down Harrison House's driveway and wandered past the porch on his way to the summer kitchen.

Next year.

With all the work on the festival, he'd completely abandoned his cooking lessons weeks ago—he didn't have time to struggle through them, and Sylvia didn't have time to run interference on his kitchen disasters. He'd been run ragged—they all had—getting the festival up in such a short time, but despite the pressure, despite the almost round-the-clock projects, despite the constant demands on his time, he'd never felt so… free.

The difference. Oh, my god, the difference. Doing something he loved, something he was *good* at, something he *wanted* to do? He couldn't believe he'd spent so much time, effort, and *angst* on something he not only loathed and was terrible at, but that he'd only approached out of *obligation*.

I'm never doing that again. I don't have *to do that again. I never did.*

As he gazed at the summer kitchen's door—freshly painted a deep crimson courtesy of Kenny and his crew—the relief, the *joy* that fountained under Casey's heart was tempered by trepidation.

Was he really considering staying here instead of returning to Manhattan?

Not falling in with Bradley's little dom act was a no-brainer, of course. But bailing on the city? On the restaurant? On Uncle Walt's dreams?

He felt like he was balanced on the ledge overlooking the quarry waters, blue and sparkling and inviting so far below. Did he scuttle back onto the safety of the rocks, or take the leap, soar into the air, and take the plunge? *Trust* that the chill water would be bracing rather than numbing, that he'd swim and not sink?

When he'd stormed out of Bradley's room, he'd declared that he was home already, and it certainly *felt* as though Home had embraced him. But had they really? Would he have a place here in town—by Dev's side—once the festival was over and summer faded into fall?

His throat tightened and his chest ached with *yearning* to make it so. Sure, he was staying in Dev's cottage every night now, but most of his belongings were still in his room at Harrison House. Dev hadn't *technically* asked him to move in. Maybe once Home was out of financial danger, he'd want his space to himself again.

Casey walked past the summer kitchen and hunkered down, resting his arms on his knees. He wasn't the only one teetering on the edge of something momentous. This festival could be the tipping point for Home, but right now it was all potential.

One more day.

Across the field stood the stage that was poised to welcome the musicians tomorrow, including Dev's old band—and *how* had he not known that Dev was a founding member of POV? Booths already lined Main Street, ready for the vendors' arrival. Bunting had appeared overnight, stretched across the green, announcing Home Grown Tastes and Tunes.

Casey made a mental note to thank Kenny for that touch. He'd intended to commission something like it from Artists United, but Kenny had volunteered to spearhead the decorations, including wrangling the contentious artists. He'd turned into an awesome partner for infrastructure, just as Pete had for logistics. The entire town had embraced the new event.

I fit in here. I do. I'm not extraneous *like I was to my dad and even to Uncle Walt. And I'm not leaving unless they chase me out with a pitchfork.*

Harrison House was too big for one person, but even if Dev didn't want Casey in the cottage, there were other vacant properties. Casey could sell his co-op in Manhattan and buy one of them. One way or another, he was staying.

And one way or another, he was holding onto the relationship he was building with Dev.

A horn blared insistently from the driveway, jolting Casey out of his reverie. He lurched to his feet.

"That had better not be Bradley," he muttered.

When he cleared the side of the house, though, instead of Bradley's Lexus, a stretch limo stood in front of the porch. The liveried driver, a decidedly sour expression on his face, was unloading luggage from the trunk while a familiar man—all tight tank, tattoos, leather pants, and sulky bad boy rocker looks —leaned into the driver's door.

Nash freaking Tambling—Dev's ex, as Casey now knew— laid on the horn again. "Where the fuck is everybody?"

A guy in a loose tie, the sleeves of his dress shirt rolled up, blotted his forehead with a handkerchief as he trotted down the porch steps. "Take it easy, Nash. I'm sure they'll be here soon. We weren't scheduled to arrive until—"

"I don't give a shit, Joe." He glared at shirt-sleeve guy. "You're our fucking manager. So fucking manage it."

Casey pasted on a smile and hurried over to Joe. "Hello. You must be Joe Rintoul." He held out his hand. "I'm Casey Friel. We spoke on the phone."

Joe shook Casey's hand, his palm damp. "Right, right. Are our rooms ready? We're a little early."

Casey managed—just—to keep from wiping his hand on his jeans. "Not to worry. I'm sure we can get you settled soon. You'll be staying here at Harrison House."

Nash sneered at Casey. "Is all the staff as incompetent as you? Maybe the *rest* of the band is staying here"—he cast a dismissive glance at Harrison House—"but I'll be staying elsewhere."

"Really?" Casey glanced between Nash and Joe as three other men boiled out of the rear of the limo. "Did you decide to stay in Merrilton instead? If so, I hope you've already booked your rooms, because from what I hear, there's not a reservation to be had within twenty miles."

Nash scowled. "Of course I'm not staying in Merrilton, although it's better than this dump."

"What are you talking about, Nash?" One of the others—a bear of a white guy with shaggy blond hair who Casey recognized from the band's publicity stills as Owen Mosley, POV's drummer—bounded over and shook Casey's hand. "This is *awesome*. I loved this house when we stayed here with Dev. He claimed there wasn't a ghost in the attic, but I swear I heard a window banging and ghostly footsteps overhead."

So that's how Randolph Scott is getting in. Casey made another mental note, this one to close off the informal cat door as he returned Owen's firm grip.

"I've been staying here for a couple of months and haven't noticed any ghosts yet." None of Randolph Scott's victims had attempted to reach out from the other side, thank goodness. "Welcome."

"Thanks. Do I get my old room back? The old nursery? The one over the side porch?"

"That's the plan."

A tall, lanky guy with skin paler than Casey's and a lugubrious expression worthy of Eeyore wandered over and held out his hand. "Eli Stack."

Casey shook. "Bass player, right?" His fingertips certainly had the calluses for it.

Eli nodded and wandered away to stare at a lilac bush.

Owen waved a hand. "Don't mind him. He hasn't cracked a smile since 2011 when Esperanza Spalding beat out Justin Bieber for the Best New Artist Grammy."

Casey glanced at the third guy, a slender Asian man with the face of a warrior monk who was standing diffidently to one side, glancing furtively at Nash, who was still scowling at the house. Casey couldn't place him, since he hadn't been in any of the publicity stills. Nash was the front man, the vocalist since Dev wasn't in the band anymore. Maybe this guy was the guitarist who'd taken Dev's place?

Owen beckoned him over. "This is—"

"Harry!" Nash said, glancing over his shoulder at the man before he had a chance to join Owen and Casey. "Did you bring my headphones?"

Sunlight glinted off Harry's wire-framed glasses when he flinched at Nash's abrupt tone. Irritation flickered across his narrow face. "No, Nash. Because it's not my job to pack for you."

"Great." Nash scowled and crossed his arms. "What am I supposed to do without my headphones?"

"No worries, Nash," Joe said. "I'll pick some up for you in town."

"I like *my* headphones. They probably don't have the right brand anywhere closer than Boston."

Joe made some kind of response, but Casey tuned out the conversation and turned to smile at Harry.

"Welcome to Home, Harry. I'm Casey."

Harry grinned crookedly, a smile that transformed his high-cheekboned face from ascetic to an almost glowing beauty. "It's Haru, actually. Haru Inada. Guitarist and backup vocals."

Owen slung an arm across Haru's shoulders. "Don't be so modest, H." He leaned toward Casey and lowered his voice into a conspiratorial whisper. "He's a kickass songwriter. Got a dozen tunes lined up for our next album."

Haru glanced sidelong at Nash, whose snit had taken a breather while Joe was engaged in a low-voiced phone conversation. "That's not—"

"We're releasing a retrospective next." Nash broke off a hydrangea bloom and began stripping it of its delicate lavender petals. "Tried and true hits from our first tours."

Haru pressed his lips together in a taut line and Owen raised his eyebrows.

"Tried and true, Nash?" Owen said with a laugh. "Tried at all those dive bars we used to play in back in the day. They're terrific tunes, but we don't have the rights. Not to record them."

The expression on Nash's face might technically be a smile, but it made Casey's back creep as though ghostly mice were staging a rally on his skin.

"Trust me," he drawled, tossing the half-denuded hydrangea onto the ground. "We'll have the rights locked by this time on Sunday. Fuck, maybe within the hour, if this idiot will move his ass and carry our bags upstairs and announce our arrival."

Casey blinked. Did Nash always speak to limo drivers that way? He couldn't expect *Joe* to schlep his luggage around, could he? That surely wasn't in a manager's job description.

Nash shifted his glare from Owen to Casey. "Well?"

Oh. I get it. I'm the idiot in question.

He swallowed a retort and pasted on a smile. After all, he'd grown up in an atmosphere of starfuckery. The context had been food, not performing arts, but the reasoning was the same: Kowtow to the talent, because they're the moneymakers.

With a sigh, Casey bent down and grabbed the handle of the nearest guitar case.

"Not that, you asshole." Nash strode over and yanked the case out of Casey's hand. "*Never* touch an artist's instrument without permission."

"Dude," Owen said. "You just *told* him to carry your shit upstairs, which is pretty outrageous, even for you. Besides, you haven't touched a guitar in months." He frowned. "In fact, do you even *have* a guitar?"

"Shut the fuck up, Owen. Of course I have a guitar."

"Ooohhh." Owen's expression cleared. "I get it. That's not *your* guitar. That's—"

"Hey, babe?" Dev's voice carried from around the corner. "I hope you don't think I overstepped, but I—" Dev rounded the lilac bush and practically ran Eli down. "Whoa!" His eyes widened. "Eli?"

"—Dev's guitar," Owen finished.

Nash shoved the guitar against Casey's chest and let go so Casey had to fumble to catch it before it fell onto the gravel.

Then Nash sauntered toward Dev with an expression like Randolph Scott's when he'd scored one of Sylvia's crab cakes.

"No need to apologize, *babe*." Nash wrapped his arms around Dev's neck. "Now that we're together again, I'm sure we can work everything out."

Chapter Twenty-Six

Dev met Casey's eyes over Nash's head as he peeled Nash's arms away and sidestepped him, only to get tackled by Owen.

"Dude!" Owen pounded him on the back as though Dev were part of his drum kit. He stepped back and grinned up at Dev. "How's life as a lumberjack?"

"I'm not a lumberjack, you nut." Dev returned Owen's grin but limited himself to a couple of bro backslaps. Owen had always reminded him of one of the more enthusiastic puppies at Ty's shelter, and despite being on the downhill side of his thirties and built like a fireplug, he still did. "Good to see you. Welcome to Home."

Owen buffeted his shoulder. "It's been too long, dude. Way too long. Why'n'cha ever come to one of our shows? Joe sent you tickets every time we played on this coast."

Dev didn't reveal by so much of a flicker of an eyelash that Joe had done nothing of the sort, probably on Nash's orders. "Mmmphmmm."

"And dude…" He leaned closer, lowering his voice to what he probably imagined was a stage whisper, but after decades behind his drums, between amp towers, was more of a stage bellow. "LA is *awesome*. You gotta come."

"Thanks, man. Appreciate the offer." Dev turned to Eli, whose personal style as well as his stage presence had always rivaled Equinox Mountain—unmovable and remote, yet somehow magnetic. He held out his hand. "Eli."

Eli didn't shake—he was probably in touch-avoidance mode today—but he inclined his head and murmured, "Dev," before turning back to the lilac bush.

Studiously ignoring Nash seething next to him, Dev faced the unknown man in the driveway. "Hi. I'm Dev, and you must be —"

"That's Harry," Nash said, and then sidled closer and hissed, "your *replacement*. Your *total* replacement, know what I mean? But that's why we're here, right?"

Dev's smile cranked closer to a grimace when he caught Casey's startled blink. He dialed his expression into something more welcoming—he hoped—and stepped away from Nash. "Nice to meet you, Harry."

"It's Haru, actually," Casey said. "Haru Inada." He smiled at Harry—who, apparently, wasn't Harry at all, but trust Nash to ignore other people's preferences. "Have I got that right?"

Haru nodded, but his smile was tight. "You do." He held out a hand to Dev. "It's an honor to meet you at last, although I feel like I know you already." When Nash snorted, pink tinged Haru's high cheekbones. "From your music. Your songs. Your style."

"Which you still haven't managed to master," Nash said. He invaded Dev's space again and placed a hand on his lower back, just above the curve of his ass. "Now, why don't we cut the bullshit? Take me to my *real* room." He leered. "The one I'm sharing with you."

Haru's smile vanished and his expression turned almost painfully blank.

Fuck, did Nash just *do* that?

If Nash's not-so-subtle insinuations were accurate, Haru was his new boyfriend as well as POV's lead guitarist, and Nash had just thrown him under the bus in front of his bandmates, his manager, the fucking *driver*, and a couple of—to Haru—perfect strangers.

Same old Nash.

"Dude," Owen muttered.

Dev edged away from Nash again, took Casey's hand and gazed down into his eyes. "I was about to tell you. I moved all your stuff over to the cottage." He kissed Casey's forehead, earning a delighted hoot from Owen and a snarl from Nash. "Is that okay? You're there every night, anyway."

Casey's smile was a little shaky. "That's fine."

"We'll put Nash in your old room. Eli can have the green bedroom, Owen—"

"Oh! Oh! Casey said you put me in the nursery, right?" Owen turned to Haru. "You should share with me. It's a huge room. Three beds. And the haunted attic is right overhead."

Dev lifted his eyebrows. "Don't let Owen snow you," he said to Haru. "Harrison House is *not* haunted."

"It so is," Owen said to Haru out of the corner of his mouth.

"We'd arranged for each of you to have your own room," Casey said, "but if you'd rather share—"

"Come on, dude." Owen nudged Haru in the ribs. "We've shared worse rooms on tour."

Haru glanced at Nash, whose frowning attention was still on Dev. "I—"

"How about this?" Casey said. "I'll take you all up and show you what we've got arranged for you. Since you'll be the only ones staying here, you're free to mix and match accommodations however you like." He spread his palms. "None of the rooms have an en suite, so other than window placement and furniture arrangement, they're equally comfortable." Casey bent to pick up a suitcase.

"Leave that, Casey," Dev said. "Time enough for *everyone*"— he emphasized the word—"to cart up their luggage after they know where they'll be sleeping."

"All right. This way." Casey trotted up the porch steps, with Eli trailing morosely at his heels, Haru following after a last glance at Nash, and Owen bounding ahead to open the door for all of them.

Nash watched them go, but didn't move. *Typical*. That was Nash. No rules applied to him that didn't align with his own agenda. "So," Nash drawled, "that's *my* replacement? You couldn't do better? Jesus, Dev, do you know how insulting that is?"

Dev planted his feet wide and crossed his arms. "If we're talking insults, how about the way you treated Haru just now?"

Nash scoffed. "Oh, please. He got what he wanted. A year of my dick and a chance to play onstage with POV. He's got no complaints."

"How do you know?"

Nash's brow puckered. "What do you mean?"

"How do you know he's got no complaints? You don't even call him by his proper name."

Nash scrunched his face like he was staring into a follow spot. "What are you talking about? You expect me to call him *babe?*" He infused the word with a barrel of mockery. "If you think that kind of shit will convince your boy toy that he's anything but temporary, you're delusional."

Heat beat behind Dev's eyes and his fingers curled into fists. "For one thing, what I call Casey is none of your business. For another, I'd expect you to call the band's lead guitarist, and, not incidentally, *your own boyfriend,* by his actual name. How do you introduce him on stage?"

Nash looked honestly confused. "I don't. He's just part of the band."

Dev raised his eyebrows so far his forehead cramped. "You're shitting me. Even when we played at the worst dive bar in Modesto, we introduced everyone by name."

Nash waved Dev's words away. "That was your idea. After you left, I didn't see the point. People are coming to *our* concerts to see *us*, so they know who we are. We don't need introductions."

"Unbelievable," Dev muttered.

Nash's expression changed, turning almost flirty. "Forget about Harry."

"Haru," Dev said, not moving.

"Whatever." Nash sauntered toward him. "Now that we're together again, he's irrelevant anyway." He reached for Dev, but Dev blocked him.

"We are not together. Where the fuck did you get that idea?"

"Oh come on." Nash edged forward again, causing Dev to back up until his heels hit the steps and he lost his balance.

Nash grabbed his arms to steady him, but didn't stop there. He yanked Dev against his chest and ground their hips together. "Yeah, that's more like it."

"Fuck's sake, Nash, get off me." Dev freed himself and sidestepped, pivoting so he had the whole of Harrison House's front yard at his back, the better to stage a hasty escape. "We've been over for a long time."

Nash shook his head, his expression almost pitying. "Dev, Dev, Dev. As soon as I heard about this so-called festival of yours, I got the message, loud and clear."

"Since I didn't tell *you* about the festival—on purpose, I might add—I'm not sure what message you think I was sending."

"That you wanted it all back—the band, your life, me." He spread his arms. "Well, here I am."

Dev huffed. "So you think that instead of, I don't know, just talking to you, I'd stage an event involving dozens of food vendors and musicians, not to mention the participation of my entire town and the cooperation of businesses as far away as Boston and Burlington, just to get back with you?"

Nash grinned. "As a grand gesture, it's impressive." He cast a dismissive glance at Harrison House. "Although it would have been better if you'd held the thing at someplace less downscale."

Temper fraying, Dev counted slow breaths through his nose. *One. Two. Fuck it.* "Here's the thing. I didn't invite you to this festival."

"I know." Nash winked. "Very sly. But then you always were."

"Are you delusional? I always told you exactly what I thought."

"Please. What you spewed in our last convo was a fucking joke, and you know it. Come back *here*? Leave music behind? Leave *me* behind?"

Dev gritted his teeth. "I came back because my brother and grandfather were killed, something you treated as though they'd done it just to inconvenience you."

"It fucking well was an inconvenience," Nash shot back. "We had Joe on the line, wanting to represent us. Three different labels vying to sign us based on our demo. And then you bolted."

"You make it sound like I left with no word. I *told* you what I needed, but you ignored me."

"What *you* needed? What about what the *band* needed? What *I* needed? You never once thought about *that*, did you?"

Dev rubbed the bridge of his nose. "I thought that as my boyfriend, you'd at least try to comfort me. Help me weather the loss." Although by that time, Dev had pretty much realized that Nash wouldn't offer anything more than lip service.

"I was very sympathetic!"

"You said, *Oh, that's too bad.* And then asked if we were out of coffee."

"I thought coffee would make you feel better! You're always cranky before your second cup."

"It was eleven o'clock at night!"

"So?"

"I don't fucking—" Dev carded both hands through his hair. "You know what?" He dropped his arms. "Never mind. The point is that this festival has precisely nothing to do with you. It barely has anything to do with me. It's about Home. Its businesses. Its *people*. Since you're on the music roster, that makes you part of the festival, but it doesn't make you part of my life. Not anymore. That door is closed for good."

For an instant, uncertainty flickered across Nash's face and his brows pinched together. But then his expression cleared and he chuckled. "Nah. If you were really done with me, you'd have pulled all the rights to your songs. But you didn't. You let us play them live."

"I didn't want to penalize the *band*. I told you that before I left. Multiple times."

Casey's tart words came back to him then: *Telling somebody something doesn't do much good if they don't listen.*

He studied Nash, eyes narrowed. Maybe Dev needed to frame this in terms Nash would understand, that would hit him in the one spot he never ignored.

His wallet.

"You know," Dev drawled, "now that you mention it, maybe it's time to renegotiate. Your manager has been emailing me for months about releasing the recording rights."

Nash's smile was triumphant. "I knew it. I told the guys I'd have this sewn up by—"

"You and I are done, but if the band wants to record my music, fine." He grinned. "As long as I get the royalties."

Dev left Nash gaping at him and strode across the lawn, but before he rounded the corner of the house, he turned. "And by the way, for your information? Casey is worth a hundred of you."

Chapter
Twenty-Seven

"Oh, wow!" Owen raced down the long room to the dormer at the far end and flopped onto the bed under the window. "This is exactly how I remember it." He sat up. "Come on, Eli. You have to stay in here with me."

Casey glanced at Haru, who was pointedly not invited. "You're certainly welcome to stay in this room, any of you who'd like to, but we do have private rooms available for each of you. I can show them to you if you like."

Eli looked around, his gaze catching on the beds centered under the other four dormers. "Single beds," he said.

"Well," Casey said diffidently, "it *is* called the nursery for a reason. Dev and his brother had their own rooms, but they stayed in here when they had friends over or when their cousin visited."

Owen snorted. "So what if the beds are single? It's a great place to jam. It's not like you and I are fucking, and Harry's gonna be in with Nash, anyway."

"Actually," Haru said, "I'd like to see that private room, if you don't mind."

Owen gaped. "But—"

"Sure." Casey forced a smile for Haru's benefit. He hadn't missed the way Nash had abandoned Haru and zeroed in on Dev. Neither had Haru, although apparently it had zoomed right over Owen's head. Eli... Casey couldn't tell, particularly since the guy was now communing with the striped wallpaper on the north wall.

"The rooms are all on this floor, and nobody else is staying here now, so you're welcome to switch up however you like. Once I give you the tour, I'll show you the kitchen and the common areas. The pantry and fridge are stocked with drinks and snacks. If you need anything we don't have, the Market is just down the street." He upped the wattage of his smile. "Breakfast is on your own, but your lunches and dinners will be prepared by Chef Sylvia Grande, so if any of you have any allergies or preferences, just let me know and I'll relay the information to her."

Owen flopped back down on the bed and laced his hands over his belly with a contented sigh. "I'm happy here. You guys go on."

To Casey's surprise, Eli set his guitar case—*although I suppose it's a bass case*—in the dormer alcove closest to the door, removed his ankle boots, and settled against the bed's headboard with a paperback he'd pulled out of his jacket pocket.

Casey turned to Haru. "I guess it's you and me, then. This way, please."

He led Haru out into the hallway. "Bathroom is right here." He pointed to the staircase. "There's another one up on the third floor to the right of the stairs." He nodded at what was formerly his door. "This…" A couple of butterflies executed a rhumba in his middle, because Dev had moved him out of Harrison House, and into his cottage. *Does that mean it's our cottage now?* "This is Nash's room."

"Is it?" Haru murmured.

Casey took a breath and exhaled slowly. "Haru, I'm not sure what Nash thinks is going to happen, but I know Dev. He is *not* going to hook up with Nash because he and I are"—what were they exactly?—"a thing. And I know for a fact that Dev is *not* okay with cheating."

Haru's smile was wry. "Wish I could say Nash felt the same."

"It won't matter. Not where Dev's concerned. Whatever you and Nash decide is up to you, of course, but whatever Nash decides, please believe that neither Dev nor I will hold it against you."

"How can you be so sure?" Haru's tone was bleak. "I've been living with Dev's ghost since the moment I joined the band." He turned his head sharply, sending his shiny black hair swinging a shampoo-commercial-worthy arc to settle on his shoulders. "Sorry. This isn't your problem."

"Maybe not," Casey said slowly. "But I've discovered lately that problem-solving is something I'm kinda good at. So if you want to talk or grab a coffee? You've got my number. It's in the welcome email I sent you after we signed the contract." He frowned. "Unless that only went to your manager?"

"No." Haru faced Casey again. "Well, yes, it did. But he forwarded it to all of us. Thanks. I might take you up on that."

Casey nodded decisively. "Good." He led the way around the stairwell to the southeast bedroom, which, for some reason, was called Charlotte's Room.

"There are two other bedrooms on this floor. The green room, next to Nash's, and the room in the middle. This one's my favorite, though, because it's got windows on two sides, and one of them overlooks the oak trees in the front yard." He grinned as he threw open the door. "It's like living in a tree house. And the other window faces east, so you get really lovely morning sun." He bit his lip. "Although I suppose musicians are more likely to be night owls than early birds. Would you rather —"

"No. This is wonderful." Haru set his guitar case inside the door and gazed around at the full-sized bed with its white wrought iron headboard, the vintage nightstand—another of Kenny's finds—and matching bureau. "Thank you." He ran a hand over the trailing star quilt in the purples and greens of the lilac bushes. "If you don't mind, I'd like to rest for a bit now."

"Of course. Just let me know when you're ready for that tour."

Casey stepped back onto the balcony and closed the door softly. "Whew." He padded to the stairs and headed down, nearly colliding with a scowling Nash on the landing. "Oh. Hello. Would you like me to show you your room?"

"No, I don't want you to show me a fucking room that I shouldn't be in anyway." He narrowed his eyes. "Whatever you think you know about Dev, whatever you think you're doing with him, you're wrong. By this time tomorrow, you'll be back on the bus to whatever podunk town you came from and he'll be plowing my ass like one of these fucking cornfields."

Casey blinked. "Uh…"

"What's the matter?" Nash sneered. "Don't tell me you haven't had his dick in you yet. That's the only reason he'd waste any time on you, and now that I'm here, you're irrelevant." He shoved past Casey and marched up the stairs. At the top, he leaned over the banister and jabbed a finger in the direction of the front door. "Go on. Head back to Podunksville now and save yourself some embarrassment."

Out of the corner of his eye, Casey caught the door to Charlotte's Room closing and winced. Haru had probably heard that entire exchange. Rather than get into a pointless conversation with Nash—or any conversation, for that matter—Casey simply turned and walked downstairs.

He was heading for the kitchen when a big brown hand reached out of the dining room archway and grabbed his arm. "Eeep!"

Dev hauled Casey against his chest and kissed him, hard and hot. When he pulled back, his gaze on Casey's face was intense but unreadable. "Come with me."

"O-okay."

Dev laced their fingers together and hauled Casey across the kitchen. They banged out the door, Dev's longer legs eating up the distance across the field so Casey had to trot to keep up.

When they reached Dev's cottage, Dev flung the door open and pulled Casey into the center of the living room. He took a huge breath before taking Casey's shoulders in a surprisingly gentle grip.

"Nash Tambling is full of shit."

Casey had to bite the inside of his cheek to keep from smiling. "I'm aware."

"I don't want him. In fact, I'd just as soon never see his stupid face again."

Casey winced. "I'm sorry. If I'd known—"

"No!" Dev grimaced. He stroked Casey's hair. "I don't blame you. You didn't know. If I'd had any notion that Nash would get it into his head that this whole thing was for his benefit, I'd have warned you. But I figured he'd moved on." His expression turned fond, and he trailed a finger along Casey's cheek. "I certainly have."

"Dev—"

"Remember Bradley the non-fiancé?"

Casey snorted. "How could I forget?"

"It's like that."

A laugh caught Casey by surprise, and he gasped through it helplessly while Dev's expression darkened.

"What's so damn funny?"

"Bradley," Casey wheezed. "Nash. They'd make a *terrific* couple. They're both equally certain that the universe revolves around them and that anyone would be lucky to have them. And since they never listen to what anybody else says, they'd never realize the other wasn't paying proper homage."

"Fuck them," Dev growled.

"No, but if we could arrange for them to fuck *each other*—"

"Casey." Dev's grip tightened on Casey's shoulders and he gave them a tiny shake. "I don't want to talk about them anymore, but I want you to understand. I don't regret leaving Nash behind, and I don't regret leaving the band."

Casey gazed up at him. "But do you regret leaving music?"

"Honestly?" Uncertainty clouded Dev's gaze, as though he wasn't used to people asking for his opinion.

No, as though he wasn't used to people asking about his pain.

"Yes. Honestly."

"Honestly." He swallowed. "Okay." He pulled Casey against his chest and rested his cheek against Casey's hair. "After the accident, it was like music was... I don't know... invisible. Gone. I didn't even listen to it anymore." He kissed the top of Casey's head. "But then you came. And I..." His chuckle rumbled under Casey's cheek. "I wrote a song about you."

The rhumbaing butterflies staged an encore. "About me? Really?"

"Yeah. First one in eighteen months."

He tilted his head so he could look up at Dev. "I kept hearing snatches of guitar music the week I first got here. Was that it?"

"Yeah."

The butterflies switched to disco. "Can I hear it?"

Dev grimaced again. "I'm not sure you want to."

"Are you kidding?" Casey bounced on his toes. "A song about me? Of course I want to hear it."

Dev rubbed the back of his neck. "You might want to rethink that. I, uh, wasn't exactly being reasonable after Bradley's unexpected appearance in the summer kitchen."

"Oh." His heart settled. A little. Because *Dev* wrote a song about *him*. "Is it a screw-you song?"

"More like an unrequited love song with screw-you overtones."

Casey flattened his palms over Dev's pecs. "I'd still like to hear it. If you're willing to play it for me."

Dev took a shaky breath. "It's still pretty rough."

"I don't care. If you've been divorced from music for almost two years, you can't expect to be perfect right out of the gate." Casey crossed to the window, retrieved Dev's guitar from its stand, and held it out. "Please?"

Dev hesitated briefly, but then took the guitar with a shaky breath. "Okay. If you're sure."

"Absolutely." Casey settled onto the sofa, his hands between his knees, while Dev sat in the Kennedy rocker, a twin to the one in Harrison House's living room.

After fiddling with the pegs for a couple of minutes until he was apparently satisfied that the guitar was in tune—or else was simply done stalling—Dev glanced up at Casey once, then lowered his gaze to his fingers on the strings.

There you stood,
Smiling, haloed in the light.
And, no excuses, I knew better,
But surrendered to the sight.
You said nothing, and why would you,
When I never asked the price?
I'd been stranded since forever
With my heart encased in ice.

Wait for it...
The smile that hides a bite.
Wait for it...
The shadow in plain sight.
Wait for it...
The wrong disguised as right.
The warning signs of your designs
All poised to escalate.

I should have
Asked when I first met your kiss.
But living my best fantasy
Was a chance I couldn't miss.
I ignored the burning questions
'Cause I didn't want to see,
But I took that invitation

Never dreaming you weren't free.

Wait for it...
The tarnish on the shine.
Wait for it...
The step across the line.
Wait for it...
The cracks you can't refine.
Don't even try to justify
I won't negotiate.

At Dev's voice, Dev's words, Dev's *music*, Casey's heart floated up, up, up to lodge under his collarbone, and heat flowed down, down, down to pool in his belly.

I'm in love with him. I don't care if we've only known each other for a couple of months, he's it for me. The one.

After the last note died away, Dev set the guitar back in its stand and looked up. "That's it."

Casey blinked away the tears that threatened to spill down his cheeks. "You need to write another verse," he croaked.

Then he pounced.

Chapter Twenty-Eight

Dev suddenly had his arms full of Casey and the rocker nearly toppled backwards. "Whoa."

Casey peppered Dev's face with kisses. "That was wonderful. Beautiful. Unbelievable." He leaned back, sending the rocker lurching forward, and cradled Dev's jaw in both hands. "Next time, play it for me naked?"

Dev laughed, and something that had been ratcheted tight inside him since the accident suddenly loosened. He took what felt like his first deep breath in months. "Only if you're naked, too."

"Deal." Casey wiggled his fingers under the hem of Dev's T-shirt, his hands smooth on Dev's skin. "Do you think you could still play while I give you a blow job?"

Dev smoothed Casey's curls off his forehead. "I don't know. Might need some rehearsal before I could pull that off."

Casey gazed somberly into Dev's eyes. "Rehearsal is very important for musicians. Or so I've been told. And after such a long break, you'll probably need *extra* rehearsal. In fact, we should start right now." He rucked up Dev's T-shirt but got the neck stuck on Dev's chin while leaving the sleeves behind.

Laughing, Dev managed to free one arm. "Take it easy. I don't know if I can—"

A knock at the door froze both of them, Dev with one arm trapped in his tangled shirt and Casey with one hand on Dev's pec and the fingers of the other under Dev's waistband.

Casey glanced from Dev's exposed skin to the door. "Are you expecting anyone?"

"No. But we are about to stage an event fit for two dozen Port-a-Potties. We should probably see who it is."

"Rats," Casey grumbled, but then he sighed. "But you're right. It's the responsible thing to do." He clambered off Dev's lap and pointed at Dev's nose. "But tonight. You and me, naked with the guitar. Promise?"

"Promise."

Dev pulled his shirt back on and shuffled, wincing, to the door. Judging by Casey's snicker, Dev probably looked like he had a broom handle lodged up his ass to match the one straining his fly. He shot a warning glance over his shoulder, but guffawed because Casey was tugging at the legs of his shorts, clearly trying to make room for his own erection.

He glared at Dev. "Shut up. This is your fault."

Dev grinned. "Pretty sure you started it, but I'll own it. Are you ready?"

"About as ready as you are." Casey sucked in a breath and blew it out through pursed lips—which didn't help Dev's situation *at all*, although Casey's shorts seemed to fit more loosely.

Dev peered at him, eyes narrowed. "How did you manage that so quickly?"

Casey smirked. "Just thought about Bradley. Maybe you should try the same with Nash."

"Fuck," Dev muttered. It didn't completely eliminate the problem, considering Casey was still within arm's reach, but it at least allowed him to walk more normally and open the door.

"Haru." Dev blinked at the man on the porch. He wasn't sure who he'd been expecting, but it hadn't been this guy. "How can I help you?"

Haru glanced back toward the house and then down, where a battered and all-too-familiar acoustic guitar case sat next to his feet. *Dev's old case. Fuck.*

"I intended just to stop by and return this to you, but then I heard…" Haru peered up at Dev from under his curtain of shiny black hair. "That song was amazing. Your voice is amazing. Your technique—" He swallowed. "Now I get it."

"My technique has been in suspended animation for almost two years, so I'm not sure what there is to get." He pushed open the screen. "Want to come in?"

Haru retreated to the edge of the porch. "You don't have to… I didn't mean to intrude."

"It's okay." Dev smiled and jerked his head sideways. "Join us. I know the other guys in the band, of course, but I'd like to get acquainted with you before things get too busy for me to think tomorrow."

"Thanks." Haru stepped inside and his eyes widened when he spotted Casey, whose cheeks were decidedly pink. "Oh."

Casey waggled his fingers. "Um. Hi. If you and Dev would rather chat privately—"

"No!" Haru grimaced. "I mean, please stay if you want."

"I'll get us something to drink. What would you like? Iced tea? Water? Beer?"

"Iced tea would be great. Thanks."

"Coming right up." Casey turned, and as he walked toward the kitchen, Dev noticed that the hem of his T-shirt was caught on the waistband of his briefs.

Which… Haru totally did not miss.

"Oh, god." He covered his face with the hand not clutching the guitar case handle. "I *really* intruded on something, didn't I?"

Dev chuckled. "It's fine. We can always pick up later." He gestured for Haru to sit down on the loveseat and took his own place in the rocker again. "I want to make sure you understand that. Casey and I are solid. I'm fixed here in Home." He let his glance stray toward the kitchen archway, where Casey was humming snatches of "Wait for It" as he clattered around, collecting glasses and filling them with ice. "I'm fixed with *him*." *At least for as long as he's here.*

Haru smiled a little wanly. "He seems really nice."

"He's more than nice." Dev glanced toward the kitchen again, his throat thick and his chest tighter than a drum skin. "He's a superhero," he murmured. "He's saved our summer. Hell, he probably saved the whole town." *He fucking saved* me. "Anyway." Dev faced Haru again. "While I'm happy to welcome POV to Home Grown, it wasn't my idea to invite you. I didn't contact Joe, and I didn't contact Nash, and I sure as shit didn't float the idea of rejoining the band."

"Oh, I know." Haru sighed. "Some big shot entrepreneur called Nash about the gig. I think he's the one who put the idea into Nash's head that you were looking to get back with us. With him."

Dev frowned. "Big shot entrepreneur? You know his name?"

"I don't think Nash ever said, other than that his name was a household word."

I'll bet my vintage Les Paul that it was Pillsbury. Damn it, that shithead wasn't kidding when he threatened to take it all. He hadn't just meant Dev's holdings and heritage. He'd meant Dev's heart. Dev glanced at the kitchen. No way was he telling Casey about this. He'd blame himself, just like he'd blamed himself over the antique fair.

"Mmmphmmm," Dev said.

"Then Nash started bugging Joe about it until he gave in. As for the other, I think I've been fooling myself. But when we met you outside Harrison House and he called me your replacement —"

"That was uncalled for." Dev scowled. "I never even hinted that I—"

Haru held up both palms, displaying the telltale calluses on the fingertips of his left hand. "I know that too. But you know Nash. He never needs any backup for his own agenda."

Dev snorted. "Trust me. I'm aware."

"It's just…" He sighed again. "I'd hoped that he'd eventually see me as myself, and not as *the new Dev*. Or that eventually you'd become *the old Haru*." He choked out a laugh. "Of course, that would require him to actually call me Haru instead of Harry."

"What can I say? He's a dickhead." Dev winced. "Sorry. I know you must have feelings for him."

"Feelings, yeah. But the type of feelings are pretty much in flux right now. I should have gotten a clue when he never let me change the arrangements for any of the songs you wrote. I mean"—he shrugged apologetically—"that guitar break in 'Slow Down, Sonny' wasn't exactly inspired, especially that chord change in the middle."

Dev slapped his forehead. "He kept that in? You're fucking *kidding* me. It was a *mistake*. We only included it on the demo because we didn't have money for the studio time to re-record it."

"I offered to fix it. I've got my own studio setup. But Nash refused. He claimed it proved the band was *real*."

"Proved he was a real dickhead, more like," Dev muttered. "Shit, that's so embarrassing."

"Here we are." Casey bustled in with a pitcher of iced tea on a tray with two glasses and a plate of Sylvia's macarons. He set the tray on the coffee table, angling it so that Dev and Haru could both reach it.

Dev frowned at the tray and then up at Casey. "Only two glasses? Aren't you joining us?"

He patted his back pocket. "Text from Kenny. I'm needed at the registration venue. I might be awhile, but I'll be back for dinner." He headed for the door, and, yup, his T-shirt was still caught in his briefs.

"Babe?"

Casey turned, one eyebrow raised. "Yes?"

"If you think I'm letting you go without a kiss, you're delusional." Dev crooked a finger. "C'mere."

Casey shook his head with a crooked grin. "I may be a terrible cook and have an indifferent palate, but I'll never turn down *that* treat." He trotted over and planted a warm, lingering kiss on Dev's lips.

Dev caught the back of Casey's neck and pulled him in for another kiss, although he kept it on the lower end of the heat scale since his dick had only just deflated. As Casey stood, Dev caught his hand.

"And, babe?" When Casey raised both eyebrows, Dev reached around and freed his T-shirt.

Casey's blush was a glorious thing, like sunrise over the trees. "Oh my god. I can't *believe* you let me parade around like that in front of Haru!"

"Be fair." Dev caught Casey's flailing hands and pressed a kiss into each palm. "You high-tailed it into the kitchen before I could mention it. And at least I kept you from parading around Home like that."

Casey lifted one brow. "You're all heart."

"They're very nice briefs," Haru said, his narrow face mock innocent. "Purple is one of my favorite colors."

"Seriously? You're as bad as he is." Casey kissed the top of Dev's head. "I'm leaving now before I humiliate myself any further."

Dev gazed at the door after Casey walked out until Haru cleared his throat. "Oh. Sorry." He picked up the pitcher and filled both glasses with tea.

Haru took the offered glass. "Don't be. If I'd still had doubts about how delusional Nash is about your intentions, the way you look at Casey would have smashed them like Pete Townshend with a Rickenbacker."

"Not gonna hide it and not gonna apologize." Dev brandished his own glass. "I'm not ashamed of the way I feel about him."

Haru tilted his head. "Does he know that?"

"I... think he does."

"Never said it in so many words, eh?"

Had he? Dev tried to remember. He'd considered it. The words had been right there on the tip of his tongue. Had they ever made it past his lips?

"Maybe not." He clinked his glass with Haru's. "But it's on the agenda. In fact, I know just how to do it. Did you hear any of the song I was playing before?"

"Before I barged in and killed the mood? Yeah. It's got terrific bones, but..." Haru bit his lip and shrugged one shoulder. "Sorry, but I'm guessing it's not finished?"

"Don't be sorry, because you're perfectly right." Dev grinned. "I only started noodling with it at the beginning of the summer when I had a, er, different impression of Casey's character. He told me it needs another verse. He's right, but I think a second guitar would improve it too." He gestured to the case at Haru's feet. "What about it? You up for a session?"

Haru's eyes widened. "Are you kidding? You want me to help *you* write a song?"

Dev shrugged. "Why not?" He snaked out an arm and retrieved his Gibson from the stand. "If you suck, it's not like I have to use your suggestions."

Haru laughed. "Fair point." He opened the case, lifted out Dev's old Martin, and held it toward Dev. "Are you sure you don't—"

"Nah. I'm good with this one. " Dev patted the Gibson's belly. It was older than the Martin, but it had mellowed over the years. He'd left it in Home when he'd gone on the road with POV, but he'd written his very first song with it. "You're welcome to use that one, but if you've got an axe of your own that you prefer, I'll wait for you to grab it."

Haru's expression shuttered. "I don't have one of mine with me. Nash always insisted I use this one for acoustic sets."

Dev met Haru's eyes. "Dickhead," they said together.

"All right, then." Dev played a lick. "That's the progression for the verse. What do you think?"

"What about switching to E major in the chorus?"

"Perfect." Dev bent over his guitar and they traded riffs, over and over, until the tune rang like a bell, from first note to final chord.

"Guys? Guys? *Guys?*"

Dev looked up, blinking blearily at Casey standing in the doorway. Why was his vision so dim?

"Casey?" he croaked. Fuck, his throat was raw. He reached for his iced tea, but the glass was empty. So was the pitcher. And his back was killing him. He straightened up, rolling his shoulders and twisting until his spine cracked. "Did you get your problem sorted?"

Casey reached over and flicked the wall switch, flooding the room with light. "About five hours ago. Did you guys even take a break?"

Dev exchanged looks with Haru. "Uh…" Come to think of it, his bladder was screaming at him.

Haru shook out his hands. "I didn't realize it had been so long." His eyes widened. "Shit! Was Nash looking for me? Was I supposed to rehearse?"

"No, you're safe." Casey walked over and took the Gibson out of Dev's cramped fingers. "Owen dragged Eli with him into the summer kitchen, and Sylvia's been teaching them to make eclairs all afternoon." He chuckled. "Owen's attempt to make choux pastry might actually be worse than mine. As far as Nash is concerned? I couldn't tell you, but he and Joe took the limo into town for lunch, and I don't think they've returned."

Haru glanced at the window, where the last glow of the sunset was fading over the trees. "I suppose I ought to check in."

"Time enough for that after dinner." Casey set the Gibson on its stand. "Which Sylvia has ready for all of us at Harrison House." He waggled his eyebrows. "Paella, with sausage and shrimp sourced from Kat's local vendors, and rustic raspberry tarts with fruit courtesy of Tim, the Vegetable Guy."

Dev's stomach growled. "Fuck, that sounds amazing."

"Trust me. It is." Casey glanced between Dev and Haru. "But before we go"—he screwed up his face—"I did a thing. A thing you might not *entirely* like."

Dev snaked an arm around Casey's waist and drew him in until his thighs bumped the rocker's arm. "Then you might as well tell us. No more avoidance, right?"

"Yeah, I'm working on that." He blew out a breath. "I put the two of you in the music lineup. Think you can have a twenty-minute set ready by tomorrow?" He gave them a gritted-teeth grin.

Dev and Haru exchanged glances. Dev's expression was probably gobsmacked. Haru's was downright panicked.

"But Nash," Haru croaked. "POV."

"Don't worry. I've got you mid-afternoon. As the headliner, POV's closing the show in the evening." He stroked Dev's hair, the look in his eyes both fond and fierce. "You deserve this." He lifted his gaze to Haru. "Both of you. So what do you say?"

Dev met Casey's gaze. *He believes in me. Maybe it's time I believed in myself again.* He smiled crookedly at Haru. "I'm in if you are."

Haru's grin bloomed and Dev took a moment to marvel at Nash Tambling's idiocy at treating this man as a *substitute.*

"Absolutely. Let's do it."

Chapter Twenty-Nine

"That's the last one." Kenny shut down his tablet and stretched. "All vendors present and accounted for, and all musicians at least accounted for, even if they're not present."

Casey chuckled. "Well, it's only eight-thirty in the morning. Musicians are a nocturnal race, aren't they? I don't think we can expect to spot any of them until the first set this afternoon."

Casey had left Dev snoozing away when he'd crawled out of bed at six. They hadn't had a chance for as much as a little frotting last night because Dev had come staggering to bed after two, following a marathon session with Haru at Ty's place. They hadn't wanted to rehearse at Harrison House where the rest of the band—or the glowering Nash—could hear or in the cottage where they'd disturb Casey.

Not that Casey would have minded being disturbed. Dev and Haru together made a truly marvelous noise.

"If you don't need me for anything," Kenny said, tucking his tablet under his arm, "I promised Kat I'd help at the Market."

Casey shooed him away. "Go, go. In fact, I'll come with you. We'll handle any other questions at the information tent in front of Harrison House." They walked across the dance studio's scuffed wooden floor, their movements echoed in the mirrors along one long wall. "Registration was the only thing I was worried about. Nothing's worse than a backlog when all the vendors want to do is get their stands set up for the incoming hordes. I helped out with enough conferences back in business school to know *that* much."

"Let's hope for hordes," Kenny said. "If we only get a trickle —"

"Bite your tongue!" Casey made sure the studio door locked behind them, and that the sign directing folks to the information table was in place. "It's going to be a rousing success. I insist."

Kenny grinned. "Well, in that case, who am I to rain on the parade?"

"Augh!" Casey held up his fingers in a cross to ward off the ominous words. "Don't say *rain*."

Kenny's grin morphed into a full-on belly laugh as they headed toward Main Street. "Even if it does—and every meteorologist from here to Burlington says we'll have nothing but a few fluffy clouds all day—the vendors will be safe under their awnings and the musicians under the stage canopy."

"But it might keep the audience away."

Kenny winked. "Never underestimate the passion of a tourist for food or a music aficionado for true discomfort in the quest for live performances. Remember Woodstock?"

"We're hardly Woodstock."

"Nope. We're Home." He winked again. "We've got more Port-a-Potties per capita. See you later."

Kenny trotted off down the street as Casey paused at the marquee under the Harrison House oak trees to greet Ty, who was chatting with Winnie Barrows, a retired schoolteacher who had volunteered to staff the table.

"Hey, Ty. Everything okay, Winnie?" Casey asked.

"All good." She raised a to-go cup from the Market. "Kat's keeping me supplied with tea, and Kenny's high school posse will be stopping by to give me breaks all day."

"You've got my number if you need me, right?"

"Don't worry, Casey. We've got this."

Beside Casey, Ty was squinting up at a suspicious bulge in the canvas overhead. He shot a wicked grin at Casey. "Say, Winnie? Could I borrow your cane for a sec?"

"Sure." She unhooked the curved wooden handle from the edge of the table and handed it to him.

Ty crept toward the bulge and used the cane's rubber tip to poke the bulge, which vanished only to appear about two feet away.

"Let me guess," Casey said. "Randolph Scott?"

"He prefers to supervise from on high."

"I've noticed," Casey said, remembering Randolph Scott lurking on top of his armoire.

"However…"

Ty set the cane against the canvas and drew it along as he walked toward the tent's edge. Sure enough, the bulge tracked it in a series of leaps.

"Watch this," Ty said with a grin.

"Ty Harrison," Winnie said with mock severity, "you're as bad as you were back in grade school. You and Eddie Mitchell gave me more gray hairs than all the other students combined. If it weren't for Kenny Li reining you both in, you'd have spent half your recesses in the principal's office."

"His reins worked better on Mitch than on me, but Kenny always was the best of us. Still is." He gave a mock bow. "Good thing he's not here now."

He pressed the cane against the tent again and took off, dashing around the table twice. Randolph Scott wasn't pouncing so much now as racing along the canvas, chasing the cane.

Suddenly, Ty made a dash toward the house and into the open. And Randolph Scott, not pausing in his momentum, flew off the edge of the tent to land on the grass in a crouch.

He shook his head, ears laid back, tail puffed out like a bottle brush, before he sauntered toward the porch as if he hadn't just made a total goober of himself.

"Fool cat can't resist a moving target." Ty returned Winnie's cane. "Falls for that every time. Never gets old. See you later, folks. I've got a petting enclosure set up for all those fairgoers who need a little stress relief." He walked off down the drive in a crunch of gravel.

"Casey?"

At the sound of that familiar voice, Casey's breath seized and his head snapped around. Uncle Walt was standing near the lilac bush at the corner of the house, his bewildered glance bouncing between Casey and the path toward the summer kitchen.

Casey hurried toward him, willing his lungs to resume their regular operation. "Uncle Walt?" He gave his uncle a quick hug. "Not that I'm not glad to see you, but what are you doing here?"

"Bradley invited me for the antique fair. He's been marketing it as far away as Atlantic City and he's been very satisfied by the response."

And I've been very satisfied to let him do the work of pulling more tourists to the area. Free advertising FTW. "Imagine that," Casey murmured.

"Yes. A number of investors have already expressed interest in..." He watched Pete drive past in a fifteen-passenger van he'd sourced from somewhere, *Home Grown Shuttle* emblazoned on its doors. "I don't understand." Uncle Walt's tone was plaintive. "What's going on? I expected to find you in Merrilton with Bradley, but he said your lessons were keeping you busy here so I thought I'd stop in and see your progress, but"—he gestured helplessly—"*this*. What *is* this?"

Casey linked his elbow with his uncle and gestured expansively with his other hand. "*This* is Home Grown Tastes and Tunes, the food and music festival I've helped organize here in Home."

"But... but what about your studies?" His expression brightened. "Are you cooking for the festival? One of your dad's dishes? To promote the restaurant?"

Casey sighed. "Come with me. I want to show you what we're doing here."

"But... But..."

"Uncle Walt. Trust me?"

He frowned, but nodded. "Of course, my boy."

Their arms still linked, Casey led his uncle at a leisurely stroll off the Harrison House lawn. He pointed to the sidewalk beneath their feet. "This is marble. It was quarried only a few miles down the road." He chuckled. "Imagine what a six-inch-thick, three-foot-square slab of marble would go for today, and it makes your head spin to think this was considered surplus at the time."

Uncle Walt jerked sideways and shuffled onto the grass. "Should we be walking on it?"

"Since it's not raining or icy, we're safe." Casey leaned in and whispered, "Otherwise, it can get a little slippery. But it's lasted for a century or so, so I think it'll withstand a little extra foot traffic today."

They wandered down Main Street, past food trucks already doing a brisk business even though it still lacked ten minutes before the official festival opening. He pointed out Tim, the Vegetable Guy's stand.

"This man owns a farm just over the border in Massachusetts. It's built in the Shaker style and he runs it as an immersion program."

Tim, all buff, six foot three of him, looked up from arranging rows of jewel-toned produce—bright chartreuse butter lettuce, ruby red radishes, glowing orange carrots with their eye-wateringly green tops—and nodded at Casey, a grin splitting his neat brown beard. "Morning. Looks like we've got some early birds."

Casey glanced at the stand next to Tim's, where Miranda, the weaver, was setting bundles of handwoven napkins and tablecloths. "Is that a problem?"

"Nah. We're ready." He tapped a stack of lunchbox-sized baskets on Miranda's table. "Your idea about do-it-yourself picnic baskets was brilliant."

Casey shrugged. "We sold out of the pre-orders for Sylvia's premium baskets, but there were enough sad-puppy emails from folks who missed out that I figured they'd be on board with a little DIY action. They can shop around, put their lunch together before heading to the music venue." He grinned. "And it'll give the vendors a chance to upsell."

Miranda laughed. "If I have anything left by noon, I'll eat my loom."

"Not taking that bet." He lifted a hand in farewell and led Uncle Walt further down the road. Vendor stands extended from the sidewalk halfway to each of the houses that lined Main Street.

Uncle Walt dodged a couple of women in bright pink visors, turquoise T-shirts, and fanny packs as they made a beeline for Mountain Laurel's booth.

"Do the homeowners mind that you've set up these... arrangements on their lawns?"

"Are you kidding? They fell over themselves offering to host them. We called our event Home Grown for a reason. It's intended to benefit businesses and artists from the region, as well as Home itself. The vendors are all from New England, mostly Vermont, New Hampshire, and northwestern Massachusetts."

"And you think it will succeed?"

Pete stopped the van at the curb and offloaded a dozen passengers as several other groups walked around the corner from East Road, obviously strolling in from the parking area Pete had set up behind Ty's clinic.

Casey's chest filled with warmth and satisfaction. "Yeah. Yeah, I think it will."

Uncle Walt gazed at the Market, where Kat had set up beverage service—strictly non-alcoholic—on the porch. "You arranged all this?"

"Not by myself. I had help. A lot of it." He turned to face his uncle. "The people who live in Home love this place, love its history, love what it stands for. Inclusion, fellowship, community. They're all invested in keeping it as charming as it is now." Casey sighed contentedly. "I can't wait to see what we'll do to keep Home growing and thriving in the coming years."

Uncle Walt blinked at him, a frown wrinkling his brow and turning his mouth down at the corners. "You mean you'll see the progress when you come back to visit. Once the restaurant is open."

Casey rolled his lips against his teeth and took a huge breath. *Now or never.* "No. I mean I intend to stay here. To sell my place in Manhattan and buy a house here."

"But, Casey." Panic chased across Uncle Walt's face. "The restaurant. The opening. Your legacy. You can't move away from your home."

"Come on, Uncle Walt. We need to talk."

Casey took his uncle's arm and led him to a bench under a maple tree on the green in front of the Market. With his stomach doing its best impression of a cement mixer, he angled himself to meet Uncle Walt's bewildered gaze.

"This is important, so I want you to really listen, okay?"

"Of course. I always listen to you, my boy."

"Yeah, but this time I want you to *hear* what I'm saying." Casey blew out a breath. *Here goes.* "Restaurants have *never* been home to me. Dad's kitchens were always someplace chaotic, intimidating, dangerous, even. They were also what took my father away from me. Every time I needed him or wanted him to be there for some little personal milestone of mine, the restaurant always stopped him. *You* were the one who came to my school plays, my soccer games, my high school graduation."

"I never begrudged the time spent with you, Casey," he said earnestly. "Not a single moment."

"I know. That's why I love you, why I've always wanted to make you happy. But being stuck in a kitchen for the rest of my life?" He gripped his uncle's hands. "I'm sorry, but I can't. Not even for you. Furthermore, you wouldn't *want* me to, because if you want your restaurant to succeed, you need a chef who can actually cook."

"It wouldn't be the same. It wouldn't be Chez Dontatien."

"As well it shouldn't. It was Dad's dream and now he's gone." Casey met Uncle Walt's eyes. "Tell me the truth. Do you even *want* to own a restaurant?"

"I… I…" He looked away, blinking rapidly, and exhaled on a half sob. "I miss him so much."

"I know. But isn't the best way to honor him to move on? *Build* on the legacy. Don't try to recreate the past, because you can't. Hire a new chef. Let them make the place their own. Maybe have one night as an homage to Dad, with a menu that's a nod to his food. But then say goodbye to it. To him." Casey squeezed his uncle's hand. "It's time. Don't you think?"

"Hey, babe." At Dev's call, Casey released Uncle Walt's hand and turned, his smile blooming at the sight of Dev's grin.

"Hi." He studied Dev's face as he trotted across the street toward them between a cheesemaker's stand and a Ben & Jerry's ice cream truck. For the first time since Casey had arrived in Home, for the first time since he'd seen Dev without his welding mask, Dev looked *relaxed*. At home in his own skin.

At home in Home.

Casey wasn't arrogant enough to think he was the whole cause of Dev's contentment. The apparent success of the event, with registration fees that more than covered the cost of the dang Port-a-Potties, not to mention his rediscovery of music, probably had more to do with it. But Casey liked to think he'd had at least a supporting role in putting that sparkle in Dev's eyes, the ease in his wide shoulders, the spring in his step.

"Sylvia wants to know if you've got the rosters for her interactive cooking demos."

"Oh! Right. Yes." Casey pulled out his phone and forwarded the list to Sylvia and Dev. "Sorry. I intended to do that right after registration closed down, but then Uncle Walt showed up."

Dev's eyebrows rose. "This is your uncle, then?" He held out his hand. "Pleased to meet you, sir. Dev Harrison."

Uncle Walt glanced a little frantically at Casey as he shook Dev's hand. "How do you do?"

"Dev is the direct descendant of Home's founder, the town manager, and"—Casey inhaled and took the plunge—"my boyfriend."

Dev's grin grew even wider as he wrapped an arm around Casey's waist and dropped a kiss to the top of his head. "And proud of it. He's the most remarkable man I've ever met."

"But… But…" Uncle Walt glanced between them. "What about Bradley?"

Casey leaned into Dev's side. "Bradley was never in the picture. Not *my* picture, anyway. If you want to partner with him for the restaurant, you can certainly do so. But I'd think really hard about that."

"Why?" Uncle Walt asked.

"Because the guy's a dickhead," Dev said. "A dickhead who doesn't deserve Casey. But if I'm lucky"—he smiled down at Casey, the warmth in his eyes enough to melt Casey's knees—"someday I will."

Chapter Thirty

As the time for his and Haru's performance grew closer, Dev's adrenaline-fueled energy grew, just as it had always done before any gig. With the awareness zinging through his veins he couldn't keep himself to a walk, loping across Harrison House's lawn with a wave at Winnie Barrows, the last song in their set list—one of Haru's, which he'd never had a chance to perform with POV—rolling out in his head.

They'd open with "Wait for It," and Dev's chest warmed, his smile dawning. *Casey's gonna love it.* When they got to the last verse—

The screen door banged open and Nash stormed down the steps and directly into Dev's path.

"What the fuck, Dev?"

Dev skidded to a stop in the gravel before he barreled into him and knocked him on his ass. *Not that the asshole doesn't deserve it.*

Nash's face was a mask of fury and revulsion. *Whoops. Guess he must have seen the new lineup.*

But Nash Tambling had no power over him anymore. Not when Casey had proclaimed right to his uncle's face that they were together. Not when he'd found music again.

"Afternoon, Nash."

Dev tried to sidestep him, but Nash blocked his way. "What kind of fucking rig are you running here, Dev? Are you *trying* to screw with my head? You *know* I need my space before I go on stage."

Is that what you call finding somewhere to fuck a groupie? Asking for a former friend. "You've got your own room, Nash. Go there."

"I *would*, but it's been *defiled*." He crossed his arms. "Your little boy-toy probably did it out of spite."

Dev kept his temper. Barely. "Casey is neither little, a boy, nor a toy, and he is the last person on earth who would ever be spiteful. Whatever's got your boxers in a bunch has nothing to do with him."

"No? Go upstairs then. *Look* at what he's done to my bed."

Dev really didn't want to waste time with Nash, not with the clock ticking down to his first public performance in almost two years, but he didn't want the asshole to take his beef—whatever it was—to Casey.

"Fine."

He took the stairs two at a time, Nash stomping along behind him, and stepped into the bedroom. It smelled of Nash's Tom Ford cologne with an undertone of weed. Nash shoved past him and struck an overdramatic pose, one hand on his hip and the other pointing at the pillows on his unmade bed.

"There! Are you trying to tell me that's not a pointed attack on me, a blatant attempt to scare away the competition?"

"Competition for what?" Dev murmured as he moved closer. If the pillows held what he thought they did… Yup. "Mouse tails."

"What?" Nash's face could double for the vomit emoji. "He cut the tails off mice just to punk me?"

"For fuck's sake, Nash. Casey didn't do this. It was—"

"Hey, Nash. Oh, hi Dev. Didn't expect to see you up here." Owen beamed at them from the doorway, a smug and purring Randolph Scott in his arms. "Look who decided to visit us."

Dev jerked a thumb at the cat. "There's your culprit. And you're right about one thing. It's definitely a pointed attack."

"A cat? You let your cat in my room?"

"First, he's not my cat. Second, he goes where he wants and nobody's figured out how to stop him yet. Third"—he pointed to the pillows—"he doesn't like you."

"What are you talking about?"

Dev shrugged. "Well, he had three dead mice, and he didn't even give you one. That definitely sends a message."

Nash's expression hardened. "You need to get rid of that animal. Shoot him, drown him, whatever, but get him away from me."

"Aw, Nash," Owen said, "don't go all Miss Gulch on us." He nuzzled the top of Randolph Scott's furry head. "He's just doing what cats do. You can't blame him for that."

"Maybe not." Nash turned to face Dev. "But I can blame you. If this is how you treat your guests—"

"Hold up." Dev folded his arms and drew himself up, emphasizing the four inches in height he had over Nash, something that always stuck in Nash's craw. "*I* didn't invite you. *You* demanded room and board as part of your fee. You've been here before, Nash. You know what Harrison House is like. If you didn't approve of the accommodations, you could have stayed in town."

"I expect that would have ruined his plans."

All of them—Dev, Nash, Owen, even Randolph Scott—turned at the terse comment.

Haru stood on the balcony, clearly just emerged from his room, since he held his guitar case and his hair still looked damp from a shower.

"Plans?" Owen glanced from Nash to Haru. "What plans?"

Haru advanced, although he stopped at the head of the stairs rather than joining the crowd in the bedroom.

"His plan to replace the replacement." His smile was thin. "We go on in thirty, Dev. I'll meet you by the stage." He walked down the stairs, his back straight and his tread measured. Randolph Scott mewed and pushed out of Owen's arms to scamper after him.

Owen peered down the stairs and then back at Dev and Nash. "What just happened?"

"What did he mean, you're on in thirty?" Nash demanded.

Casey stepped onto the lower landing, a grim-faced Haru on the tread below him, Randolph Scott cradled in his arms. "Manchester Blues is finishing up, Dev. It won't take long to set up for you and Haru, but if you need more time"—his gaze took in Nash's furious face, Owen's bewildered one, and Dev's, which, considering the annoyance spiking his insides probably looked like a thunderhead—"to, um, prepare, we can probably call a break."

Dev edged past Owen. If he were honest with himself, he'd have liked a few minutes, preferably alone with Casey in his arms, to reset his mood. But he'd performed under worse conditions. Hell, he'd performed with Nash for years.

"If Haru's ready, I'm ready."

"I can't *believe* this!" Nash stormed after Dev and caught his arm at the top of the stairs. "If you perform with anybody, it should be *me*."

Dev raised an eyebrow. "Don't you mean with Persistence of Vision?"

"Isn't that what I just said?"

"Dude," Owen said. "Seriously?"

Nash glared down at Haru. "And you. If you perform with him, I'll… I'll *sue*. You have a *contract*."

"Actually," Haru said, "I don't. I'm just the *replacement*, remember? You pay me like a session musician."

"Dude. *Seriously?* What the hell?" Owen punched Nash in the biceps. "Harry's been part of the band since… since… well, since Dev."

Haru's smile was crooked. "That's where you're wrong, Owen. I was never part of the band. I was just there to stand in for Dev until Nash finished sulking and made a play to get him back."

"I don't *sulk*," Nash said.

Casey lifted both eyebrows. "Really? *That's* what you took away from that statement?"

Haru's smile turned more genuine as he faced Casey. "Guess that's because he can't say any of the rest of it was false."

"Or else," Casey said, "he's just a self-centered jerkface who can't believe everything's not about him. Trust me. I know the type."

"Shut the fuck up," Nash snarled. "You're *nothing*. Both of you. You"—he jabbed his finger at Haru—"can forget about POV because you'll never play with us again. And you?" He crossed his arms and smirked down at Casey. "Dev will drop you in a heartbeat now that I'm back."

"Funny thing about that," Owen said, brow wrinkled in thought. "You're back. But Dev didn't drop Casey. Also, how are we gonna play our gig tonight without Harry? I mean, Haru."

Nash shot him an irritated glance. "Dev will step in, of course."

"No, I won't." Dev shook off Nash's grip and stepped down onto the first stair tread. "And if you don't stop being such an entitled dickwad, I'll take back the rights to the POV songs. You won't have anything *to* play."

Nash gaped at him. "You... You can't. They're *our* songs."

"No, they're not. I wrote them for the band, yes, but *I* wrote them. Not you. They're copyrighted under my name, but I never insisted on rights or royalties because I considered that I owed it to Owen and Eli not to fuck up their careers. POV is not only you. And it wasn't only me, either. But threaten Haru, threaten to walk on this gig when POV is the headliner, and I'll take 'em back in a hot minute. Your choice." He strode down the stairs, stopping on the landing to give Casey a kiss. He grinned at Haru. "Ready to do this?"

Haru nodded. "Absolutely."

"Hey, guys?" Owen leaned over the banister, a hopeful grin on his round face. "Need a drummer?"

Dev laughed. "Not this time. But we'll talk."

He and Haru descended the rest of the stairs and walked out the door. As they crunched down the driveway toward West Road and the path the performers took to the rear of the stage, Dev cast a sidelong glance at Haru.

"You okay?"

Haru took a moment, gazing up at the trees overhanging the road; at Madame Ivanova's empty house and studio, set back among a stand of maples, its green shutters barred; at the glint of water in the millpond behind Kenny's place.

"Yeah. Yeah, I am."

He took a deep breath and exhaled slowly. If Dev had to peg his expression, he'd call it... peaceful. Contented. Dev should recognize the look by now—he'd seen it in the mirror every day since that picnic at the quarry.

Dev grinned. "Then what do you say we rock and roll?"

Haru grinned back. "You're on."

Chapter Thirty-One

"This is *your* fault." Nash stalked down the stair toward Casey while Owen watched, wide-eyed, from the balcony. "You staged this whole thing just to humiliate me. You and that... that fucking furball."

Casey backed against the landing wall, clutching Randolph Scott to his chest as a low growl rumbled in the cat's throat.

"The only thing I did was comply with the contract your manager provided. Home Grown didn't contact *you*. You contacted *us*. So from where I stand"—*with a seriously pissed off cat in my arms*—"it looks like you did all the staging yourself. It's your bad luck that the other players didn't follow your script." Randolph Scott's growl rose to a yowl. "And if I were you, I'd stand back. Randolph Scott *really* doesn't like you, and you know nothing about cats if you think anybody can control them."

Nash stopped a step above the landing, obviously trying to further intimidate Casey by *looming*. But Casey had been loomed over by Donald Friel for years. Nash Tambling was a rank amateur.

"You poisoned Dev against me."

"I didn't even *know* you until yesterday. I didn't even know Dev had been with the band. So this isn't on me. You're the one who let him go when he needed you most."

"What about *my* needs?"

Casey pushed off the wall, teeth bared in a grin that probably bordered on feral. "Frankly, my dear, I don't give a damn." He marched down the rest of the stairs and whispered to Randolph Scott, "I've always wanted to say that!"

"Dude, wait up!" Owen barreled down the stairs, passing Nash without a sideways glance. "Are Dev and Haru really playing together?"

"Yup. In less than twenty minutes now."

"Awesome! Let's go see."

Casey let Owen bound out the door ahead of him and then looked up at the seething Nash. "If you don't want to disappoint your fans and trash your own reputation, I suggest you find Haru after his set. If you apologize *very* nicely, you might still have a guitarist for what might be POV's last performance. Now, you'll have to excuse me. My boyfriend is about to play a song he wrote for me and I don't want to miss it."

"What about my bed?" Nash shrieked. "My pillows?"

"Extras are in the linen closet," Casey called over his shoulder as he set Randolph Scott down. "Make your bed and lie in it." He opened the door and let the cat scamper out ahead of him.

"Dude!" Owen beckoned to him from the driveway. "We don't want to miss 'em."

"Don't worry. I know a shortcut."

He led Owen down the path toward the summer kitchen, where the aroma of rustic fruit tarts wafted out the open windows and a burst of laughter followed them into the woods behind the building. When Casey reached the willow tree and pushed inside, with both Owen and Randolph Scott sticking to his heels, he found Ty and Kenny already there.

"Hey, guys."

Kenny grinned. "I see you've discovered the best seat in the house, too."

Heat rushed up Casey's throat when he remembered exactly how he'd discovered it and what he was doing the last time he was here. "I, um, may have. Did we miss anything?"

"Nope," Ty said. "They're just setting up."

Kenny chuckled. "My high school shop guys are chuffed to be roadies. They think it makes them extra cool."

"Roadies are the best." Owen gestured to himself. "I'm Owen Mosley. Drummer."

Ty nodded a greeting. "Ty Harrison. Town vet."

Owen turned to Kenny and thrust out his hand with a wide grin and a double bounce on his toes.

With a slightly panicked glance at Casey—yeah, Owen's enthusiasm could be a lot—Kenny shook Owen's proffered hand. "Kenny Li. Handyman."

"Seriously?" The look on Owen's face was something usually reserved for kids at Christmas when they discovered a new bike under the tree. "You can *fix* things?"

"Yeah." Kenny exchanged a mystified glance with Casey and Ty. "This is New England. Our motto is 'Use it up, wear it out, make it do, or do without.' So fixing things is kind of our way of life."

"That's awesome. The only thing I can fix is guacamole. Oh, and margaritas." He smiled a little shyly. "No patience."

"Owen," Casey said with a smile, "I suspect you're a product person at heart."

"I think I'm more a guy who hires the right person to do the job." He bumped Kenny's shoulder with his own. "'Cause when it comes to fixing shit? I know that's sure not me." He glanced at Ty and said kindly, "I'm sure vets do great stuff too."

Casey was tempted to see if he could fan Owen's obvious attraction spark. Kenny was so nice. He deserved a great boyfriend, and while Owen was more like one of the big, exuberant puppies in Ty's shelter, he had a good heart.

But then Dev and Haru walked on stage and sat on the tall stools behind a pair of mics and he tabled that thought for later.

He stepped forward and parted the willow fronds so his view was unobstructed. Since the tree was off to stage left, they didn't have a full frontal view, but they were closer than they'd have been if they stood at the back of the crowd. From here, he could see Dev's face in three-quarter profile and the back of Haru's head, since he was sitting facing Dev rather than the audience.

"Haru needs to cheat out," Owen muttered. "Nash always insisted that he and Eli stand facing *him* at center stage."

"Nash is a dickhead," Ty said.

Owen turned to him, blinking like he'd just awoken from a nap. "Hunh. You know, I guess he is. We just got so used to thinking of him as The Talent—"

Ty scoffed. "Probably because that's the way he thinks of himself."

"No argument there. Ah." Owen nodded in satisfaction as Dev murmured something to Haru and he changed position to be more open to the audience. "That's better."

"Afternoon, folks," Dev said, and his voice, amplified by the sound system, sent a definite feedback loop through Casey's nerves. "I'm thrilled you've joined us here for Home Grown Tastes and Tunes." He grinned. "In case you haven't noticed already, this is the Tunes portion of the event, but I hope all of you will sample the Tastes from our vendors before you head home today." He made a production out of peering out at the audience. "I see some of you have already discovered the joys of Home Grown picnics." The audience's laughter was accompanied by a smattering of applause and a few cheers. "Next to me is Haru Inada, whom you might recognize. He'll be back later this evening when he takes the stage with Persistence of Vision." More heartfelt applause and cheers erupted.

Haru leaned into his mic. "He forgot to mention his name. This is Dev Harrison, one of the founders of POV, town manager of Home, and one of the people who organized this event."

Dev gave a mock bow over the belly of his acoustic guitar as the applause grew. "Thank you for the welcome. Now, Haru and I have some songs to share with you. This first one is brand new. It's called 'Wait for It' and I wrote it for a very special person. Casey, this one's for you."

They launched into the song and Casey could barely breathe. It had been lovely when Dev had sung it for him the first time, but now, with the two guitars lines twining with each other and Haru's voice, a mellow tenor, harmonizing with Dev's scrumptious baritone, it was heartbreakingly beautiful.

"Damn," Owen murmured. "They need to record that. They'll make a mint."

On stage, as the song neared the end, Dev turned and met Casey's eyes. *He knows where I am. He knew the whole time.* Then, instead of finishing, the song went on.

Now you're back,
Steadfast, demanding that I hear
Without judgment, so I listen
Till at last the facts are clear.
I've been a fool, and that's on me.
Can you possibly forgive?
I promise I'll do better, love,
For as long as we both live.

Wait for it...
The unexpected twist.
Wait for it...
The sign I almost missed.
Wait for it...
The words I can't resist.
The big reveal that you still feel
That I was worth the wait.

"Damn," Ty said, a catch in his voice as he gripped Casey's shoulder. "Just *damn*."

"He wrote another verse," Casey croaked as the audience surged to their feet. His heart felt so full it couldn't possibly fit in his chest. "He wrote another verse for me."

Ty swiped a hand under his eyes and then grabbed Casey in a tight hug. "Thank you." He let go and stumbled back, narrowly missing Randolph Scott's tail. "I've, uh, gotta go. I'll... yeah. Bye." He hurried away.

The rest of the set went by in a blur. Dimly, Casey realized they'd divided the set into roughly three categories—Dev's songs, Haru's songs, with a couple of unusual covers, including a jazzed up, a cappella version of "Moonlight in Vermont," with Haru beat-boxing instead of an instrumental break.

When they rose at the end of the set, the applause was thunderous and the cheers could probably be heard in Merrilton. Dev and Haru bowed and waved, then Dev slung an arm across Haru's shoulders and they walked offstage, each gripping the neck of their guitar.

"Holy shit," Owen said. "Haru's songs are *epic*. I don't know why Nash won't let the band play them." When Casey raised both eyebrows, Owen patted the air. "Right, right. Nash is a dickhead. I'll have the T-shirts made up by Monday." He winked. "I'll put you down for two."

"Mmmphmmm."

Casey, still dazed from the performance, turned at the sound of that quintessential Home grunt to find Pete standing next to him, munching a rustic raspberry tart. Pete nodded at Casey.

"For a fool kid, you did all right." He turned and sauntered away, Randolph Scott trotting beside him, clearly hoping for crumbs.

"Wow." Kenny's whisper was somehow loaded with awe. "He called you a fool kid."

Casey, who had been a little resentful that Pete had tempered his compliment with that back-handed epithet, turned to him. "Is that good?"

"He only calls people fools if he considers them part of the town. Otherwise, they're just flatlanders." He grinned and tapped Casey's biceps with his fist. "Guess you're home."

Casey gazed at the stage, where Dev and Haru had returned to take another bow at the audience's insistence. "Yeah." He was pretty sure his heart was floating in the air over his head by this time. "I guess I am."

Chapter Thirty-Two

Soaring on post-performance endorphins, a rush he'd nearly forgotten, Dev handed off his guitar to one of Kenny's high school roadies. He gave Haru a hug—not the bro-backslap kind, but a real one.

"Great show, man, even if I do say so myself."

Haru returned the hug and then stepped back. Judging by the size of his grin, he was flying as high as Dev. "I think the audience said it first."

"We've gotta do it again."

Haru's grin faded a little, turning wistful. "Do you mean it?"

"I do." Dev looked down at him. "But I've got to tell you, I'm fixed here in Home. I don't want to tour. I don't want to deal with the assholes in the music business anymore. Making music? Yeah. Being a rock star? No." He chuckled. "Not that I think I'd ever get there, but—"

"Don't sell yourself short." Haru moved out of the way as the Teenage Mutant Ninja Roadies hauled the next act's equipment onstage. "But I'm right there with you on the touring and the industry shit. We wouldn't have to go that route, though. I told you I've got my own recording equipment?" When Dev nodded, Haru bit his lip. "It's a little more than that. Like a lot. I've produced albums for other local artists. That's what I did before Nash hired me for POV."

Unbelievably, Dev's post-performance rush stepped up a level. "Really? You'd be willing to do that?"

Making music, recording music, capturing the spark of performance for others, even when they weren't actually present... That was a dream he'd followed from the time he'd stepped onstage with his guitar at his first grade school talent show. He thought he'd lost it when he left POV to take up the Harrison mantle in Home. If he could have that again...

Dev came back to earth with an almost audible crash. "But you've got the POV touring schedule. And like I said, I'm fixed here in Home."

Haru looked out at the sliver of the field visible from their spot in the wings. "I'm pretty sure I'm out of POV. In fact, I'll quit before Nash has the chance to fire me."

"Are you sure?"

He nodded. "I'm sure. I've found something I like better." He sighed, a sound of deep contentment. "I've found Home."

"You're serious? You want to stay?" Dev grinned and clasped Haru's hand. "That's fantastic. I've got several houses you could —" Dev spotted Casey standing next to the willow tree. "Hold that thought, okay? We'll talk."

Leaving a bemused Haru, Dev ran down the steps at the side of the stage and raced across the grass. He caught Casey up in a hug and whirled in a circle.

"Dev," Casey said, laughing. "Put me down."

Dev looked into Casey's face, his heart so full he felt like he could light Main Street all summer long. "Not yet." He danced around in a circle some more.

"Okay, but at least stop twirling me around. I'm getting dizzy."

Dev stopped immediately, setting Casey back on his feet, but keeping his arms around his waist. "Sorry."

Casey laced his fingers behind Dev's neck, his eyes practically glowing. "Don't be. You were wonderful. And that song?" He blinked rapidly. "Crap, now I'm gonna cry in front of all these people."

"Don't cry, Casey." Dev smoothed the soft curls off Casey's forehead and kissed each of his eyes. "I never want you to be sad."

"I'm not sad, you doofus. I'm... I don't know. Thrilled. Touched." He laid his palm along Dev's cheek. "Happy. And so, so proud of you."

"Me?" Dev scoffed. "All of this was your doing. If it had been up to me, I'd have been up to my ass in Port-a-Potties for no reason."

Casey shook his head. "It wasn't me. It was all of us. You. Kenny. Ty. Pete, Kat, Sylvia." He chuckled. "The high school kids. Everybody pitched in. Everybody wants to save Home." He lifted on his toes and kissed Dev's lips gently. "And you're its heart, Dev. Home wouldn't be home to any of us without you."

Flying again.

Dev carded his fingers through Casey's hair and tilted his face up at the perfect angle for a deeper kiss or seventeen. Casey's little whimper, his taste—of raspberries and sunshine— his lips so soft under Dev's, the way he opened so sweetly for Dev's tongue, the—

"Uh, guys?"

Still intoxicated by Casey kisses—the perfect capper to post-performance euphoria—Dev dimly heard Haru's voice and... was that applause? The next act was probably taking the stage, so he ignored it and pulled Casey closer, so they were pressed together from chest to groin.

"Guys?"

The feel of Casey against him, the softness of his hair under Dev's fingers, the sweetness of his mouth. God, *this* was home.

"*Guys!*"

Reluctantly, Dev lifted his head to glare at Haru, tucking Casey's head against his chest. "What?"

"You've, um, kind of got an audience." Haru cut his eyes to the side, and Dev realized that the applause wasn't for the next act—the musicians were standing next to the stage, grinning like loons. Every face in the audience was turned toward him.

Toward him and Casey.

"Oh my god," Casey murmured. "Crying in front of everybody is nothing. Dev, we practically humped each other!"

"Nonsense." Dev kissed the top of Casey's head. "We didn't go *that* far." Barely. Although if Haru hadn't stopped them, Dev wasn't sure what would have happened. But since the audience was applauding, cheering, and hooting, he just raised one hand in acknowledgement and, keeping Casey tucked safely against his larger body, covered the short expanse of grass and into the shelter of the willow tree.

Unfortunately, the space inside the leafy green curtain was more populated than Dev liked. Kenny grinned and gave them a thumbs-up. "Nice encore, Dev."

Dev gave him the finger, but the grin that threatened to split his face probably canceled the effect.

"My dudes!" Owen punched Dev's biceps and then held his fist out for Haru to bump. "Fan-fucking-tastic set. You've seriously gotta record those tunes."

His arm still firm around Casey's waist, Dev glanced at Haru. "I, uh, think we might have floated the possibility?"

Haru shrugged. "I'm there if you are."

Dev looked down at Casey. "Haru's interested in moving to Home, along with his music production equipment."

"Really?" Casey asked, almost breathlessly. "Do you do video production, too?"

Haru glanced from Casey's eager face to Dev. "Yeah. But nothing too elaborate."

"That's perfect." Casey beamed at him. "I've got a couple of ideas I want to run by you. Maybe we can chat later?"

"Sure." Haru's hopeful smile faded, and he set his jaw. "But first, I've got to get through my farewell performance with POV."

"Duuuude," Owen groaned. "You're leaving the band? Why?" He held up both hands. "Nope. Don't say it. I know." He looked at Casey. "Dickhead, am I right?"

Dev bristled. "Watch it, Owen. Casey isn't—"

"Settle down, big guy." Casey patted Dev's chest. "He's talking about Nash."

"Oh. That's okay then."

Owen's shoulders sagged. "Damn. That means the band's breaking up."

"You could get another guitarist," Haru said. "You did before."

"Maybe. But who'd write the songs?" He tapped Casey's shoulder. "And who wants to work with a dickhead?" He glanced between Dev and Haru. "Don't suppose you two would be looking for a drummer?"

Dev shared a look with Haru. "I don't know, Owen. We haven't really gone much further than the possibility. We won't tour. No industry events or perks. And whatever we do would be based here in Home."

Owen glanced sidelong at Kenny. "There's worse places to be." He linked elbows with Haru. "Come on. If it's our last appearance, let's make it a good one." He dragged Haru out from under the willow and toward the woods.

"Did he..." Kenny looked at Dev and Casey. "Was he *flirting* with me?"

Dev chuckled. "Kenny, my man, if you can't tell, then you've been single for way too long."

"Tell me about it," Kenny muttered. "I better go check on my high school crew. See you guys later. And Dev? Seriously great set." He grinned. "Welcome back."

Dev frowned after him. "What does he mean? I've been here for almost two years."

"I think, sweetheart, that he means welcome back to *you*." Casey gazed up at Dev, his eyes serious, and placed his palms on Dev's chest. "I don't blame you for leaving the band or for returning to Home." His expression darkened. "And lord knows I'm ecstatic that you left the dickhead in the dust. But music and Home aren't mutually exclusive." He patted Dev's chest. "The magic is in you. You carry it with you wherever you go, with or without your instruments, as long as you set it free. *That's* what Kenny meant."

Thank god he'd already performed, because Dev's throat was so tight he couldn't have done anything other than croak.

When Dev left the band, it had seemed like an either/or decision. He'd been treating POV and music as though they were synonymous, but they weren't, just as—like Casey had brilliantly put it, igniting a giant fucking lightbulb over Dev's head—Home and music weren't mutually exclusive.

He'd been caught in some kind of toxic denial triangle for almost two years: Can't have Home and POV, can't have music without POV, therefore can't have Home and music.

Yes, he'd been juggling the grief of loss—his brother, his grandfather, *and* music—with stepping into a role he'd never expected to fill and for which he was woefully unprepared.

But then *Casey*.

Casey had shown Dev that he could *recombine* his responsibilities and his passions into a new dynamic that—if he didn't fuck it up again—could make him better at both.

Dev wrapped his arms around Casey and buried his face in Casey's soft hair. "God, I love you," he choked out. "I'm going to miss you so much when you go."

"What if," Casey said, his voice muffled by Dev's chest, "you didn't have to miss me? What if I stay?"

Dev's heart bounced against his collarbone. *What?* He raised his head and searched Casey's face. "You'd do that? You'd stay for me?"

"No." Casey shook his head, and Dev's heart plummeted. "I'd stay for *us*. I'd stay for what we can do here—and not just for the town and its people, but for what we can do, both together and separately, for ourselves." He gazed up at Dev, his lips curved in a soft smile, his eyes warm. "You're on the cusp of something, Dev. We both are. Of remaking our lives into something we can love, something we can be proud of, something *meaningful*."

With the tip of one finger, Dev traced Casey's face from temple to chin. "I see how this benefits me. But what about you? Your life is in Manhattan."

"Wrong." Casey caught Dev's hand against his cheek. "My *residence* was in Manhattan, but I wouldn't call my existence there a *life*, at least not one I chose. But this? Home? You? *This* is home. *This* I choose." Uncertainty flickered across his face, and he bit his lip. "That is… if you want me to."

Dev whooped, his grin so wide his cheeks hurt. He grabbed Casey around the waist again and danced in a circle.

"Dev," Casey said crossly. "What did I say about the twirling? I get motion sick."

"Can't have that." Dev strode to the willow's trunk and pressed Casey's back against it. "How's this? Too lumpy?"

Casey wriggled, causing some very distracting friction when he wrapped his legs around Dev's waist. "No. But this hideaway isn't as private as you might think."

"I know." He kissed Casey once, just a soft press of lips, and set him down. "We'll go back to our house and lock the door. *Then* I'll show you exactly how happy I am that you've found a home in Home. With me."

A muffled mew at their feet was followed by a soft *plop*.

Casey clenched his eyes shut and clutched Dev's biceps. "Oh my god. Did Randolph Scott just drop a dead mouse on *my* shoe?"

Dev glanced down. "Yep." He kissed Casey's eyelids until they fluttered open. "But that's a good thing."

Casey's brows drew together in the least intimidating—and dearest—scowl in the world. "How do your figure?"

"Because if Randolph Scott shares his treats with you, then you really are home."

Chapter Thirty-Three

Two months later.

"Dev?" Casey emerged from the cottage bathroom in a cloud of steam, a towel around his waist, and padded into the bedroom.

Hmmm. No Dev. Nobody but Randolph Scott stretched out on the bed with Lizzie and Xander draped over him in the extreme kitten exhaustion that always followed their morning zoomies.

"Thanks for babysitting the kids, big guy. You know they get lonely if Dev and I aren't around." He scratched Randolph Scott's ears and got a rumbling purr in response. "Although I think you see them more as fashion accessories, since brown tabby coordinates so well with your fur."

Casey saw it as a win-win, actually. The kittens that he'd adopted after he'd officially moved in with Dev—surprisingly, Uncle Walt had adopted their brother, Huck—would also keep Randolph Scott from indulging in mouse murder, which was absolutely crucial today.

He briefly considered heading in search of Dev with only the towel for clothing, since that could result in some *very* interesting uses of furniture, not to mention the floor and walls, but they had a jam-packed agenda today, and Home's residents considered *doors* a suggestion rather than an actual boundary. Although after Kenny had walked in on Dev and Casey, er, in medias res, as it were, he at least knocked first.

Casey opened the walk-in closet. After Kenny had outfitted it with new rods and drawers and shelves, it held both Casey's and Dev's clothes very comfortably, especially since neither one of them were precisely fashion plates. Today, though, Casey wanted to take a little more care with his appearance.

Because today was an extra special day.

So instead of his usual uniform of worn jeans and a sweatshirt, he donned his best pair of chinos, a pin-striped button-down, and the forest green cashmere V-necked sweater that was so soft Dev couldn't keep his hands off it whenever Casey wore it.

Dev's hands always calmed Casey's nerves—that is, when they weren't driving him out of his senses. But Dev was a master at understanding when Casey needed soothing rather than arousal, and today was definitely a soothing kind of day.

He pulled on the hand-knitted socks he'd bought from one of the knitters at Simple Gifts and wiggled his toes, smiling at the pattern of red, orange, and gold leaves that matched the colors on the trees all over Home.

Leaf-peeper season, Pete called it with a grunt and grumble, but considering he'd been waxing the Home Grown van all week, not to mention shining up his Uber/Lyft car, Casey didn't take his grousing too seriously.

He slipped on his loafers and trotted out to the living room. Dev was standing at the window, facing the field, his phone to his ear.

"You sure it's okay? Kenny said he can install whatever storage you need, and knows a guy who can upgrade the electrical if— Okay, cool. I'll let him know you're good to go, then." Dev chuckled. "Looking forward to it. Later."

"Was that Haru?" Casey wrapped his arms around Dev's waist and leaned his chin on his shoulder.

"Yep. He's all settled in. Finished setting up his studio last night. Owen's been helping him, when he hasn't been underfoot at Ty's clinic or haunting Make It Do and driving Kenny bonkers." He turned in the circle of Casey's arms and smiled down at him. "Hey."

Casey kissed him. "Hey, yourself."

"You look great." He smoothed his hands down Casey's back. "I love this sweater."

Casey smirked at him. "I know." He bit his lip. "Does it bother you that POV broke up?"

"Honestly? No. It wasn't my band anymore. Hadn't been for a long time. I'm just glad Haru, Owen, and Eli found soft landings though."

"I can't believe Eli's off at a retreat somewhere."

"He's not *at* a retreat, babe. He's *running* the retreat. Meditation through music or something." Dev twirled one of Casey's curls around his finger. "Call me vindictive, but I can't say I'm sorry that Nash's solo career fizzled like a wet sparkler."

"Vindictive," Casey said, deadpan.

Dev tugged on the curl. "Smartass."

"I still think we should have set him up with Bradley."

"Now who's being vindictive?" When Casey raised his hand, Dev laughed. "You ready for today?"

"As I'll ever be. What are you looking forward to?"

Dev's grin turned filthy. "Peeling you out of this sweater, not to mention your shirt and pants." He waggled his eyebrows. "Are you wearing those new briefs? The mesh ones?"

Casey arched an eyebrow. "You'll have to wait to find out." He so was, although he had to order them by the dozen because Dev had a tendency to tear them off. Sometimes with his teeth. "But that's not what I meant. What are you looking forward to with Haru?"

"We're recording our first track today." He kissed Casey. "Wanna know what it is?"

"Judging by the sounds emanating from the practice room at Harrison House—which, by the way, are completely audible from here and maybe all over Home—I'd say…" He still got a little jangle in his belly whenever he thought about it. "I'd say it's 'Wait for It.'"

"Yup. Do you want…" Dev's voice went a little hoarse, and he cleared his throat. "That is, would you like to be there? In the studio?"

Jingle jangle. "You wouldn't mind?"

"Are you kidding?" Dev's arms tightened around him. "Babe, I wrote the song for you. And even Haru says that I perform it better when you're in the audience." He nuzzled Casey's neck and whispered, "He says the love shows in my voice."

Okay, now that wasn't fair. He glared at Dev so the prickle behind his eyes wouldn't spill over and poked his chest with both forefingers.

"There should be a town ordinance that nobody's boyfriend is allowed to say things like that to them right before they walk out the door for a *very important event*." Casey looked down his nose—hard to do with a boyfriend who was half a head taller. "You're the town manager. You should take care of that."

Dev's smile was wicked. "Why? Heart pounding? Knees weak?" He murmured into Casey's ear again. "Cock hard?"

"Stop it. Stop it right now." Wincing, Casey slapped both palms on Dev's chest and pushed him away—although he fisted a hand in Dev's fisherman's sweater and tugged him back for a last—very quick!—kiss. "We can't be late. Sylvia would be devastated. You wouldn't want to do that to her."

Dev sighed and stepped away. "You're right. Sorry. We'll have time later." He held out a hand. "Let's go."

Casey laced his fingers with Dev and they stepped out of the cottage together. A chilly breeze hit them the minute they stepped onto the porch, cutting right through Casey's sweater.

"Brrr. Maybe I should bring a jacket. Vermont is a lot colder in October than Manhattan usually is."

"Nah," Dev said as he closed the door behind them. "Once we're out in the sun, you'll be glad of the breeze."

"If you say so. Clearly, I'll have to toughen up if I expect to make it through my first legendary Vermont winter."

Dev chuckled as he led Casey down the steps and across the sunny meadow toward Harrison House. "It's not so bad as long as you're dressed for it. Don't let Pete's apocalyptic stories scare you."

"It's not Pete's stories. It's Kenny's." Casey shivered. "Pete says nothing but *mmmphmmm*, which might be more terrifying. I mean, what's he *not* saying?"

"Don't worry, babe." Dev dropped a kiss atop Casey's head. "I'll keep you warm."

"I'll hold you to that."

When they reached the summer kitchen, Casey knocked on the door and peeked inside. Sylvia, wearing a rust-colored duster over her chef's whites, was pacing in front of her office door, cell phone to her ear.

"You can tell him from me that I never poach anybody." She spotted Casey and raised a hand in greeting. "At least not without brandy or a nice court bouillon. It was Deborah's own decision to stay here after she finished the advanced class last month. If he doesn't want to lose key staff, he should start treating them better. And honestly, Walt, why is he complaining to you?" She winked at Casey. "Just because you've been recommending my classes, it's not like you've been *encouraging* people to jump ship at all the Pillsbury Dickboy's restaurants. Will we see you soon? Okay. Good. Ciao." She flicked the screen with her thumb and tucked the phone into her pocket. "Chalk another one up for your uncle. He's relentless."

Casey hadn't been all *that* shocked when Uncle Walt had severed his business relationship with Bradley. He'd actually listened and taken Casey's warnings to heart. But when he and Dev had bonded over losing their brothers unexpectedly, he'd gone a step further and started to *weaponize* the connections he still had in the restaurant business and begun systematically dismantling Bradley's little empire from the inside. Between that and taking over management of the Harrison investment portfolio—much to Dev's heartfelt relief and gratitude—Casey suspected he'd be relocating to Home when he retired in a few years.

Casey peered behind Sylvia into the office. "Where *is* Deborah?"

"She's been on site since before dawn. Supervising, she claims, but I suspect she won't be able to resist getting in on the action." Her smile turned more natural and more than a touch eager. "Ready?"

"Absolutely."

She patted her hair. "Do I look all right?"

Casey smoothed one errant silver strand behind her ear. "Perfect. Besides, you know the fans love it even more when one or both of us looks a little frazzled. It makes them feel better about their own efforts."

He and Sylvia, with Haru as camera operator and producer, had launched a web channel called *Cooking for the Culinarily Clueless*, which featured Sylvia attempting to teach Casey how to make dishes of varying difficulty. They posted two episodes a week featuring recipes simple enough for beginners to master without too much trouble, and every other week they added another with a more challenging dish.

When they discovered that the audience's—half a million subscribers and growing!—favorite episodes were the ones where Casey crashed and burned in a major way, they'd added another feature: Any viewer who wanted to pay a premium could request a particular recipe. They'd done two so far, and the response had been fantastic.

And they'd channeled all the proceeds into the venture that was launching today.

"Are you nervous?" he asked her.

"Not really." She smiled at Dev when he held the door for her. "Are you?"

Casey nodded, but when she frowned, he held up both hands. "Not about your part. I know you'll be brilliant. I'm just worried that nobody will discover that brilliance. I want this to work."

Dev captured both their hands. "It will. You've each done a terrific job with promotion. Aren't Summer Kitchen's sessions booked solid from now until April?"

"Well." Casey crossed his fingers lest he jinx them. "Yes."

"And vendors have already started calling for spots in next summer's Home Grown?"

"Yeeesss." He'd had three messages waiting on his phone when he woke up today, making that an even dozen this week alone and it was only Tuesday.

"And isn't Shira *begging* you to partner with the resort and make the antique fair a joint annual event after Bradley bailed on her?"

Casey gave Dev a narrow-eyed look. "Also yes. But this is different."

"Don't think of it as different. Think of it as.... as Home *growing*. It'll be great." He kissed Casey softly. "I'll stake my town management career on it."

"I'd feel much better about that if you actually *wanted* a town management career," Casey said tartly.

"You know," Dev said as they headed down Main Street, "it's actually... growing on me."

Casey rolled his eyes. "Don't quit your day jobs, Dev. Music and town management are one thing, but your stand-up chops need serious work."

Dev just laughed, but as they cut between the Market and the Historical Society, Casey held his breath until they stepped out onto East Road.

Then he choked when he tried to inhale into lungs already full.

The road in front of Ty's clinic/shelter was full of people, the crowd spilling off the sidewalk in front of their destination: a neat, clapboard bungalow that until six weeks ago had been empty. But now, a rainbow *Grand Opening* banner was swagged over its wide plate-glass front window. The hand-lettered wooden sign above its double front doors was a collaboration between Kenny and the Artists United co-op:

Home Cooking.

And beneath it in smaller letters: *Open for breakfast and lunch, seven days a week.*

Dev smiled down at Casey. "See? What did I tell you?"

"Oh my god." Casey clutched Dev's hand with both of his, belly tumbling. "We've only got fifteen tables. How are we going to fit everybody in?"

Sylvia gave a contented sigh. "Same as at any popular restaurant. First come, first served. And since it's time to let the first diners in, you'll both need to excuse me. I'm sure Deborah's got things well in hand, but I want to lend my support." She strode off down the street, cutting down the alley to reach the kitchen entrance.

Casey leaned into Dev. "You think it'll really work?"

Dev tucked Casey closer against his side. "Home hasn't had a restaurant since the Inn closed. The locals will support it during the off-season, and the tourists will flock here in the fall and summer. Who knows? We might get the ski crowd in the winter too, if the roads don't get too bad." He placed a finger under Casey's chin and tilted his head up. "It's a good thing you did, Casey."

Casey met Dev's loving gaze. "It wasn't just me. It was all of us. And it won't take one restaurant, one successful festival, or even the surge in Summer Kitchen's popularity to save Home. Not entirely."

"Maybe not." Dev took Casey's hand and drew him toward the restaurant. "But it's a start. Now let's go have breakfast. I'm pretty sure Sylvia saved us a table."

About

Camera
Shy

Never assume…

…that your uber competent personal assistant will *get it* when you announce your (fake) engagement to him during a live on-air interview with your archnemesis.

Never waver…

…from your plan to punish your arrogant celebrity boss for his presumption by turning your (fake) wedding into a reality competition for event planners.

Never admit…

…that the feelings blossoming between the two of you through seven (fake) engagement celebrations, six (fake) bachelor parties, five (fake) wedding party luncheons, and four (fake) rehearsal dinners are about as (real) you can get.

Camera Shy is a boss/employee, fake-engagement, right-in-front-of-your-nose romantic comedy featuring a former child model-turned-PA who is *so done* with cameras, a cocky LGBTQ activist/talk show host who *does not* lose, more scarves than midwinter in Boston, and banter. So. Much. Banter.

Read on for a sneak peek!

Sneak Peek of

Camera Shy

Curtis scuttled back to stand next to Dustin at the podium as the lights above the audience dimmed and the monitors flickered to life. Standing behind camera two, Xavier held up his hand, fingers spread. "And we're live in five…" He folded a finger down. "Four… three…" He folded the last two fingers down silently as the show theme played and camera one focused on Ari.

"Good afternoon, and welcome to *Ari Dimitriou on Life*. Today, my special guest is none other than Jesse Sandusky. Journalist. Activist." Ari smiled directly at the camera. "Antichrist."

Dustin smothered a moan and lowered his forehead to the podium. *And so it begins.* He sighed and raised his head, glancing between the set and the monitors, as camera three, which usually did both audience reaction shots and one-shots of the guest du jour, caught Jesse chuckling amiably, his arms draped across the back of the sofa reserved for guests, as if to say, "I've got nothing to hide."

"I see you haven't gotten any less dramatic since we last chatted, Ari."

"And apparently you haven't gotten any less self-important." Ari picked up a hardcover book from the table that was the only thing separating him from Jesse. "I believe you've published a book since then." He flashed the dust jacket at the camera, then dropped the book on the floor on the far side of his chair.

"Yep." Jesse rested one ankle on the opposite knee. "Some people—a lot of people, judging by my NYT bestseller status—are open to alternate perspectives." He grinned. "Want to hear the reader demographics, Ari? How many books I've sold to queer people? How many queer people have written to me, praising my courage?"

Ari folded his hands on his knee. *Uh oh.* But it might still be okay, as long as Ari didn't get that smile—

Ari smiled.

Dustin curled his fingers into fists. *Okay, as long as he doesn't look at Jesse from under his brows—*

Ari lowered his chin and peered at Jesse from under his brows.

Oh, god. Here we go.

"You know what I've found, Jesse? It seems queer people are just as apt to be assholes as straight people, even to each other. You're a case in point."

"Thank you, Ari. Your opinion means so much to me. But you know…" Jesse's grin stretched wider. "If a person—queer or straight—isn't interested in *my* opinions, they don't need to buy my book."

"Don't be disingenuous. You have a platform. A voice. A following."

"Glad you finally admit that."

Ari didn't acknowledge the interruption. "Most queer people lack that kind of public privilege. Yet you used your… notoriety to speak out against their right to marry. Their right to be treated equally."

"And you shouldn't be imprecise, Ari. I never said anybody deserved unequal treatment. My stance is that marriage shouldn't be the yardstick by which we measure the legitimacy of any relationship. I wasn't arguing against marriage for couples of the same gender. I was arguing against marriage for couples of *any* gender."

"That's not how the conservative pundits saw it. They used you—your words, your articles, your sound bites—as counter arguments. You even appeared on Fox News, for Chrissake."

Jesse's grin matched Ari's at his most sharklike. *Dueling Great Whites. Just shoot me now.* "Jealous? They've never invited you to guest, I believe."

A muscle in Ari's jaw twitched, which camera one probably caught in full close-up glory.

"You're incredibly arrogant to believe that you can speak for what all LGBTQ people want. What they can expect. What they deserve."

"But you're doing the same. You're using your voice to declare that they should want the same things as straight people —who, I might add, don't necessarily want the confines of marriage either."

"I'm not saying they *should* do any one thing or another. Only that they shouldn't be *denied* a particular legal status that confers certain rights and privileges under our laws."

"Bullshit."

Curtis leaned close to Dustin and murmured, "Can he say that on the air?"

"There's a ten-second delay," Dustin whispered back. "They can bleep out anything inappropriate in the control room."

On the set, Jesse pointed both index fingers at Ari. *Stick 'em up.* "You're perpetuating an archaic construct. Buying into the impression that the ultimate union is one that's solemnized by the farce of institutionalized monogamy."

"You're saying that you and I, as gay men—"

"I'm bi, actually."

Ari bared his teeth in the deadly smile Dustin knew all too well. *Uh oh.* "You and I as *queer* men don't deserve the same consideration as men who identify as straight?"

"Not at all. I'm just saying it's against our nature, whether we're queer or straight. Male biology is configured to spread sperm as widely as possible. Our brains are hard-wired for promiscuity."

"I don't accept that notion. The brain is a highly adaptable organ."

"But the penis is not."

Half the audience laughed. The other half booed. Curtis turned to Dustin, his eyes wide. "Can he say *that* on the air?" Dustin just sighed.

Jesse settled back on the couch, spreading his arms again. "You know, Ari, I've noticed something. You're such a cheerleader for marriage, and yet you prove my point for me."

Ari propped his elbows on his chair arms, steepling his fingers. "That's highly unlikely."

"No? If the tabloids are to be believed"—Jesse grinned at the camera again—"and if it's in the *National Enquirer*, it's *gotta* be true, am I right?—you party with a different man every week."

Dustin gripped the edge of the podium. He'd *warned* Ari how his personal life might reflect on his political and professional stance. But had Ari listened? No, he had not, this morning's impromptu brunch being a prime example.

"Just because I haven't gotten married yet doesn't mean I won't." But the defensive edge to Ari's voice and the way he laced his fingers together set off Dustin's mental *Danger!* klaxon.

"Really." Jesse's eye glinted in the harsh studio lights. "How old are you again?"

"Thirty-five. It's not a secret."

"Uh huh. And how many men have you dated?"

"I'm not one for keeping score. It's disrespectful."

Jesse held his palms out like he was serving something up on a platter. "You heard it here first, folks. The man who claims true love is everyone's Holy Grail can't even count the number of times he *hasn't* found true love. But then why settle for one true love when perpetually looking is obviously more to your taste?"

Ari's eyebrows twitched, but he didn't scowl. *Not enough for the camera to catch, anyway.* "There's no timetable on finding love."

"Obviously. Come on, man. How many places"—he made air quotes—"have you looked for this mythical true love?"

"I prefer not to say."

"I'll make it easy on you. I won't ask for a full count, or even a year-to-date tally. How about how many *today?*" Jesse pulled out his phone and held it up, screen out. Camera three zoomed in, and there on the monitor—grainy but unmistakable—was Ari's unscheduled brunch. Taran was completely hidden behind a potted palm, but the intent behind Ari's amatory smile was obvious.

For an instant—and there's no way the camera didn't catch it —an expression skittered across Ari's face that was all too familiar on this show, although never before on its host: the look of a hunted, cornered rat.

But then it disappeared, replaced by the *I'm-just-about-to-nail-you* grin.

"You know, Jesse…"

And that's how it started. With Ari's casual drawl, leading up to the fatal zinger that left virtual blood on the studio floor. Dustin scrubbed his hands through his hair. *Wonder who'll be on cleanup duty today?*

"You've forced my hand."

What? Dustin edged out from behind the podium. Was Ari *conceding?* He never conceded.

"Have I?" Jesse uncrossed his ankle. Any minute now he'd spread his legs, because nothing says *I win* like a good crotch shot.

"I've been keeping this under wraps because my fiancé is a private person, and I had no desire to expose him to the glare of publicity."

Fiancé? Dustin gripped the metal rail on the corner of the riser, the square edges biting into his palm. *Who? Not Taran. Please not Taran.* But if it was Taran, why did Ari have Dustin cancel the dinner reservation?

"But he's here in the studio today."

Dustin scanned the audience. Many of them were part of Ari's Army, the volunteers who helped him with his LGBTQ activism. Press, too. Dustin counted at least four that he knew of, although there could be more. Dustin couldn't recognize them all by sight, considering how assiduously he dodged anybody who might come armed with a camera. *"Come" being the operative word, thank you for that phobia, Walker.*

"Who's the lucky guy?" Sure enough, Jesse spread his knees wide, the better to frame his package and play *my-dick-is-bigger-than-yours.* "Don't keep us in suspense."

The audience cheered. Because of course they did. Dustin kept a close eye on Ari's face. Was he going to dodge again? If so, he'd made a grave error by admitting his fiancé was here somewhere. But Ari's triumphant smile didn't dim.

Then he turned and looked right at Dustin. "Dustin? I'm sorry, sweetheart, but our secret's out. Come over here and greet our audience."

Free Stories

Follow E.J. on Ream (https://reamstories.com/ejr) or subscribe to her newsletter (https://ejr.pub/news-from-ej) to get these stories for free!

The following QR codes will get you there with your smartphone camera or other code reader.

Second First Date

Rusty has a plan to win Cas again...

A Mythmatched companion story that takes place immediately following the last chapter of Vampire with Benefits.

Rusty's Really Bad Day

Something is terribly wrong—and it's up to Rusty to put things right.

A Mythmatched companion story that takes place after Howling on Hold.

A Very Quest Solstice

It's our first holiday together, and I'm determined to make it special for Lachlan. Only problem? I know zip about how selkies celebrate, so I don't even know which winter holiday to pick.

With Lachlan out on a fishing charter, I try to tease some suggestions from my friends, but they're surprisingly unhelpful. And when we get a tip about a Disappeared sighting, my opportunity for more research evaporates.

I guess I'll just have to improvise. Again.

Dammit.

A holiday coda which builds on characters and situations from the first four Quest Investigations books. It takes place the month following Death on Denial *and is not intended to stand alone.*

First Flight

Will Seb overcome his fear of heights and take to the air with Nevan and Lulu?

A Mythmatched companion story that takes place between Chapter 33 and the Epilogue of Assassin by Accident.

Possession in Session

When an outcast demon is thrust into a medical technician training program, are death and destruction sure to follow?

After centuries of being bound to one greedy magician after another, Auni-jel-Chandu broke free and retreated to Sheol, outcast even among other demons. But then the Realm Accords passed, and suddenly he's thrust into the Sheol Retraining Initiative as the newest supernatural medical technician student at United Memorial Hospital (aka St. Stupid's).

Uh oh.

Wash Hernández might be a dud witch—he'd never been able to attract a familiar, so he's as magic-null as any human—but as a St. Stupid's orderly, he's still able to assist supernatural beings who need medical care. But when he meets a bewildered naked demon wandering the hospital corridors and forms an instant connection, he's not certain who needs help the most.

a message from
♥ *ej*

Dear Reader,

Thank you so much for reading *Summer Kitchen*, the first in my new Saving Home series. I'm so happy you've taken this journey with me! I'd be immensely grateful if you'd take a moment to leave a review at the retailer and any other site you use for reviews. Believe me, reviews make an *enormous* difference to the health and well-being of books (and not incidentally, to their associated authors!).

I'll be returning to Home in the future, but in the meantime you can pop on over to my website, https://ejrussell.com, for the deets on all my books: my other rom-coms, both paranormal and contemporary; my paranormal mysteries; my supernatural suspense; my science fantasy; and my one lone historical. If you're an audio fan, you can find the audio scoop there too. *Summer Kitchen*, for instance, is narrated by the wonderful Greg Boudreaux. (The QR code on the next page will get you there with your smartphone camera or other code reader.)

Would you like exclusive content and ARC giveaways, not to mention gratuitous dance videos? Then I'd love for you to join me in E.J. Russell's Reality Optional, my Facebook fan group (https://facebook.com/groups/reality.optional). My newsletter is the place to get the latest dish on new releases, sales, and more. I promise I only send one out when I've got…well…news. You can subscribe here: https://ejrussell.com/newsletter.

All my best,
—E

Also by
ej

Paranormal Romance
Mythmatched Universe
Fae Out of Water Trilogy
Cutie and the Beast
The Druid Next Door
Bad Boy's Bard

Supernatural Selection Trilogy
Single White Incubus
Vampire With Benefits
Demon on the Down-Low

Other Mythmatched Romances
Howling on Hold
Possession in Session
Witch Under Wraps
Cursed is the Worst
The Skinny on Djinni
Assassin by Accident (part of Carnival of Mysteries)

Mythmatched Companion Stories
Rusty's Really Bad Day (free to newsletter subscribers)
Second First Date (free to newsletter subscribers)
First Flight (free to newsletter subscribers)

Quest Investigations Mysteries
Five Dead Herrings
The Hound of the Burgervilles
The Lady Under the Lake

Death on Denial

At Odds with the Gods (A Mythmatched / Purgatory Playhouse crossover)

Art Medium Series
The Artist's Touch
Tested in Fire
Art Medium: The Complete Collection (omnibus edition)

Legend Tripping Series
Stumptown Spirits
Wolf's Clothing

Enchanted Occasions Series
Best Beast
Nudging Fate
Devouring Flame

Royal Powers Series (shared world)
Duking It Out
Duke the Hall
King's Ex

Magic Emporium Series (shared world)
Purgatory Playhouse

Science Fiction
Sun, Moon, and Stars Series
Partnership
Principles

Interdimensional Time Bureau
Monster Till Midnight

Historical Romance
Silent Sin

Contemporary Romance
Camera Shy
Summer Kitchen
The Thomas Flair
Mystic Man
For a Good Time, Call… (A Bluewater Bay novel, with Anne Tenino)

Christmas Kisses (holiday shorts)
The Probability of Mistletoe
An Everyday Hero
A Swants Soiree

Geeklandia Series
The Boyfriend Algorithm (M/F)
Clickbait

Writing as Nelle Heran
(traditional cozy mystery)

Crafty Sleuth Series (with C.K. Eastland)
Die Cut
Mixed Media
Found Objects (*coming soon*)

About the
Author

E.J. Russell (she/her), author of the award-winning Mythmatched paranormal romance series, writes LGBTQ+ romance and mystery in a rainbow of flavors. Count on high snark, low angst, and happy endings.

Reality? Eh, not so much.

She's married to Curmudgeonly Husband, a man who cares even less about sports than she does. Luckily, C.H. also loves to cook, or all three of their children (Lovely Daughter and Darling Sons A and B) would have survived on nothing but Cheerios, beef jerky, and Satsuma mandarins (the extent of E.J.'s culinary skill set).

E.J. also writes traditional cozy mystery as Nelle Heran. She lives in rural Oregon, enjoys visits from her wonderful adult children, and indulges in good books, red wine, and the occasional hyperbole.

News & Social Media:
Website: https://ejrussell.com
Ream: https://reamstories.com/ejr
Newsletter: https://ejrussell.com/newsletter

Acknowledgements

I've got some thank-yous to spread around. Meg DesCamp—thank you for coming full circle with me on Home and the guys, from brainstorming back in the day to final edits (and look—I've put two em dashes in this sentence just for you!). Thanks to Catherine Thorsen for story evaluation and direction; to the Crit Posse (L.C. Chase, Amy Aislin, and Lee Blair) for the suggestions and encouragement while I was slogging through revisions; to Cate Ashwood for the adorable cover; to NOLA Kim, my amazing PA, for… well… everything; of course to the family (Jim, Hana, Nick, Ross, and Billy) with love for cheerleading, support, and always buying my books on release day.

And, always and forever, thank you to my readers for accompanying me on this journey. You're the reason I can continue to follow my heart, and I appreciate you more than I can say.

9 781947 033924